THE TERROR

A small cannister from the missing nuclear sub *Starbuck* comes to Dirk Pitt from the sea. Inside, a final message, a testament of doom—and of terror...

> *There is no explaining this hell...we entered the fogbank...explosion...torrents of water... We lie at the bottom...They've come again! Mother of Christ! We can't hold them but a few hours more! They have nearly broken through ...No good! No good! We shall all be dead....*

THE VORTEX

Somewhere below the foggy Pacific seascape, crippled within the shark-infested depths, lies *Starbuck*—America's most devastating deep-diving weapon...a nuclear time-bomb set for destruction within hours... a prize that international forces are now racing to possess.

PITT'S MISSION

Penetrate the Vortex. Neutralize the enemy. Resurrect *Starbuck*.

BUT TIME IS RUNNING OUT.
PITT HAS ONLY ONE SHOT AT SUCCESS.
AND HIS SUPERIORS HAVE ALREADY
WRITTEN HIM OFF.

PACIFIC VORTEX!

PACIFIC VORTEX!

CLIVE CUSSLER

BANTAM BOOKS
TORONTO · NEW YORK · LONDON · SYDNEY

PACIFIC VORTEX!
A Bantam Book / January 1983

ISBN 0–553–22866–8

Published simultaneously in the United States and Canada

Bantam Books are published by Bantam Books, Inc. Its trademark, consisting of the words "Bantam Books" and the por-
trayal of a rooster, is Registered in U.S. Patent and Trademark
Office and in other countries. Marca Registrada. Bantam
Books, Inc., 666 Fifth Avenue, New York, New York 10103.

FOREWORD

Not that it really matters, but this is the first Dirk Pitt story.

When I mustered up the discipline to write a suspense/adventure series, I cast around for a hero who cut a different mold. One who wasn't a secret agent, police detective, or a private investigator. Someone with rough edges, yet a degree of style, who felt equally at ease entertaining a gorgeous woman in a gourmet restaurant or downing a beer with the boys at the local saloon. A congenial kind of guy with a tinge of mystery about him.

Instead of a gambling casino or the streets of New York, his territory became the sea, his challenge, the unknown.

Out of the fantasy, Dirk Pitt materialized.

Because this was his first adventure, and because it does not weave the intricate plots of his later exploits, I was reluctant to submit it for publishing. But at the urging of my friends and family, fans and readers, Pitt's introduction is now in your hands.

May it be looked upon as a few hours of entertainment and, perhaps, even a historic artifact of sorts.

CLIVE CUSSLER

PROLOGUE

Every ocean takes its toll of men and ships, yet none devours them with the voracious appetite of the Pacific. The mutiny on the *Bounty* took place in the Pacific, the mutineers burning the ship at Pitcairn Island. The *Essex*, the only known ship to be sunk by a whale (the basis of Melville's *Moby Dick*), lies under the Pacific's waves. So does the *Hai Maru*, blown to bits when an underwater volcano erupted beneath her hull.

Despite all this, the world's largest ocean tends to be a tranquil place; even its name means peaceful and mild of temper.

Perhaps that is why the grim thought of disaster couldn't have been further from Commander Felix Dupree's mind as he climbed onto the bridge of the nuclear submarine *Starbuck*, just before nightfall. He nodded to the officer on watch and leaned over the rail to gaze at the effortless ease in which the bow of his ship pushed aside the marching swells.

Men usually respect the sea: they are even awed by its serenity. But Dupree was not like most men; he was never overcome by the spell. Twenty years at sea, fourteen of them spent in submarines, he was hungry —hungry for recognition. Dupree was captain of the

world's newest and most revolutionary submarine, but it wasn't enough. He yearned for more.

The *Starbuck* was built in San Francisco from the keel up, as no other sub had been built before; every component, every system in her pressure hull, was computer designed. The first of a new generation of underwater ships—the beginning of a submerged city capable of cruising at one hundred twenty-five knots through the timeless depths two thousand feet beneath the sunlit surface. The *Starbuck* was like a thoroughbred jumper at her first horse show, chafing at the bit, ready to show her stuff.

But there was to be no audience. The Department of Underwater Warfare ordered the trials to be conducted in the strictest secrecy, in a remote area of the Pacific, and then without an escort vessel.

Dupree was chosen to command the *Starbuck* on her maiden trial because of his outstanding reputation. The Data Bank, his classmates at Annapolis had called him: program him with facts, and then watch his mouth spit out the logical answers. Dupree's skills and talent were well-known among submariners, but personality, influence, and a flair for public relations were the necessary ingredients for advancement in the Navy. Since Dupree possessed none of these traits, he had recently been passed over for promotion.

A buzzer sounded; the officer on watch, a tall raven-haired lieutenant, picked up the bridge phone. Unseen by the voice on the other end, he nodded twice and hung up.

"Control room," he said briefly. "Echo sounder reports the seafloor has risen fifteen hundred feet in the last five miles."

Dupree turned slowly, thoughtfully. "Probably a small range of submarine mountains. We still have a

mile of water beneath our keel." He grinned and
added, "No worry about running aground."

The lieutenant grinned back. "Nothing like a few
feet for insurance."

The lines around Dupree's eyes wrinkled with a
smile as he slowly turned back to the sea. He lifted
a pair of binoculars which hung loosely around his
neck and peered intently at the horizon. It was a
gesture born from many thousands of lonely hours
spent searching the oceans of the world for other
ships. It was also a useless gesture; the sophisticated
radar systems on board the *Starbuck* could detect an
object long before the naked eye could. Dupree knew
that, but there was something about studying the sea
that cleansed a man's soul.

Finally he sighed and lowered the binoculars. "I'm
going below for supper. Secure the bridge for diving
at 2100."

Dupree lowered himself through the three levels
of the conning tower—or sail, as the modern Navy
called it—and dropped into the control room. The
Executive Officer and another man, the navigator, were
bent over the plotting table, studying a line of depth
markings. The Executive Officer looked up at Dupree.

"Sir, we seem to have some strange readings here."

"Nothing like a mystery to end the day," Dupree
replied good-naturedly.

He moved between the two men and stared down
at a sheet of finely printed chart paper illuminated by
a soft light from the frosted glass tabletop. A series of
short dark lines crisscrossed the chart, edged with
carelessly written notations and mathematical form-
ulas.

"What have you got?" Dupree asked.

The navigator began slowly. "The bottom is raising

at an astonishing rate. If it doesn't peak out in the next twenty-five miles, we're going to find ourselves rubbing noses with an island, or islands, that aren't supposed to exist."

"What's our position?"

"We're here, sir," the navigator answered, tapping his pencil at a point on the chart. "Six hundred seventy miles north of Kahuku Point, Oahu, bearing zero-zero-seven degrees."

Dupree swung to a control panel and switched on a microphone. "Radar, this is the captain. Do you have anything?"

"No, sir," a voice replied mechanically through the speaker. "The scope is clear... wait... correction, Captain. I have a vague reading on the horizon at twenty-three miles, dead ahead."

"An object?"

"No, sir. More like a low cloud. Or maybe a trail of smoke; I can't quite make it out."

"Okay, report when you confirm its identity." Dupree hung up the microphone and faced the men at the plot table. "Well, gentlemen, how do you read it?"

The Executive Officer shook his head. "Where there's smoke, there's fire. And where there's fire, something's got to be burning. An oil slick, possibly?"

"An oil slick from what?" Dupree asked impatiently. "We're nowhere near the northern shipping lanes. The San Francisco to Honolulu to Orient traffic is four hundred miles south. This is one of the deadest spots in the ocean; that's why the Navy picked it for the *Starbuck*'s initial tests. No prying eyes." He shook his head. "A burning oil slick doesn't fit. A new volcano rising from the Pacific floor would be a closer guess. And that's all it would be—a guess."

The navigator pinpointed the radar's fix and drew a circle on the chart. "A low cloud on or near the surface," he thought out loud. "Highly unlikely. Atmospheric conditions are all wrong for such an occurrence."

The speaker clicked on. "Captain, this is radar."

"This is the captain," Dupree answered.

"I've identified it, sir." The voice seemed to hesitate before it went on. "The contact reads as a heavy bank of fog, approximately three miles in diameter."

"Are you positive?"

"Stake my rating on it."

Dupree touched a switch on the microphone and rang the bridge. "Lieutenant, we have a radar sighting ahead. Let me know the minute you see anything." He rang off and turned to the Executive Officer. "What's the depth now?"

"Still coming up fast. Twenty-eight hundred feet and climbing."

The navigator pulled a cotton handkerchief from his hip pocket and dabbed it to his neck. "Beats the hell out of me. The only rise I've heard of that comes close to this one is the Peru-Chili Trench. Beginning at twenty-five thousand feet beneath the surface of the sea, it climbs at a rate of one vertical mile for every one horizontal mile. Until now, it was considered the world's most spectacular underwater slope."

"Yeah," the Executive Officer grunted. "Won't marine geologists have a ball with this little discovery?"

"Eighteen-hundred fifty feet," the voice from the echo sounder droned unemotionally.

"My God!" the navigator gasped. "Up a thousand feet in less than half a mile. It just isn't possible."

Dupree moved over to the port side of the control

room and placed his nose within a few inches of the glass encasing the echo sounder. According to the digital display, the sea bottom was depicted as a long zigzagged black line climbing steeply toward the red danger mark at the top of the scale. Dupree placed a hand on the shoulder of the sonar operator.

"Any possibility of a foul-up in calibration?"

The sonar operator flipped a switch and stared at an adjoining window. "No, sir. I get the same set of readings from the independent backup system."

Dupree watched this upward trail for a few moments. Then he stepped back to the plot table and looked at the pencil marks showing his ship's position in relation to the rising seafloor.

"Bridge speaking," a robotlike voice came through. "We've got it." There was some hesitation. "If I didn't know better, I'd say our contact was a scaled-down version of a good old New England fog bank."

Dupree clicked the microphone. "Understood." He continued gazing at the chart, his face unreadable, his eyes thoughtful.

"Shall we send a signal to Pearl Harbor, sir?" the navigator asked. "They could send a recon plane to investigate."

Dupree didn't answer immediately. One hand idly drummed the edge of the table, the other hung loosely at his side. Dupree rarely, if ever, made snap decisions. His every move went by the book.

Many of the *Starbuck*'s crew had served under Dupree on prior assignments, and although they didn't exactly offer him their blind devotion, they did respect and admire his ability and judgment. They trusted him to a man, confident that he would never make a critical mistake that would endanger their lives. Any

other time they might have been right. But this time they were all terribly wrong.

"Let's check it out," Dupree said quietly.

The Executive Officer and the navigator exchanged speculative glances. Orders were to test the *Starbuck* —not chase after ghostly fog banks on the horizon.

No one ever knew why Commander Dupree suddenly stepped out of character and deviated from orders. Perhaps the lure of the unknown was too strong. Perhaps he saw a fleeting vision of himself as a discoverer, sailing toward the glory that had always been denied him. Whatever the reason, it was lost as the *Starbuck*, like an unleashed bloodhound with a hot scent flowing through her nostrils, swung on her new course and surged through the swells.

The *Starbuck* was expected to dock in Pearl Harbor on the following Monday. When she failed to show, and an exhaustive air and sea search failed to find a single trace of oil or wreckage, the Navy had no choice but to admit the loss of its newest submarine and one hundred sixty men. It was officially announced to a stunned nation that the *Starbuck* was lost somewhere in the vast emptiness of the North Pacific. Shrouded in a silent mystery she vanished with all hands. Time, place, and cause unknown.

PACIFIC
VORTEX!

CHAPTER 1

Among the crowded beaches in the state of Hawaii, it is still possible to discover a stretch of sand that offers a degree of solitude. Kaena Point, jutting out into the Kauai Channel like a boxer's left jab, is one of the few unadvertised spots where one can relax and enjoy an empty shore. It is a beautiful beach, but it is also deceptive. Too often its shores are whipped by rip currents extremely dangerous to all but the most wary swimmers. Each year, as if predestined by a morbid schedule, an unidentified bather, intrigued by the lonely sandy strand and the gentle surf, enters the water and within minutes is swept out to sea.

On this beach a six-foot-three-inch deeply suntanned man, clad in brief white bathing trunks, lay stretched on a bamboo beach mat. The hairy, barrel chest that rose slightly with each intake of air, bore specks of sweat that rolled downward in snaillike trails and mingled with the sand. The arm that passed over the eyes shielding them from the strong rays of the tropical sun, was muscular but without the exaggerated bulges generally associated with iron pumpers. The hair was black and thick and shaggy, and it fell halfway down a forehead that merged into a hard-featured but friendly face.

Dirk Pitt stirred from a semisleep and, raising him-

1

self up on his elbows, stared from deep green glistening eyes at the sea. Pitt was not a casual sun wor-
shipper; to him, the beach was a living, moving thing,
changing shape and personality under the constant
onslaught of the wind and waves. He studied the
swells as they rolled in from their storm-rocked birth-
place thousands of miles at sea, rising and increasing
their velocity when their troughs felt the shallow bottom. Changing from swell to breaker, they rose higher
and higher—eight feet, Pitt judged—from trough to
crest before they toppled and broke, pounding themselves into a thundering mass of foam and spray. Then
they died in small, swirling eddies at the tideline.

Suddenly Pitt's eyes were attracted by a flash of
color beyond the breakers, about three hundred feet
from the shoreline. It was gone in an instant, lost behind a wave crest. Pitt kept gazing with intent
curiosity at the spot where the color was last visible.
After the next wave rose and crested, he could see it
again gleaming in the sun. The shape was undis-
tinguishable at that distance, but there was no mistaking the bright fluorescent yellow glint.

The smart move, Pitt deduced, would be to simply
lay there and let the force of the surf bring the unknown object to him; but he pushed sound judgment
from his mind, rolled to his feet, and walked slowly
into the surf. When the water rose above his knees,
he arched his body and dove under an approaching
breaker, timing it so that he only felt the surge crash
over his kicking feet. The water felt as heated as a
tepid hotel room bath; the temperature was somewhere between seventy-five and seventy-eight degrees.
As soon as his head cleared the surface, he began to
stroke through the swirling foam, swimming easily,

allowing the force of the current to carry him into deeper water.

After several minutes, he stopped and treaded water, searching for a hint of yellow. He spotted it twenty yards to his left. He kept his eyes keyed on the strange piece of flotsam as he narrowed the gap, only losing sight of it momentarily when it dropped in the advancing troughs. Sensing that the current was pulling him too far to his right, he compensated his angle and slowly increased his strokes to avoid the dangerous threat of exhaustion.

Then he reached out and his fingers touched a slick, cylindrical surface about two feet long, and eight inches wide, and weighing less than six pounds. Encasing the object was a yellow waterproof plastic material with U.S. NAVY printed in block letters on both ends. Pitt locked his arms around it, relaxed his body, and surveyed his now precarious position some distance beyond the surf.

He scanned the beach, searching for someone who might have seen him enter the water, but the sand was empty for miles in either direction. Pitt didn't bother to examine the steep cliffs behind the shore; it was hopeless to expect anyone to be scaling the rocky slopes in the middle of the week.

He wondered why he took such a stupid and foolhardy risk. The mysterious yellow flotsam had given him an excuse to dare the odds, and once started, it never occurred to him to turn back. Now the merciless sea held him securely.

For a brief moment he considered trying to swim in a straight line back to shore. But only for a brief moment. Mark Spitz might have made it, but Pitt felt certain he'd never have won all those gold medals at

the Olympics while smoking a pack of cigarettes a day
and consuming several shots of Cutty Sark Scotch
every evening. Pitt decided to concentrate instead on
beating Mother Nature at her own game.

Pitt was an old hand at rip currents and undertows;
he had bodysurfed for years and knew their every
trick. A man could be swept out to sea from one
section of the shore, while a hundred yards away
children cavorted in the diminishing waves without
noticing the slightest tug from the current. The
unrelenting force of a rip current occurs when the
longshore flow returns to the sea through narrow,
stormgrooved valleys in offshore sandbars. Here the
incoming surf changes direction and heads away from
land, often as rapidly as four miles an hour. Now the
current had nearly expended itself, and Pitt was
certain he had but to swim parallel to the shoreline
until he was out of the sandbars, and then head in at
a different point along the beach.

The menace of sharks was his only worry. The
sea's murder machines didn't always signal their
presence with a water-slicing fin. They could easily
attack from beneath with no warning, and without a
face mask Pitt would never know when the slashing
bite was coming, or from what direction. He could
only hope to reach the safety of the surf before he
was placed on the menu for lunch. Sharks, he knew,
seldom ventured close to shore because the swirling
turbulence of heavy wave action forced sand through
their gills; this discouraged all but the hungriest from
a handy meal.

There was no thought of conserving his energy now;
he struggled through the water as if every man-eater
in the Pacific Ocean was on his tail. It took nearly
fifteen minutes of vigorous swimming before the first

wave nudged him toward the beach. Nine more breakers marched by; the tenth caught the buoyancy of the cylinder and held it, carrying Pitt to within twelve feet of the tideline. The instant his knees touched sand again, he rose drunkenly like an exhausted shipwrecked sailor and staggered out of the water, dragging his prize behind him. Then he dropped thankfully onto the sun-warmed sand.

Wearily, Pitt turned his attention to the cylinder. Underneath the plastic covering was an unusual aluminum canister. The sides were ribbed with several small rods that resembled miniature railroad tracks. One end held a screw cap, so Pitt began twisting, intrigued by the great number of revolutions, before it finally dropped off in his hand. Inside was a tight roll of several papers, nothing else. He gently eased them into the daylight and began studying the hand-written manuscript exactingly penned among titled columns and lines.

As he read over the pages, an ice-chill hand touched his skin, and in spite of the ninety-degree heat, goose-flesh broke out over his body. More than once he tried to draw his eyes away from the pages, but was stunned by the enormity of what he held in his hands.

Pitt sat and gazed vacantly out over the ocean for a full ten minutes after he read the last sentence in the document. It ended with a name: ADMIRAL LEIGH HUNTER. Then, very slowly, Pitt gently inserted the papers back in the cylinder, screwed on the cap, and carefully rewrapped the yellow cover.

An eerie, unearthly blanket of silence had fallen over Kaena Point. As the breakers rolled in, their roar somehow seemed muted. He stood and brushed off the sand from his wet body, packed the cylinder under his arm, and began jogging up the beach. When

he reached his mat, he quickly wound it around the object in his hands. Then he hurried up the pathway leading to the road alongside the beach.

The bright red AC Ford Cobra sat forlornly on the road. Pitt wasted no time. He threw his cargo on the passenger's seat and moved rapidly behind the steering wheel, his hand, fumbling with the ignition key.

He swung onto Highway 99, passing through Waialua and heading up the long grade that ran next to the picturesque and usually dry, Kaukomahua Stream. After the Schofield Barracks Military Reservation disappeared behind the rearview mirror, Pitt took the turnoff below Wahiawa and headed at high speed toward Pearl City, completely ignoring the threat of a wandering state highway patrolman.

The Koolau Range rose on his left, with their peaks buried underneath perpetual dark rolling rainclouds. Alongside of them the neat, green pineapple fields spread in vivid contrast against the rich, red volcanic soil. Pitt met a sudden rainstorm and automatically turned on the wipers.

At last the main gate at Pearl Harbor came into view. Pitt slowed the car as a uniformed guard came out of the office. Pitt pulled out his driver's license and his identification papers from his wallet, and signed in the visitors' logbook. The young marine simply saluted and waved Pitt through.

Pitt then asked the guard for directions to Admiral Hunter's headquarters. The marine pulled a pad and pencil from his breast pocket and politely drew a map which he handed to Pitt. He saluted once more.

Pitt pulled up and stopped in front of an inconspicuous concrete building near the dock area. He would have passed it but for a small, neatly stenciled sign that read: HEADQUARTERS, 101ST SALVAGE FLEET.

He turned off the ignition, picked up the damp package, and left the car. Passing through the entrance, Pitt mentally wished he'd had the foresight to carry a sport shirt and a pair of slacks with him to the beach. He stepped to a desk where a seaman in the Navy summer white uniform mechanically punched a typewriter. A sign on the desk read: SEAMAN G. YAGER.

"Excuse me," Pitt murmured self-consciously, "I'd like to see Admiral Hunter."

The typist looked up casually, then his eyes almost burst from their sockets.

"My God, buddy, are you off your gourd? What are you trying to pull, coming here wearing nothing but a bathing suit? If the old man catches you, you're dead. Now beat it quick or you'll wind up in the brig."

"I know I'm not dressed for an afternoon social," Pitt spoke quietly and pleasantly, "but it's damned urgent that I see the admiral."

The seaman rose from the desk, his face turning red. "Stop clowning around," he said loudly. "Either you go back to your quarters and sleep it off, or I'll call the Shore Patrol."

"Then call them!" Pitt's voice was suddenly sharp.

"Look, buddy," the seaman's tone became one of controlled irritation. "Do yourself a favor. Go back to your ship and make a formal request to see the admiral through the chain of command."

"That won't be necessary, Yager." The voice behind them carried the finesse of a bulldozer scraping a cement highway.

Pitt turned and found himself locking eyes with a tall wizened man standing stiffly within an inner office doorway. He was dressed in white from collar to shoes and trimmed in gold braid beginning at the arms and

working up to the rank boards on the shoulders. The
hair was bushy and white, very nearly matching the
tired cadaverous face beneath. Only the eyes seemed
alive, and they glared curiously at the canister in
Pitt's hand.

"I'm Admiral Hunter, and I'll give you just five
minutes, big boy, so you better make it worth my
while. And bring that object with you," he said, pointing to the canister.

"Yes sir," was all Pitt could reply.

Hunter had already spun and was striding into his
office. Pitt followed and if he wasn't embarrassed before
he stepped into the admiral's office, there was no
doubt of his discomfort now that he was inside. There
were three other naval officers besides Hunter seated
around an ancient, immaculately polished conference
table. Their faces registered astonishment at the sight
of Pitt standing half naked with the strange-looking
package under one arm.

Hunter routinely made the introductions, but Pitt
wasn't fooled by the phony courtesy; the admiral
was trying to frighten him with rank while studying
Pitt's eyes for a reaction. Pitt learned that the tall,
blond lieutenant commander with the John Kennedy
face was Paul Boland, the 101st Fleet's Executive
Officer. The heavyset captain who was perspiring
profusely, possessed the odd name of Orl Cinana, the
officer in command of Hunter's small fleet of salvage
ships. The short, almost gnomelike creature, who
hurried over and pumped Pitt's hand, introduced himself as Commander Burdette Denver, aide to the
admiral. He stared at Pitt, as if trying to remember
his face.

"Okay, big boy." That term again. Pitt would have
given a month's pay to ram his knuckles against

Hunter's teeth. Hunter's voice oozed with sarcasm. "Now if you will be so kind as to tell us who you are and what this interruption is all about, we will all be eternally grateful."

"You're pretty rude for someone anxious to know why I'm carrying this canister," Pitt answered, settling his long body comfortably in a vacant chair, waiting for a reaction.

Cinana glared across the table, his face twisted in a clouded mask of malevolence. "You scum! How dare you come in here and insult an officer!"

"The man's insane," snapped Boland. He leaned toward Pitt, his expression cold and taut. He added, "You stupid bastard; do you know who you're talking to?"

"Since we've all been introduced," Pitt said casually, "the answer is a qualified *yes*."

Cinana's sweaty fist slammed to the table. "The Shore Patrol, by God. I'll have Yager call the Shore Patrol and throw him in the brig."

Hunter struck a light to a long cigarette, flipped the match at an ashtray, missing it by six inches, and stared at Pitt thoughtfully. "You leave me no choice, big boy." He turned to Boland. "Commander, ask Seaman Yager to call the Shore Patrol."

"I wouldn't, Admiral." Denver rose from his chair, recognition flooding his face. "This man some of you have referred to as filth and a bastard and wish to cast into chains, is indeed Dirk Pitt, who happens to be the Special Projects Director of the National Underwater and Marine Agency, and whose father happens to be Senator George Pitt of California, Chairman of the Naval Appropriations Committee."

Cinana uttered something short and unprintable.

Boland was the first to recover. "Are you certain?"

"Yes, Paul, quite certain." He moved around the table and faced Pitt. "I saw him several years ago, with his father, at a NUMA conference. He's also a friend of my cousin, who's also in NUMA. Commander Rudi Gunn."

Pitt grinned happily. "Of course. Rudi and I have worked on several projects together. I can see the resemblance now. The only noticeable difference is that Rudi peers through horned-rimmed glasses."

"Used to call him Beaver Eyes," Denver laughed, "when we were kids."

"I'll throw that at him next time I see him," Pitt said, smiling.

"I hope you . . . you won't take offense to . . . to what we said," stuttered Boland.

Pitt tossed Boland his best cynical stare and simply said: "No."

Hunter and Cinana exchanged looks that Pitt had no difficulty in deciphering. If they tried to ignore their uneasiness at having the son of a United States senator sitting in their midst, they failed badly at concealing it.

"Okay, Mr. Pitt, it's your quarter. We assume you're here because of the canister. Would you explain how you got it?"

"I'm only an errand boy," Pitt said quietly. "I discovered this while sunbathing on the beach this afternoon. It belongs to you."

"Well, well," Hunter said heavily. "I'm honored. Why me?"

Pitt looked at the three men speculatively, and set the cylinder, still covered with the bamboo beach mat, on the table. "Inside, you'll find some papers. One has your name on it."

There wasn't a flicker of curiosity in Hunter's expression.

"Where did you find this thing?"

"Near the tip of Kaena Point."

Denver hunched forward. "Washed up on the beach?"

Pitt shook his head. "No, I swam out beyond the breakers and towed it in."

Denver looked puzzled. "You swam beyond the breakers at Kaena Point? I didn't think it possible."

Hunter gave Pitt a very thoughtful look indeed, but he passed it off. "May we see what you have there?"

Pitt nodded silently and unwrapped the cylinder, paying scant notice to the damp sand that spilled on the conference table. Then he passed it to Hunter.

"This yellow plastic cover was what caught my eye."

Hunter took the cylinder in his hands and held it up for the other men to examine. "Recognize it, gentlemen?"

The others nodded.

"You've never served on a submarine, Mr. Pitt, or you'd know what a communications capsule looks like." Hunter set the package down and touched it lightly. "When a submarine wishes to remain underwater and communicate with a surface ship following in her wake, a message is inserted in this aluminum capsule." As he spoke he gently pulled away the yellow plastic. "The capsule, with a red dye marker attached, is then ejected through the submarine's hull by means of a pneumatic tube. When the capsule reaches the surface, the dye is released, staining several thousand square feet of water, making it visible to the chase ship."

"The fine threads on the cap," Pitt said slowly, "they were machined to prevent leakage under extreme pressure."

Hunter gazed at Pitt expectantly. "You read the contents?"

Pit nodded. "Yes, sir."

Neither Boland, Cinana, nor Denver comprehended, or even saw, the sickness, the despair, in Hunter's eyes.

"Would you mind describing what you saw?" Hunter asked, knowing with dread certainty what the answer would be.

Several seconds passed as Pitt silently wished to hell he had never seen that damned capsule, but there was no avenue of escape. One last sentence and he would be rid of the whole discomforting scene. He took a deep breath and spoke slowly.

"Inside you will find a note addressed to you, Admiral. You will also find twenty-six pages torn from the logbook of the nuclear submarine *Starbuck*."

CHAPTER 2

The following is a summary of Commander Dupree's comments, narrated by Admiral Hunter:

> There is no explaining the hell of the last five days. I alone am responsible for the change in course that brought my ship and crew to what surely must seem a strange and unholy end. Beyond that, I can only describe as best I can, the circumstances of the disaster—my mind is not functioning as it should.

The fact that Dupree was not in full command of his mental faculties is an astonishing confession from a man whose reputation was built upon a computer-like mind.

> At 2040 hours, June 14, we entered the fog bank. Shortly thereafter, with the seabed only ten fathoms beneath our keel, an explosion ripped the ship's bow, and a roaring torrent of water burst into the forward torpedo compartment, flooding it almost instantly.

The commander did not reveal, if indeed he knew, whether the explosion came from inside or outside the *Starbuck*'s hull.

> Of the full crew, twenty-six had the good fortune to die within seconds. The three still on the bridge,

Lieutenant Carter, Seaman Farris, and Metford, we hoped had gotten clear before the ship settled beneath the surface. Tragic events proved otherwise.

If, as Dupree indicates, the *Starbuck* was riding on the surface, it seems odd that Carter, Farris, and Metford could not clear the bridge and go below in less than thirty seconds. It is inconceivable that he would have secured the hatches and left the men to their fate. It is just as inconceivable that there was no time to save them—it was not a likely possibility that the *Starbuck* sank like a stone.

Meanwhile, we sealed off the hatches and vents. I then ordered all ballast blown and hard rise on the planes; it was too late; the tearing sounds and groans forward meant the ship had plowed into the sea bottom bow on.

It seems reasonable to assume that with all ballast tanks blown, and the bow buried in only one hundred sixty feet of water, the stern section of the *Starbuck's* three-hundred-twenty-foot hull might still extend above the surface. Such was not the case.

We now lie on the bottom. The deck canted eight degrees to starboard with a down angle of two degrees. Except for the forward torpedo room, all other compartments are secure and showing no signs of water. We are all dead now. I have ordered the men to resign the game. My folly killed us all.

The most fantastic mystery yet. Allowing twenty-five feet from keel to topside, the distance from the

aft escape hatch to the surface was one hundred thirty-five feet; a moderate ascent for a man with a self-contained breathing apparatus, a device carried on all submarines for crew members. During World War II, eight men from the sunken submarine *Tang*, swam one hundred eighty feet to the surface, surviving on nothing but lung power.

The last few sentences are all the more bewildering. What precipitated Dupree's madness? Was he overwhelmed by the stress of the whole nightmarish situation? He further retreated from reality.

Food gone, air only good for a few hours at best. Drinking water gone after the third day.

Impossible! With the nuclear reactor operable—and there's no reason to believe it wasn't—the crew could survive for months. The freshwater distillation units could easily provide a more than ample supply of drinking water, and with a few precautionary measures, the life support system which purified the sub's atmosphere and produced oxygen, would have sustained sixty-three men comfortably until it ceased to function, an unlikely event. Only the food presented a long-range problem. Yet, since the *Starbuck* was outward bound the food stock should have been enough, if rationed, to last ninety days. Everything hinged on the reactor. If it died, the men died.

My way is clear, I feel strangely at peace. I ordered the ship's doctor to give the men injections to halt their suffering. I will, of course, be the last to go.

My God! Is it possible Dupree could actually order the mass murder of his surviving crew?

They've come again. Carter is tapping on the hull.
Mother of Christ! Why does his ghost torture us so?

Dupree had fallen over the edge and entered the
realm of total madness. How can it be after only five
days?

We can hold them but a few hours more. They have
nearly broken through the hatch in the aft escape
compartment. No good, no good ... [illegible]. They
mean to kill us, but we will outwit them in the end.
No satisfaction, no victory. We shall all be dead.

Who in the hell does he mean by "they?" Is it
possible another vessel, perhaps a Russian spy trawler,
was trying to rescue the crew?

It is dark on the surface now, and they have stopped
work. I will send this message and the last pages of
the log to the surface in the communications capsule.
Good chance they'll miss it at night. Our position is
[the first figures are crossed out] 32°43′15″N—
161°18′22″W.

The position doesn't figure. It's over five hundred
miles from the *Starbuck*'s last reported position. Not
nearly enough time between the last radio contact and
Dupree's final position for the *Starbuck* to travel the
required distance, even at flank speed.

Do not search for us; it can only end in vain. They
cannot allow a trace to be found. The shameful trick
they used. If I had but known, we might well be
alive to touch the sun. Please see this message is
delivered to Admiral Leigh Hunter, Pearl Harbor.

The final enigma. Why me? To my knowledge, I have never met Commander Dupree. Why did he single out me as the recipient of the *Starbuck*'s last testament?

CHAPTER 3

Pitt hunched over the bar of the old Royal Hawaiian Hotel, staring vacantly at his drink, as his mind wandered over the events of the day. They flickered past his unblinking eyes and dissolved into a haze. One scene refused to fade away: the memory of Admiral Hunter's pallid face as he read the contents of the capsule—the terrible senselessness of the *Starbuck*'s tragic fate, and the bewildering, paranoiac words of Commander Dupree.

After Hunter had finished, he slowly looked up and nodded at Pitt. Pitt shook the admiral's leathery outstretched hand in silence, mumbled his good-bye to the other officers, and, as if in an hypnotic state, slowly walked from the room. He could not remember driving through the twisting traffic flow of Nimitz Highway. He could not remember entering his hotel room, showering and dressing, and leaving in search of some opaque, unknown objective. Even now, as he slowly swirled the Scotch within the glass, his ears heard nothing of the babble of tongues around him in the cocktail lounge.

There was something strangely sinister about his discovery of the *Starbuck*'s final message, he idly reflected. There was a wary, retrospective thought that fought desperately to surface from the inner recesses

of his brain. But it faded and fell back into the nothingness from which it came.

Out of the corner of his eye Pitt caught a man further down the bar holding up a glass in his direction, gesturing the offer of a free drink. It was Captain Orl Cinana. Like Pitt, he was dressed casually in slacks and a flowered Hawaiian aloha shirt. Cinana came over and leaned on the bar beside him. He was still sweating and dabbed at his forehead and wiped his palms almost constantly with a handkerchief he carried.

"May I do the honors?" Cinana said with a smile that smacked of insincerity.

Pitt held up a full glass. "Thanks, but I haven't made a dent in the one I've got."

Pitt had taken little notice of Cinana earlier at Pearl Harbor, but now he was mildly surprised to see something he'd missed. Except for the fact that Cinana outweighed Pitt by a paunchy fifteen pounds, they could have passed for cousins.

Cinana swirled the ice around in his Rum Collins, nervously avoiding Pitt's expressionless gaze.

"I'd like to apologize again for that little misunderstanding this afternoon."

"Forget it, Captain. I wasn't exactly a paragon of courtesy myself."

"A nasty business, the *Starbuck*'s loss." Cinana took a swallow from his glass.

"Most mysteries have a way of eventually getting solved. The *Thresher*, the *Bluefin*, the *Scorpion*—the Navy never gave up until everyone was found."

"We're not repeating the act this time," Cinana said grimly. "This is one we'll never find."

"Never say never."

"The three tragedies you mentioned, Major, oc-

curred in the Atlantic. The *Starbuck* had the fatal misfortune of vanishing in the Pacific." He paused to wipe his neck. "We have a saying in the Navy about ships lost out here."

Those who lie deep in the Atlantic Sea
Are recalled by shrines, wreaths, and poetry,
But those who lie in the Pacific Sea
Lie forgotten for all eternity.

"But you have the position from Dupree's message," Pitt said. "With luck, your sonar should detect her within a week's sweep of the area."

"The sea doesn't give up its secrets easily, Major." Cinana set his empty glass on the bar. "Well, I must be going. I was supposed to meet someone, but apparently she stood me up."

Pitt shook Cinana's outstretched hand and grinned. "I know the feeling."

"Good-bye, and good luck."

"Same to you, Captain."

Cinana turned and sidestepped through the crowd to the hotel lobby entrance and became lost in the milling sea of heads.

Pitt still hadn't touched his drink. After Cinana's departure, he sensed a maddening loneliness, despite the surrounding din of voices in the crowded room. Pitt had the urge to get very drunk. He wanted to forget the name *Starbuck* and concentrate on more important matters, such as picking up a vacationing secretary who had left all her sexual inhibitions back in Omaha, Nebraska. He downed his drink and ordered another.

He was just about ready to try out his soft-tongued affability when he became aware of the touch of two

soft, feminine breasts pressing into his back, and a pair of slender white hands encircling his waist. He unhurriedly turned and found his eyes confronted by the impish face of Adrian Hunter.

"Hello, Dirk," she murmured in a husky voice. "Need a drinking partner?"

"I might. What's in it for me?"

She tightened her hands around his waist. "We could go to my place, tune in the late, late movie, and take notes."

"Can't. Mother wants me home early."

"Oh come now, lover, you wouldn't deny an old friend an evening of scandalous behavior, would you?"

"That what old friends are for?" he said sarcastically. Her hands had moved downward and he pulled them away. "You should find yourself a new hobby. At the rate you indulge your fantasies, I'm surprised you haven't been sold for scrap by now."

"That's an interesting thought," she smiled at him. "I could always use the money. I wonder what I'd bring."

"Probably the price of a well-used Edsel."

She thrust out her chest and faked a pout. "You only hurt the one you love, so I'm told."

Considering the exhaustive pace of her nightlife, Pitt thought she was still a damn good-looking woman. He remembered the soft feel of her body when he last made love to her. He also remembered that no matter how relentless his attack, nor how expert his technique he could never satisfy her.

"Not to change the subject of our stimulating conversation," he said, "but I met your father for the first time today."

He waited for a hint of surprise. There was none.

She seemed quite unconcerned. "Really? What did old Lord Nelson have to talk about?"

"For one thing, he didn't care for the way I was dressed."

"Don't feel badly. He doesn't care for the way I dress either."

He took a sip from his Scotch and gazed at her over the top of the glass. "In your case, I can't blame him. No man likes to see his daughter come off like a back alley hooker."

She ignored his last remark; that her father had come face-to-face with but one of her many lovers, didn't interest her at all. She wiggled onto the next bar stool and gazed at him with a seductive look burning in her eyes, the effect heightened by the long black hair winding around one shoulder. Her skin glowed like polished bronze under the dim lights of the cocktail lounge.

She whispered, "How about that drink?"

Pitt nodded at the bartender. "A Brandy Alexander for the ... ah, lady."

She scowled a little and then smiled. "Don't you know that being referred to as a lady is very old-fashioned?"

"An old carry-over. All men want a girl, just like the girl, that married dear old Dad."

"Mom was a drag," she said, her voice elaborately casual.

"How about Dad?"

"Dad was a will-o'-the-wisp. He was never home, always chasing after some smelly old derelict barge or a forgotten shipwreck. He loved the ocean more than he loved his own family. The night I was born, he was rescuing the crew of a sinking oil tanker in the mid-

Pacific. When I graduated from high school, he was at sea searching for a missing aircraft. And when Mother died, our dear admiral was charting icebergs off Greenland with some long-haired freaks from the Eaton School of Oceanography." Her eyes shifted just enough to let Pitt know he was onto her sore spot. "So don't bother shedding tears over this father-daughter relationship. The admiral and I tolerate each other purely out of social convenience."

Pitt stared down at her. "You're all grown up now; why don't you leave home?"

The bartender brought her drink and she sipped it. "What better deal can a girl find? I'm continually surrounded by handsome males in uniform. Look at the odds; thousands of men and no competition. Why should I leave the old homestead and scrounge for leftovers? No, the admiral needs the image of a family man, and I need old Dad for the fringe benefits that come with being an admiral's daughter." Then she looked at him, faking a shy and bashful expression. "My apartment? Shall we?"

"You'll have to take a raincheck, Miss Hunter," said a delicate voice behind them. "The captain is waiting for me."

Adrian and Pitt both turned in unison. There stood the most exotic-looking woman Pitt had ever seen. She possessed eyes so gray, they defied reality, and her hair fell in an enchanting cascade of red, presenting a vibrant contrast against the green, Oriental sheath dress that adhered to her curvaceous body.

Pitt quickly searched his memory, but with no success. He was certain he had never laid eyes on this beauty before. When he rose off the bar stool, he was pleasingly surprised to feel his heart accelerate. She was the first woman to ignite his emotions on a first

meeting since a basset hound-eyed blond in the fifth
grade who bit him on the arm during recess.

Adrian was the first to break the silence. "I'm sorry,
honey, but as they say in the old family mining claim,
you're trespassing."

Adrian seemed to enjoy the situation. To her, the
intruder was no more than a nuisance. She turned,
offering her back to the girl, and began sipping her
drink again.

The great gray eyes never strayed from Adrian.
"Your rudeness, Miss Hunter, is only surpassed by
your reputation as a tramp."

Adrian was too cool to give up an inch. She sat
immobile, staring straight ahead at the girl's reflection
in the mirror behind the bar. "Fifty dollars?" she said
loudly so all within thirty feet could hear. "Considering your amateur standing and less than mediocre
talents, you're vastly overpriced."

Several customers sitting in the immediate neighborhood of the bar were listening intently to the caustic
exchange. The women were frowning, but the men
were grinning, secretly envying the speechless male
who was trapped in the no-man's-land of the sex battle.
Pitt was adequately awed. It was a new experience to
have two lovely females trading barbs over his
possession. His ego basked in the sheer exhilaration
of the moment.

"May I speak with you in private, Miss Hunter?"
asked the mysterious girl in the green dress.

Adrian nodded. "Why not?" She turned and slid
smoothly off the bar stool, following the stranger
through the open doors that led to the hotel's private
beach. Pitt stared in rapt fascination at both pairs of
rounded hips as they rotated in a fluidlike motion that
was, or so Pitt imagined, suggestive of two beach-

balls caught in the same swirling whirlpool.

Pitt sighed and leaned limply against the bar, feeling like a spider eyeing two flies circling his net, and wishing they'd entangle somewhere else. Then he caught the open stares of his audience; he grinned and bowed, acknowledging their steadfast attention before he turned back to the bar.

There's been enough surprises for one day, he ruefully admitted to himself. Where will it all end? Heeding the call for more courage, he signaled the bartender and ordered another Cutty on the rocks— a double this time.

Fifteen minutes later, Gray Eyes returned and stood silently behind him. Pitt was so deeply lost in thought that it took him several seconds before he sensed her presence and looked up to be met by her reflection in the mirror.

Her lips moved in what could have been the beginning of a smile. "To the victor goes the spoils?" It was a question asked hesitantly.

The bruise beneath her right eye had begun the transformation from red to purple, and a small cut on her lower lip unleashed a few drops of blood that trickled down her chin, falling with precise accuracy down the cleavage between her breasts. Pitt still thought she was the most desirable woman he'd ever seen.

"And the loser?" he asked.

"She'll be in need of heavy makeup for a few days, but I think she'll survive to fight another day."

He pulled his handkerchief from a pocket, wrapped it around an ice cube fished from his glass, and touched it lightly to her lip. "Here, keep this pressed against the cut. It'll contain the swelling."

She forced a wan smile and nodded a *thank you*.

His meddling audience was back, this time with a concerted leer that bordered on infamy. Quickly, he paid off the bartender, taking the girl by the arm and dragging her from the lounge to the beach outside. Pitt scanned the shoreline but there was no sign of Adrian.

"Mind telling me what happened?"

She had to remove the ice cube to speak. "Isn't it obvious? Miss Hunter wouldn't listen to reason."

Pitt looked at her, half uncertainly, half speculatively. Why elect me, he thought. Why fight over a man she'd never met? And the jackpot question— what was her game? Pitt didn't kid himself; no movie studio would ever star him in a remake of *Don Juan*. He'd had his share of women, but never before the usual preliminaries, the artful little lies, the step-by-step manuevers. He decided not to delve into her reasons but to let the mystery heighten the intrigue.

"Shall we walk along the beach?" he asked.

"I was hoping you'd suggest that." She smiled, and immediately had him in her power. And she knew it. She shrewdly watched his eyes wander to her breasts, then down her body to her legs.

Her breasts were surprisingly small and taut in contrast with the accented curves that abounded the rest of her figure. In the moonlight and the flaming glow from the torches staked around the hotel terrace, he could see where the deeply tanned flesh, speckled by blood, plunged invitingly beneath the dress. Lower and beyond, her waist gently tapered to a firm, flat stomach which then exploded into a brace of pneumatic hips that fought to escape the tight seams of their green prison. She looked Indian, but the flaming

red hair that fell to the small of her back did not attest to it.

"If you keep staring at me, I'll be forced to charge you admission."

Pitt made an effort to look shyly embarrassed but didn't pull it off. "I thought art galleries were free."

She squeezed his arm. "Not if you wish to purchase something."

"I like to browse. I rarely buy."

"So you're a man of principles."

"I have a few, but they don't apply to women." Her perfume was getting to him, a fragrance that somehow seemed familiar.

She stopped, clinging to him for support, and removed her shoes, wriggling her toes in the cool sand of Waikiki Beach. They strolled on in silence for a few minutes, she tightened her grip on his arm and pulled herself close as they walked.

Her eyes glinted in the dim light and she said in a low voice, "My name is Summer."

Pitt said nothing as he enclosed her in his arms and lightly kissed her on her swollen lips. And suddenly the warning bells were clanging in his mind, but the warning came too late; the pain burst on him first. His mouth dropped open and a gasp that started deep down in his throat erupted into the quiet air as Summer thrust her knee into his groin.

What caused the cells in his brain to order such a lightning reaction he would never know: through the haze of the shock he barely saw his fist lash out in a blurring reflex action and catch Summer solidly on the right side of her jaw. She swayed drunkenly for an instant and then crumpled silently onto the sand.

The hidden, unsuspected resources, ready to be called upon in a moment of desperation, kept Pitt

from sliding into an unconscious void. The agony in his lower body forced him to suck in air in great wheezing gasps. He slowly sunk to his knees beside the inert form of the girl, clutching his groin and swaying in pain.

Pitt clenched his teeth together until his jaws ached, damming back any outcry from the agony. He dug his knees into the soft sand and swayed back and forth. Discovered hunched over an unconscious girl holding his hands tightly between his legs could result in embarrassing questions. Fortunately, except for a circle of beachboys and hotel guests who were seated around a small fire about two hundred feet away, the beach was vacant.

Four minutes passed; four minutes during which the grinding torment finally faded to a dull, throbbing ache. It was then he noticed something gleaming in Summer's hand, something glasslike reflected by the flames of the flickering tiki torches. He crawled over to the girl, crouched over her quiet form, and gently pulled a hypodermic syringe from between her loosely clasped fingers.

Pitt was at a loss. In the faint light Summer looked no more than twenty-five, gentle and sweet. Holding the syringe, he wondered what it held as he dropped the liquid-filled glass tube carefully into his breast pocket.

He leaned over, awkwardly heaved the girl over his shoulder, and rose shakily to his feet. It had suddenly occurred to him that she probably had a couple of friends lurking about in the shadows; he wasn't about to wait for the posse to block the pass. His hotel was a good three blocks away, so he balanced his load, steadied himself, and began limping stiffly across the sand.

His one hope of getting past the roving crowds of tourists who wandered the sidewalks at night was to skirt through the heavy foliage of the gardens. He certainly didn't want to meet cruising policemen or a do-gooder vacationer who might conjure up the notion of playing Herbert Hero and rescuing little Eva from the villainous Simon LaPitt.

Along the sidewalks it would have been an easy walk of five minutes, but it took Pitt twenty by way of the backyard jungle. He paused in the shadows, catching his breath and waited for a group of drunken party goers to stagger out of view. He savored the delicate fragrance that whispered about Summer's body. This time he recognized it as plumeria, not an uncommon scent in the Hawaiian Islands, but it was the first time Pitt had sensed its presence on a woman.

His hotel was just across the street now, the lights behind the lobby door beckoning with womblike safety. At the first lull in traffic, Pitt covered the distance on the run, his face strained from the ache in his groin and his lungs tortured from the physical effort of carrying a deadweight over a four-hundred-yard obstacle course in the dark. He threaded his way quickly around the parked cars at the curb, edged up to the doorway of the building, and cast a wary eye in the lobby.

His luck deserted him momentarily. A cleaning woman was vacuuming the carpet outside the elevators, a huge dark-skinned behemoth of a Hawaiian woman with an *I'll-scream-for-a-cop-look*. He moved around the corner and trotted down the ramp leading to the underground garage. Except for a sprinkling of cars stationed throughout the dim, concrete interior, the garage was empty. He found an open elevator,

entered, and pushed the panel button and then leaned against the heavy teak railing that ran along the closetlike walls.

Pitt was a damp mass of sweat now; the exertion and the humidity of the night had combined to push him within a hairline of total exhaustion. As he stood there, stooped under Summer's weight, he managed to catch his breath. The elevator hummed monotonously and cooperated by not opening on any other floor than the one Pitt had selected.

The panel light blinked 10. Pitt's luck stuck by him —the hall was clear in both directions. Groping clumsily in his pants pocket for several frustrating seconds, he finally managed to extract a key and shove it into the lock of a carved rosewood door marked 1010.

A plushly decorated suite was a luxury Pitt could hardly afford on his salary, but he justified its existence under the excuse that it was his first vacation in three years.

He entered the bedroom and dumped Summer unceremoniously on the bed. Another time, staring down at a woman who was so delicate and smooth, he would have felt desire. Not tonight. Mentally, emotionally, and physically, Pitt had had it. The day began and ended as one grueling endurance run. Pitt left Summer blissfully unconscious and entered the bathroom where he undressed and took a shower.

Nothing made sense. Why would a perfect stranger want to kill him? His only beneficiary was his little white-haired mother, and unless she'd given up charity teas and hooked rugs, and had taken up with the Mafia, she'd have no motive. Besides, he grinned to himself at the sheer fantasy of it all, what proof did

he have that the hypodermic syringe held poison?

A drug? That was a semicredible possibility. But again, why? He knew no military codes he could think of, no nuclear bomb secrets, no classified missile locations, no top secret plans for the destruction of the world. His thoughts wandered back to Summer's magnificent beauty. Then he finally forced his mind back to the reality of the moment, closing the tap and stepping out of the shower stall. He slipped a robe over his broad shoulders and, returning to the bedroom, placed a damp washcloth over the girl's forehead, noting with a tinge of sadistic pleasure that she would wear a healthy-looking bruise on her jaw in the morning.

He shook Summer roughly by both shoulders. Slowly, reluctantly, not wanting to part with the contentment of oblivion, and murmuring incoherently in a soft voice, her big gray eyes crept open. Awaking in a strange place would have startled most women. Not Summer. She was tough. Pitt could almost see the circuits of her mind burst into sudden operation. Her eyes darted about the room, first to Pitt, then to the door, to the balcony, and back to Pitt again. She stared at him casually, but a little too casually to be genuine. Then she raised her hand and lightly touched her jaw, wincing at the contact.

"You hit me?" It was more a question than a statement.

"Yes." He grinned. "And now that I have you on home ground, I think I'll rape you."

At last her eyes came wide. "You wouldn't dare."

"How do you know I haven't already?"

She almost fell for it; her hand began moving down across her lower stomach and then suddenly stopped. "You're not that perverted."

"Who said I was?"

She looked at Pitt in a very peculiar way. "I was told . . ." She stopped herself and avoided his eyes.

"You should be more careful," Pitt said reproachfully. "Believing nasty old rumors and running up and down Waikiki Beach jabbing hypodermic needles into defenseless men can get you into a heap of trouble."

She stared at him for a few seconds, her lips moving as if she were about to reply, but uncertainty slowly welled in those fantastic gray eyes. "I don't know what you mean."

"No matter." Pitt turned his back on her and reached for a telephone. "I'll let the police figure your game. That's what honest citizens like me pay them for."

"A mistake." Her voice suddenly turned hard and cold. "I'll scream rape and with these marks on my face, who will they believe, you or me?"

Pitt picked up the telephone and began punching the numbered buttons. "There's not the slightest doubt that they'd believe you. That is, until Adrian Hunter testifies in my defense. She probably has a few marks of her own." Pitt turned his attention to the phone. The voice that answered on the other end of the line surrendered after the fifth hello and hung up. At the dial tone, Pitt said: "Hello, I'd like to report an assault . . ."

That was as far as he got. Summer leaped off the bed and pushed the receiver down. "Please, you don't understand." Her voice was low and desperate.

"That's the understatement of the evening," Pitt said angrily. He grabbed her by the shoulders, squeezing hard and staring unblinking, only a few inches from her widening pupils. "Kick a man in the balls and jam a hypodermic needle into his back and then act like

34 PACIFIC VORTEX!

little Miss Rebecca of Sunnybrook Farm when you
screw up. Just what in hell is your game?"

She started to struggle, then relaxed almost immediately. "You gangster!" Her voice was a savage
whisper.

The obsolete expression caught Pitt off guard. Slowly he released his hold and stepped back. "That's me,
one of big Al Capone's torpedoes, fresh off the boat
from Chicago."

"I wish to heaven I'd . . ." She broke off and crossed
her arms and massaged the reddening skin on her
shoulders. "You are a devil."

Pitt felt no hate in return, only a touch of remorse
as he noted the angry masses of red welts where his
fingers had dug into her flesh.

There was a long pause before she spoke. "I'll tell
you what you wish to know." Despite the subtle
change in tone, there was nothing soft in the coldness
in her eyes. "But first, could you help me to the bathroom. I feel . . . I think I'm going to be sick."

Pitt extended his hand and grabbed her wrist, feeling her muscles tighten under his grip. Suddenly she
braced one foot against the railing of the bed and
threw every ounce of her slender body into a shoulder
block to Pitt's stomach. She caught him off balance; he
fell backward over a chair, crashing to the floor and
taking the bedstand lamp with him. Pitt had hardly
collided with the shag carpet when Summer jerked
open the sliding door and vanished out onto the
balcony.

Pitt made no effort to rise, but leaned back and
relaxed into a more comfortable position on the floor.
Ten seconds passed. He could hold it back no longer;
he began to laugh. "Next time you exit a man's tenth-

floor apartment, you'd best carry a parachute."

She slowly stepped back into the bedroom, her lovely face livid with rage. "There is an evil word for you."

"I can think of at least a dozen," he said, smiling politely.

She moved to the other side of the room, putting as much space as the room allowed between them, and lowered herself into a chair, her eyes exploring his. "If I answer your questions, what then?"

"Nothing," Pitt said quietly. "When you tell a story I can swallow without gagging, you're free to leave."

"I don't believe you."

"My dear girl, I'm not the Boston Strangler or Jack the Ripper, and I assure you, I'm not in the habit of abducting innocent virgins from Waikiki Beach."

"Please," she implored softly, "It was not my intent to harm you. I must work for my government just as you must work for yours. You have information I was ordered to obtain. The content of the syringe was an ordinary solution of scopolamine."

"Truth serum?"

"Yes. Your reputation with women made you a prime suspect."

"You're not making sense."

"The United States Navy, or at least its intelligence section, has reason to believe one of Miss Hunter's lovers has been trying to gain classified information concerning her father's fleet operations. I was ordered to investigate your involvement with her. That's all there is to it."

That wasn't all there was to it. There was no doubt in Pitt's mind that she was lying. He also knew that she was trying to buy time. The only classified in-

formation that Adrian Hunter possessed was how the Navy's up-and-coming crop of future admirals rated on her personal lovemaking scale.

As Pitt rose from the floor and moved in front of her, she saw the brutal gleam in his eyes and she visibly tensed. Confused and angry, Pitt found himself sensing a strong degree of compassion toward the girl. He gazed at the red hair tousled over one eye, and the long slender hands reclining loosely on an inviting lap.

"I'm sorry it turned out this way," he said. "Damned sorry." He felt a little foolish. "Too bad you ruined a good thing. You're not with Naval Intelligence, dear heart. You're not even a bona fide American. Hell, nobody's used the term *gangster* in this country since the 1930s. You also failed your secret agent test. No professional would have bought that phony telephone call to the police, but you did. Anyway, the Navy isn't in the habit of allowing their female operators to run loose among villain types minus a backup crew armed to the teeth within screaming distance. You don't carry a purse, and your dress is too tight to hide a transmitter to warn the watchdogs when the going gets nasty." The shock treatment was working too well. Her face drained of all color and she truly looked sick.

He went on. "And, in case you think I might be as pure and virginal as you are, you're sadly mistaken. I checked you over from hair to painted toenails when I carried you here from the beach. The only thing you've got on under that dress is a tiny holster for the syringe, taped to the inside of your left thigh."

Summer's eyes were glazed with revulsion. Pitt couldn't remember when a woman had looked at him like that. She turned and stared at the bathroom as

if she were making up her mind to throw up in the
sink or on the shag carpet. The sink won. She rose unsteadily from the chair and reeled into the bathroom,
slamming the door.

He soon heard the sound of water gushing as the
commode was flushed; then the faucet on the sink was
turned on. Pitt walked over to the balcony and gazed
at the twinkling lights of Honolulu in the distance,
while far below, the ocean breakers droned against
the beach. He lingered at the balcony perhaps a little
too long.

He was jolted back to reality by the sound of
running water in the bathroom; the flow was too constant, too prolonged for normal routine. It took him
three steps to reach the door—locked from the inside.
No time for a theatrical "are you in there" line. Bal-
ancing on one leg, he kicked hard at the lock with the
other, revealing an empty room.

Summer was gone. Her only trace was a trail of
knotted bath towels, tied to the shower curtain railing
and stretching over the windowsill. Casting an anxious
eye below, he saw the last towel dangling only four
feet above a chaise lounge on the balcony belonging to
the room beneath his. No lights were showing, no
shouts of alarm from the tenants. She had escaped
safely. For that he was thankful.

He stood there recalling her face—a face that was
probably compassionate and tender and gay.

Then he cursed himself for letting her get away.

CHAPTER 4

It was early morning. Thin, ghostly trails of vapor were left behind from a light rain that had come and gone during the night. The humidity would have been stifling but for the tradewinds that swept clean the sodden atmosphere and dispersed it over the blue ocean beyond the encircling reefs. The sandy strip of beach that curled from Diamond Head to the Reef Hotel was empty, but already tourists were beginning to trickle from the great glass and concrete hotels to begin a day of sightseeing and shopping excursions.

Lying crosswise on the sweat-dampened sheets of his bed, a naked Pitt gazed out the open window at a pair of myna birds who were fighting over a disinterested female perched in a neighboring palm tree. Black feathers flew in profusion as the birds squawked riotously, creating a disturbance heard for nearly a block. Then, just as the miniature brawl was about to reach its final round, Pitt's door chime sounded. Reluctantly, he slipped on a terrycloth robe, walked yawning to the door, and opened it.

"Good morning, Dirk." A short, fire-haired man with a protruding face, stood in the hall. "I hope I'm not interrupting a romantic interlude?"

Pitt stretched out his hand. "No, I'm quite alone. Come on in."

The little man crossed the threshold, looked unhurriedly about the room, then stepped out on the balcony, taking in the splendid view. He was nattily dressed in a light tan suit and vest, complete with watch and chain. He had a neatly trimmed Ahab, the whaler's red beard, with two evenly spaced white streaks on each side of the chin, presenting a facial growth that was strikingly uncommon. The olive face was beaded with perspiration either from the humidity or from climbing the stairs, or both. When most men wove their lives through the channels of least resistance, Admiral James Sandecker, Chief Director of the National Underwater and Marine Agency, hit every barrier, every obstacle in the shortest line from point A to point B.

Sandecker turned and nodded over his shoulder. "How in hell do you get any sleep with those damned crows screeching in your ears?"

"Fortunately, they don't fly amok until the sun's up." Pitt motioned to the sectional couch. "Get comfortable, Admiral, while I get the coffee going."

"Forget the coffee. Nine hours ago I was in Washington. The jet lag has my body chemistry all screwed up. I'd prefer a drink."

Pitt pulled out a bottle of Scotch from a cabinet and poured. He glanced across the room only to be met by Sandecker's twinkling blue eyes. What was coming? The head of one of the nation's most prestigious governmental agencies didn't fly six thousand miles just to chat with his Special Projects Director about birds. He handed Sandecker a glass and asked, "What brings you from Washington? I thought you were buried in plans for the new deep-sea current expedition?"

"You don't know why I'm here?" He was using his

quiet cynical tone, the one that always made Pitt involuntarily cringe. "Thanks to your meddling in affairs that don't concern you, I had to make a special trip to bail you out of one mess and throw you into another."

"I don't follow."

"A talent I know only too well." There was the slight hint of a derisive smile. "It seems you aggravated a hornet's nest when you showed up with the *Starbuck*'s message capsule. You unknowingly set off an earthquake in the Pentagon that was picked up on a seismograph in California. It also made you a big-man-on-campus with the Navy Department. I'm only a retired castoff to those boys, so I wasn't offered a peek behind the curtain. I was simply asked by the Joint Chiefs of Staff, courteously, I might add, to fly to Hawaii posthaste, explain your new assignment, and arrange for your loan to the Navy."

Pitt's eyes narrowed. "Who's behind this?"

"Admiral Leigh Hunter of the 101st Salvage Fleet."

"You can't be serious?"

"He personally requested you."

Pitt shook his head angrily. "This is asinine. What's to stop me from refusing?"

"You force me to remind you," Sandecker said calmly, "that in spite of your status with NUMA, you're still carried on the active rolls as a major in the Air Force. And, as you well know, the Joint Chiefs frown upon insubordination."

Pitt's eyes looked resentfully into Sandecker's. "It won't work."

"Yes it will," Sandecker said. "You're a damn good marine engineer, the best I've got. I've already met with Hunter and I minced no words in telling him so."

"There are other complications," Pitt didn't sound very confident, "that haven't been considered."

"You mean the fact that you've been laying Hunter's daughter?"

Pitt stiffened. "Do you know what that makes you, Admiral?"

"A sly, old devious son of a bitch?" Sandecker asked. "Actually, there's much more to this business than you've taken the trouble to notice."

"You sound ominous as hell," Pitt said, unimpressed.

"I mean to," Sandecker replied seriously. "You're not joining the Navy to learn a new trade. You're to act as liaison between Hunter and myself. Before this thing's over with, NUMA will be involved up to its ears. NUMA has been ordered to help the Navy with whatever oceanographical data they demand."

"Equipment?"

"If they ask for it."

"Finding a submarine that disappeared six months ago won't be a picnic."

"The *Starbuck* is only half the act," Sandecker said. "The Navy Department has compiled thirty-eight documented cases of ships over the past thirty years that have sailed into a circular-shaped area north of the Hawaiian Islands and vanished. They want to know why!"

"Ships disappear in the Atlantic and Indian oceans too. It's not an unheard-of occurrence."

"True, but under normal circumstances, marine disasters leave traces behind; bits of flotsam, oil slicks, even bodies. Wreckage will also float ashore to give a hint of a missing ship's fate, but no such remains have turned up from the ships that vanished in the Pacific Vortex."

"The Pacific Vortex?"

"That's the name the seamen in the maritime unions coined for it. They won't sign on a ship whose course takes them through the area."

"Thirty-eight ships," Pitt repeated slowly. "What about radio contact? A ship would have to go down in seconds not to transmit a Mayday signal."

"No distress signals were ever received."

Pitt didn't say anything. Sandecker simply sipped his Scotch, offering no further comment. As if on cue, the myna birds began their noisy antics again, shattering the brief silence. Pitt shut them from his mind and stared steadfastly at the floor; there were a hundred questions swirling around in his head, but it was far too early in the morning for him to conjure up theories on mysterious ship disappearances.

After the silence had dragged on a bit too long, Pitt spoke: "Okay, so thirty-seven ships will never reach port again. That leaves the thirty-eighth, the *Starbuck*. The Navy has the exact position from the capsule. What are they waiting for? If they locate the remains, their salvage ships won't require an act of God to raise her from ten fathoms."

"It's not all that elementary."

"Why not? The Navy raised the submarine F-4 from sixty fathoms right here on Oahu off the entrance of Pearl Harbor. And that was back in 1915."

"The armchair admirals who do their thinking through computers today, aren't convinced that the message you found is genuine. At least not until they've had time to analyze the handwriting."

Pitt sighed. "They suspect the dumb ass who brought in the capsule of perpetrating a hoax."

"Something like that."

Pitt forced back a laugh. "So that, at least, explains the transfer. Hunter wants to keep an eye on me."

"You made the mistake of reading the capsule's message. This alone takes you from the ranks of innocent bystander, and classifies you as top secret material. Also, the 101st Fleet wants to borrow our new long-range FXH helicopter. None of the Navy's pilots are checked out on it. You are. And, if an un-friendly nation got it in their heads to try and locate and salvage Uncle Sam's newest and most advanced nuclear sub before we do—it's first come, first serve in international waters—you're a sitting duck for their undercover agents to kidnap in order to discover the *Starbuck*'s position."

"It's nice to be known and loved," Pitt said. "But you forget; I'm not the only one who knows the *Starbuck*'s final resting place."

"Yes, but you're the easiest to come by. Hunter and his staff are safely confined to Pearl Harbor, working around-the-clock in an attempt to clear up the puzzle." The admiral paused, stuck a massive cigar in his face, lit it, and puffed meditatively. "Knowing you like I do, my boy, an enemy agent wouldn't have to use muscle. They'd simply send their most seductive Mata Hari to the nearest bar and let you pick *her* up."

Sandecker noticed the sudden look of pain that gripped Pitt's face but he went on.

"I might add, for your own information, that the 101st Fleet is one of the finest undercover salvage operations in the world."

"Undercover?"

"Talking to you is like floundering on a reef," San-decker said with forbearance. "Admiral Hunter and his men have raised a British bomber from the water only ten miles from the Cuban shore right under the nose of Castro. Then they salvaged the *New Century* off Libya, the *Southwind* in the Black Sea, the *Tari*

Maru within sight of the lights of China. In each case the ships were all salvaged by the 101st before the nations whose waters the vessels sank in, knew the score. Don't underestimate Hunter and his gang of underwater scrap mongers. They're second to none."

"The *Starbuck*," Pitt said, "why all the cloak and dagger?"

"For one thing, Dupree's final position is an impossibility. The only way the *Starbuck* could possibly be where his message said it lay, was for the ship to fly. A feat marine architects haven't as yet accomplished. Not with ten thousand tons of steel, at any rate."

Pitt looked steadily at Sandecker. "It's got to be out there. Underwater detection systems are far more advanced now. It doesn't figure that the *Starbuck* remains lost, or that a massive search turned up absolutely nothing."

Sandecker held up his empty glass and stared at it. "As long as there are seas, ships, and men, there will be strange unsolved mysteries. The *Starbuck* is only one."

CHAPTER 5

Pitt stood under the shower nozzle; the steaming hot water opening his pores. After finishing under a heavy spray of cold water, he stepped out, toweled, and shaved the stubble from the night before, taking his time. He hadn't the slightest intention of arriving at Hunter's headquarters on time. Mustn't spoil the old bastard my first day on the job, he thought, grinning in the mirror.

He decided on a white suit with a pink shirt. As he went through the intricacy of tying his tie, it occurred to him that it might not be a bad idea to carry a little protection. Summer had failed, but nevertheless, Pitt began to see the odds of his living to a ripe old age fade with each passing hour. He wasn't about to compete in hand-to-hand combat with highly trained, professional intelligence agents.

The Mauser, Model 712 Schnell Fueur Pistole Serial Number 47405, could only be described as a positively bloodthirsty firearm. It was a unique handgun due to its ability to fire one shot at a time or, automatically, like a machine gun. It was the perfect weapon to induce terror into any poor unfortunate who found himself gazing helplessly into its muzzle.

Pitt casually tossed the gun onto the bed and reached into the suitcase again, retrieving a wooden

shoulder holster. The narrow end had a metal railing that slid on a notch in the broomstick-styled grip, converting the gun into a carbine for long-distance targets; it also served as a grasp when firing on full automatic. Pitt then inserted the gun into the holster and, along with a fifty-shot clip, wrapped the ugly killing machine in a beach towel.

Before the elevator reached the lobby, it obediently halted at every other floor to take on new passengers until it could hold no more. Pitt wondered to himself what thoughts his fellow riders might entertain if they'd had any inkling of what he carried under the towel. After the throng bumped shoulders as they spilled into the lobby, Pitt remained and punched the panel button marked B and rode down to the basement parking area. He unlocked the AC Cobra, shoved the Mauser into a narrow space behind the driver's seat, and climbed in behind the wheel.

He eased the car up the exit ramp and joined the traffic flow of Kalakaua Avenue, aiming its blunt snout toward the northern end of the city. The palm trees lining the street leaned their arched trunks over the block-long rows of contemporary-designed shops and offices, while the sidewalks snaked in a dense-moving column of tourists dressed in brightly colored shirts and dresses. The sun was strong and the savage glare bounced off the asphalt, causing Pitt to squint before he groped over the narrow dashboard for his sunglasses.

He was already over an hour late for his meeting with Hunter, but there was something he had to do, some small hunch in the back of his brain that begged for a chance to be heard. He didn't quite know what he expected to find as the tires crunched the red

volcanic pebbles that lined the driveway, but he had driven two miles out of his way and there was no reason not to see it through. He parked the car and walked past a small, neatly carved sign that read: BERNICE PAUAHI BISHOP MUSEUM OF POLYNESIAN ETHNOLOGY AND NATURAL HISTORY.

The main hall, with its balconies circling the upper levels, was crowded with neatly spaced exhibits of outrigger canoes, stuffed fish and birds, replicas of primitive grass huts, and strange, ugly carvings of ancient Hawaiian gods. Pitt spotted a tall, white-haired, proudly erect man arranging a collection of shells in a glass case. George Papaaloa had the true Hawaiian look, the wide brown face, the jutting chin, large lips, misty brown eyes, and a graceful way of effortlessly moving his body. He looked up and, recognizing Pitt, he waved.

"Ah, Dirk. Your visit makes my day one of joy. Come into my office where we can sit down."

Pitt followed him into a neat Spartan office. The furniture was ancient, but refinished in a varnished sheen, and the books lining the walls were free of dust. Papaaloa sat down behind the desk and motioned Pitt toward a Victorian settee.

"Tell me, my friend, have you discovered King Kamehameha's final resting place?"

Pitt leaned back. "I spent the better part of last week diving along the Kona Coast and found nothing that resembled a burial cave."

"Our legends say he was placed in a cavern beneath the water. Maybe it was one of the rivers."

"You know better than I, George, that during the dry season your rivers are nothing more than dry gulches."

Papaaloa shrugged. "Perhaps it is best that his burial place is never found and that his remains lie in peace."

"No one wants to disturb your king. There is no treasure involved. Kamehameha the Great would be a great archaeological find. Nothing more. And, instead of some damp old cave, his bones would rest in a fine new tomb in Honolulu, revered by all."

Papaaloa's eyes looked sad. "I wonder if our great king would appreciate being gawked at by you *haoles*."

"I think he could tolerate we mainland *haoles* if he knew that eighty percent of his kingdom was now populated by Orientals."

"Sad, but true. What the Japanese failed to take with bombs in the forties, they took with cash in the seventies and eighties. Someday it wouldn't surprise me to get up and see the rising sun waving in the tradewinds over the Iolani Palace." Papaaloa looked at Pitt steadily, his face expressionless. "There isn't much time left for my people. Two, maybe three generations and we will be totally melted into the other races. My heritage dies with me. I am the last of my family with pure Hawaiian blood." He waved his arm around the room. "That's why I have made this place my life's work. To preserve the culture of a dying race, my race."

Papaaloa stopped, gazing off vacantly out a small window at the Koolau Mountains. "My mind wanders more as I get older. Now then, you didn't come here to hear an old man ramble on. What's on your mind?"

"I want to know something about an area of the sea called the Pacific Vortex."

Papaaloa's eyes narrowed. "Pacific Vor...ah yes, I know the place you mean." He looked thoughtful

for a few moments and then spoke softly, almost in a whisper.

> A ka makani hema pa
> Ka Mauna o Kanoli Ikea
> A kanaka ke kauahiwi hoopii.

"Hawaiian is a very musical tongue," Pitt said.

Papaaloa nodded. "That's because it has only seven consonants: *h*, *k*, *l*, *m*, *n*, *p*, and *w*. There can be no more than one consonant to a syllable. Translated in English the poem means:

> When the south wind blows
> The mountain of Kanoli is seen
> And the summit seems peopled.

"Kanoli?" Pitt asked.

"A mythical island to the north. According to legend, many centuries ago a family tribe left the islands far to the southwest, probably Tahiti, and traveled in a large canoe across the great ocean to join other tribesmen who had immigrated to Hawaii decades before. But the gods were angry at the people's flight from their homeland, so they changed the position of the stars, causing the navigator of the canoe to lose his way. They missed Hawaii by traveling many miles to the north where they sighted Kanoli and landed there. The gods had truly punished the tribe, for Kanoli was a barren island with few coconut and fruit trees, taro plants, and no cool, clear streams of pure water. The people made sacrifices and cried out to the gods for forgiveness. Their pleas went ignored, so the people threw off their cruel gods and worked very hard under the harshest of obstacles to

make Kanoli a garden. Many died in the attempt, but after several generations the people of Kanoli had built a great civilization out of the volcanic rock of the island, and, pleased at their accomplishment, they proclaimed themselves as their own gods."

Pitt said: "Sounds like the trials of our Pilgrims, Quakers, and Mormons."

Papaaloa uttered a long negative sigh. "Not the same. Your people kept their religion as a staff to lean on. The natives of Kanoli saw themselves as better than the gods they had once worshiped. After all, had they not built a paradise without them? They had overstepped the bounds of mortals. They began to raid Kauai, Oahu, Hawaii, and the other islands, killing and pillaging, taking the fairest of women back as slaves. The primitive Hawaiians were helpless. How could you fight men who acted and fought like gods? Their only hope was their faith in their own deities. They prayed for deliverance and they were heard. The gods of the Hawaiians caused the sea to rise up and bury the evil Kanolians forever."

"My people also have a similar legend of a land being swallowed by the sea. It was called Atlantis."

"I've read of it. Plato describes it quite romantically in his *Timaeus and Critias*."

"It seems you're an authority on myths other than Hawaiian."

Papaaloa smiled. "Legends are like knots on a string; one leads to another. I could tell you of tales handed down through the centuries in many faraway lands that are very nearly identical to, but predate, those of the Christian Bible."

"Clairvoyants predict Atlantis will rise again."

"The same is said of Kanoli."

"I wonder," Pitt muttered, "how much truth lies behind the legend."

Papaaloa leaned his elbows on the desk and gazed at Pitt over clasped hands.

"Strange," he said slowly, "most strange. He used the same words."

Pitt looked up questioningly. "He?"

"Yes, it was a long time ago. Right after World War Two. A man came to the museum every day for a week and studied every book and manuscript in our library. He was also researching the legend of Kanoli."

"There must have been others through the years who found the story interesting."

"No, you are the first since the other."

"You have a razor-sharp memory, my friend, to recall someone that far back."

Papaaloa unclasped his hands and stared at Pitt hesitantly. "I never forgot the incident simply because I never forgot the man. You see, he was a giant with golden eyes."

Beyond puzzlement lies frustration, the neutralizing cloud hiding the next move. When a man enters that cloud, he is a man outside himself, a man who moves and acts instinctively. It was in such a state that Pitt found himself half an hour before noon, minutes after leaving George Papaaloa at the museum.

His mind was confused, shifting gears back and forth, trying desperately to piece the first two parts of the puzzle together. An old gray Dodge truck pulled out of the museum's parking lot and followed close behind. Pitt was ready to dismiss the trailing truck as fantasy—his subconscious was beginning to see enemy agents, complete with trench coats and beady eyes,

lurking behind every clump of philodendron. But as he drove toward Pearl Harbor, the truck stayed with him around every corner as if tied by a rope.

Pitt made another turn and increased his speed slightly, his eyes now on the rearview mirror. The truck also turned, lagged a bit, and then accelerated, closing the gap to its previous position. Pitt snaked the AC through traffic for two miles and then swung onto Mount Tantalus Drive. He drove smoothly around the hairpin curves that curled up the fern-forested mountainside of the Koolau Range, gradually pushing the gas pedal a millimeter closer to the floor with each turn. Glancing in the mirror, he studied the driver of the truck who was fighting with the wheel in a fanatical attempt to stay with the elusive little red car.

Then the unexpected happened. With no telltale warning of a blasting report, a bullet smacked into the sideview mirror on the door, shattering the tiny circular glass and then passing through. The game was getting rough. Pitt stomped on the accelerator and put some distance between him and the pursuing Dodge.

The son of a bitch was using a silencer, Pitt cursed silently. It had been a stupid move driving out of town. He'd have been relatively safe in downtown traffic. Now his only hope was to get back to Honolulu before the next shot took the top of his head off. With a little luck he might happen onto a cruising police car. But Pitt was stunned by the next glance in the mirror. The truck had pulled to within ten yards of the AC's bumper.

The road reached the two-thousand-foot crest and started the sharp descent in a series of meandering arcs to the city below. Pitt roared onto a mile-long

straightaway and the truck made an effort to close. Pitt held his speed constant in readiness for the next corner, crouching as low as the confining interior of the AC would allow. The needle on his speedometer was touching seventy-five as the pursuing driver crossed the centerline of the road and pulled abreast. Pitt shot a look out the window; he never forgot the picture of the black, long-haired man who grinned back at him through irregular, tobacco-stained teeth. It was only a flicker in time, but Pitt saw every detail of the pockmarked face, the black burning eyes, the huge hooked nose covered by swarthy walnut skin.

All Pitt could feel was frustration; frustration at not being able to shoot back, to blow that bastard's face to pieces. He had a perfectly good machine gun resting behind his seat not ten inches away, and he couldn't even reach it. A contortionist four feet tall might have been able to get his hands on the Mauser's grip, but not six-foot three-inch Pitt.

The next option was to simply stop the car, get out, lean back in and grab the gun from behind the seat, unwrap the towel that covered it, pop off the safety, and begin firing. The only problem was the timing. The old truck was too close. The hook-nosed driver could have stopped his truck and pumped five shots into Pitt's guts before he'd even reached the towel-unwrapping stage.

The road ahead swept sharply to the left into a dangerous hairpin corner marked by a yellow sign whose black letters proclaimed: SLOW TO 20. Pitt drifted through the curve at fifty-five. The truck couldn't handle the centrifugal pull and lost ground, dropping back momentarily before the driver called on his ample supply of horsepower.

Plan after plan shot through Pitt's mind, each new

one discarded along with the ones before. Then, as he braked for the next corner, he began to apply still heavier pressure to the accelerator while watching the rearview mirror, studying the movements of the truck's driver as he began to pull even with the AC once more.

It was small consolation that the man was not aiming a gun at Pitt's cranium. He meant to force Pitt off the road, over a steep cliff that fell several hundred feet to the valley below.

Another two hundred yards and they would meet the next curve, yet Pitt maintained his speed. The gray Dodge inched closer to the sports car's front fender. One final nudge and Pitt would be airborne. Then, with only a hundred more yards to go, Pitt mashed the accelerator down hard, held it, and suddenly let up and braked. The abrupt maneuver caught the grinning stalker off guard. He had also increased his speed, attempting to stay even with his quarry, working again toward the position that would send Pitt hurtling over the cliff edge. Too late! They were on the curve.

Pitt kept braking hard; he downshifted, and threw the car around the bend, the tires shrieking in frictional protest across the pavement. The AC was in a four-wheel drift, the back end beginning to break away. A quick twist to the right and the skid was compensated and then, accelerating again, Pitt shot onto the next straight. A glance in the mirror showed that the road behind him was empty. The gray truck had vanished.

He slowed down, relying on gravity and momentum to carry the car for the next half mile. Still no sign of the truck. Cautiously, Pitt spun a U-turn and drove back toward the curve, ready to crank another hundred-eighty-degree turn if the old Dodge should

suddenly come into sight. He reached the curve, stopped the car, and got out, walking to the edge of the road.

The dust far below was settling very slowly upon the tropical underbrush. At the bottom of the drop, just beyond the base of the steep-sided cliff, the remains of the gray truck lay with its engine torn from the frame. The driver was nowhere to be seen. Pitt had almost given up searching when he spotted an inert form high on a telephone pole about a hundred feet to the left of the wreckage.

It was a grisly sight. It looked as though the driver had tried to leap clear before the old Dodge began its flight over the precipice. He'd missed the edge and had fallen, tumbling through the air for nearly two hundred feet before he struck a telephone pole perched in a concrete base. The body was impaled on a metal foot spike used by telephone repairmen for line maintenance. As Pitt stood entranced, the bottom section of the pole slowly turned from brown to red as if painted by some unseen hand; like a flank of beef hanging on a meathook.

Pitt drove down Mount Tantalus past the Manoa Valley lookout until he reached the nearest house. He went up onto the vine-covered porch and asked an elderly Japanese woman if he might use her telephone to report the accident. The woman bowed endlessly and motioned Pitt to a phone in the kitchen. He dialed Admiral Hunter first, quickly relating the story and giving the location.

The admiral's voice came over the receiver like an amplified bullhorn, forcing Pitt to hold the blast a few inches from his ear. "Don't call the Honolulu police," Hunter bellowed. "Give me ten minutes to get our security men on the wreckage before the local

traffic investigators foul up the area. You got that?"

"I think I can manage it."

"Good!" Hunter went on without touching on Pitt's sarcasm. "Ten minutes. Then move your tail out to Pearl Harbor. We've got work to do."

Pitt acknowledged and hung up.

Pitt waited ten minutes, answering a multitude of questions about the crash shot in rapid fire by the little Oriental woman. Then he picked up the phone again and asked the operator for the Honolulu police. When the gravel-throated voice requested his name after he volunteered the location, he said nothing and quietly replaced the receiver in its cradle.

He thanked the owner of the house and backed away into the safety of his car. He sat there behind the wheel for a good five minutes, sweating from the humidity of the tropical heat and the unyielding leather of the bucket seat.

Something didn't jell; something he'd missed came back to tug at his mind, some line of thought that couldn't be translated.

Then suddenly he had it. He started the car quickly and left twin streaks of Goodyear rubber on the worn asphalt as he sped back toward the wreck site. Five minutes to the telephone, twenty minutes spent dawdling as though time meant nothing, three minutes back, twenty-eight minutes in all, wasted.

He should have guessed there'd be more than one of them on his trail. The AC skidded to an abrupt stop and Pitt ran once more to the edge of the drop.

The wreckage was just as he'd left it, all twisted and torn like a child's smashed toy. The telephone pole was as he left it too, standing forlornly in the center of the palisade, its crossbars clutching wires that

stretched off into infinity. The footspikes were still there too. But the driver's body had disappeared. Only the red stain remained, clotting and crystalizing under the onslaught of the morning sun.

CHAPTER 6

A Quonset hut—it looked more like the dilapidated office of a salvage yard—was the saddest excuse for an operations building since the Civil War. The rusting corrugated roof and cracked, dust-coated windows were encompassed by an unkempt sea of weeds. But at the paint-chipped and weathered door, Pitt was barred by a marine sergeant armed with a holstered automatic Colt .45.

"Your identification, please." It was more a demand than a request.

Pitt held up his ID card. "Dirk Pitt. I'm reporting to Admiral Hunter."

"I'm afraid I must see your orders, sir."

Pitt wasn't in the mood for gung ho procedure. Marines irritated him, all puffy-chested, eager for a fight, looking for any excuse to break out in a chorus of the "Marine Hymn."

"I'll show my papers to the officer in charge and no one else."

"My orders are . . ."

"Your orders are to check identification cards against a list of people who may enter the building," Pitt said coldly. "No one gave you permission to play hero and check papers." Pitt motioned at the door. "Now, if you'll be so kind."

The red-faced sergeant looked as though he could not decide whether to haul off and punch Pitt in the mouth. But he hesitated a moment, studied the icy expression on Pitt's face, turned, opened the door behind him, and nodded for Pitt to follow.

The interior of the Quonset hut was empty but for a couple of overturned chairs, a dusty file cabinet, and several faded newspapers scattered over the floor. The place smelled musty and cobwebs were dangling from the ceiling. Pitt was thoroughly puzzled until the sergeant stopped near the back of the deserted room and stomped twice on the wooded flooring. Hearing a muffled acknowledgment, he lifted a perfectly concealed trapdoor and motioned Pitt to descend down a dimly lit stairway. Then he stepped aside as the concealed door dropped behind him, barely missing Pitt's descending head by a few inches.

Shades of Edgar Allan Poe, Pitt thought. At the bottom of the stairs he pushed aside a heavy curtain and stepped into a carnival of noisy activity. Before him was a large underground bunker stretching almost two hundred feet. The overhead fluorescent lights revealed an operations room to end operations rooms. From paneled wall to paneled wall lay a thick beige carpet covered by desks, computers, and teletype machines that would have easily meshed into the plushest offices of Madison Avenue.

A bevy of attractive girls in prim and proper naval uniforms unsmilingly manned most of the desks, some furiously typing away at their respective video displays, some moving with fluidlike grace around the row of computers that stood in the center of the room. Twenty male officers in Navy whites stood in isolated groups examining computer readout sheets or jotting down a series of complex notations on the green chalk

boards which covered the walls. The whole scene looked like a high-class betting parlor. The only thing missing was the monotonous voice of a race announcer.

Admiral Hunter caught sight of Pitt, straightened, smiled his sly fox-toothed smile, and strode forward with his hand outstretched.

"Welcome aboard the new headquarters of the 101st, Mr. Pitt."

"Most impressive."

Hunter casually waved around the vast room. "Built during World War Two. Hasn't been used since. I couldn't bear to see it go to waste, so I moved in."

Hunter took Pitt's arm and steered him over to a partitioned office in one corner of the bunker which they entered. The deeply set face, the authoritative expression, and the intense eyes made Hunter a perfect prototype for the gimlet-eyed task force commander who was about to attack an unseen enemy over the horizon. Which was precisely what he was.

"You're exactly two hours and thirty-eight minutes late," Hunter said firmly.

"Sorry, sir. The traffic got a bit sticky."

"So you told me over the phone. I wish to compliment you for your call. I'm grateful for the fact that you contacted me first. Good thinking."

"I'm only sorry I blew it by leaving the scene of the crash."

"Don't sweat it. I doubt if we'd have learned much from the body except a possible identification. Most likely your friend in the truck was only a local hoodlum paid for the job of putting you in a cemetery."

"Still, there might have been something . . ."

"Agents," Hunter interrupted sarcastically, "seldom leave notes describing their operations pinned on the shirts of their hired help."

"By agents, you mean the Russians?"

"Maybe. We have no proof as yet, but our intelligence people seem to think that the Russians have an organization nosing around the neighborhood trying to dig up the *Starbuck*'s final position so they can grab their hooks into her first."

"Admiral Sandecker mentioned such a possibility."

"A damn good man." There was satisfaction in Hunter's voice. "He showed me your personnel file this morning. I must admit in all honesty, I was caught unprepared by the contents. Distinguished Flying Cross with two clusters, Silver Star, plus several other commendations and a Purple Heart. Frankly, I had you down as a rip-off artist."

Hunter picked up a pack of cigarettes from his desk and offered them to Pitt.

The old bastard, Pitt thought, is actually making an attempt at courtesy. "You probably noted that there was no mention of a Good Conduct Medal." Pitt passed on the cigarettes.

Hunter regarded Pitt with searching eyes. "I noticed." He took a cigarette and struck a light, then leaned over the desk and pushed a switch on his intercom. "Yager, round up Commanders Denver and Boland, and send them in here." He broke off, turned, and jerked down a wall map of the North Pacific Ocean. "The Pacific Vortex, Major, ever hear of it?"

"Not until this morning."

Hunter rapped his knuckles against a spot on the map north of Oahu. "Here, within a diameter of four hundred miles, almost forty ships have sailed into oblivion since 1956. Extensive search operations turned up nothing. Before then, the sinkings diminish to a normal loss factor of one or two every twenty years." Hunter turned from the map and scratched his ear.

"There's been a lot of study on this one. We've run every available shred of information through the computers in hopes of coming up with a plausible solution. So far, we've only dredged up far-out theories. Cold hard facts are damn few and far between ..."

A soft knock on the door interrupted Hunter; he looked up as Denver and Boland walked into the room. They both stared blankly at Pitt for a moment, before recognition slowly stirred in their eyes.

Denver was the first to react. "Dirk, it's good to have you on the team."

Pitt grinned. "This time, I dressed for the occasion."

Boland simply nodded in Pitt's direction, mumbled a greeting, and sat down.

Hunter pulled a linen handkerchief from his hip pocket and dabbed it to his mouth to remove a bit of tobacco from his tongue. After staring at the small brown particle for a moment, said: "We haven't had much time to get fully organized, Mr. Pitt, but we've pretty much got things running on an even keel. Our computers are linked with every security agency in the country. I'm counting on you to coordinate our operation with your people in Washington. We'll need answers and we'll need them fast. If you require anything, request it from Commander Boland."

"There is one thing," Pitt said.

"Name it," Hunter snapped back.

"I'm only low man on the totem pole around here. Until this morning, I'd never heard of any of this. I'll be of little service to you without some idea of what's behind all this talk about a mysterious vacuum in the sea that gobbles up ships."

Hunter looked thoughtfully at Pitt. "My apologies." He paused, then went on very quietly indeed. "I take it that you're aware of the Bermuda Triangle."

Pitt nodded, muttering an affirmative.

"The Triangle," Hunter continued, "isn't the only area in the world where unexplainable things happen. The Mediterranean Sea has its share. And though it has received less publicity, the Romondo region of the Pacific southeast of Japan has been claiming more ships over the last two centuries than most of the oceans combined. Which brings us to the last and most unusual area: the Pacific Vortex."

"Personally, I think it's a lot of crap," Pitt said sharply.

"Oh, I don't know," Boland replied. "There are a lot of respected scientists who feel there is something to it."

"So you're a skeptic?" Hunter asked Pitt.

"I'm strictly along for the ride. I believe only what I can see, smell, and touch."

Hunter looked and sounded resigned. "Gentlemen, it makes no damned difference what our opinions are. It's the facts that count; and that's what we're going to pursue as long as I command the 101st Fleet. Our job is to salvage. And right now, our primary job is to find and raise the *Starbuck*. We got entangled in this Pacific Vortex myth only because of the strange circumstances surrounding the message from Commander Dupree. If we can clear up the mystery of the *Starbuck's* loss while solving the disappearance of other ships over the years, so much the better for the maritime freight and shipping industries. If the Russians or Chinese get their hands on her before we do, it's going to piss off a lot of people in Washington."

"Particularly the Navy Department," Boland added.

Hunter nodded. "The Navy Department and every scientific research lab and engineering firm that worked for years planning and constructing the most advanced

nuclear submarine afloat. The people who poured their sweat and labor into the *Starbuck* won't take it kindly if it turns up tied to a Soviet pier in Vladivostok."

"Are there any similarities between the *Starbuck*'s disappearance and the other ships and planes that have been lost?" Pitt asked.

"I'll answer your question, Major." Boland's tone was cutting. "To begin with, unlike the Bermuda Triangle, there are no instances of aircraft lost over the Pacific Vortex. And secondly, when there are no survivors, lifeboats, bodies, or floating debris, there is no way to make a connection. The only link between the submarine and the other missing vessels is that they all disappeared within a well-defined sector of the Pacific Ocean."

Denver leaned over and touched Pitt on the arm. "Except for the message capsule you discovered on the Kaena Point Beach, there is only one other piece of evidence seen by man."

Pitt said: "Admiral Sandecker mentioned such an exception."

"The *Lillie Marlene*," Hunter said quietly. "An incident that is even more extraordinary than the *Mary Celeste*." Hunter opened a drawer and fumbled around for a moment. "There isn't much to it, only a few pages." He handed a file folder to Pitt and, in the same motion, hit the intercom and grunted into it. "Yager, bring us some coffee."

Pitt settled into his chair, noted the title on the folder, and began reading:

The Strange Disaster of the S.S. *Lillie Marlene*
On the afternoon of July 10, 1968, the S.S. *Lillie Marlene*, a former British torpedo boat converted to

a private yacht, left the port of Honolulu and set a course northwest of the island of Oahu for the express purpose of filming a lifeboat scene for a movie under the direction of Herbert Verhusson, internationally recognized film producer and registered owner of the ship. The sea was calm and the weather fair with a few scattered clouds; a wind blew from the northeast at approximately four knots.

At 2050 hours on July 13, the Coast Guard station at Makapuu Point and the Naval Communications Center at Pearl Harbor, picked up a distress call from the ship, followed by a position. Air rescue at Hickam Field was alerted, and Naval and Coast Guard ships set out from Oahu. After the Mayday calls continued for twelve minutes, there was silence, broken by the final and mysterious words from the *Lillie Marlene:* "They come out of the mist. The captain, first mate dead. Crew fighting. No chance. Too many. Passengers first to go. No one, even women, spared." Then came an incoherent sentence. "A ship sighted on the southern horizon. Oh God! If only it arrives in time. Mr. Verhusson dead. They're coming for me now. No more time. They hear the radio. Do not blame the captain. He could not have known. They are pounding in the door now. Not much time. I do not understand. The ship is moving again. Help! For God's sake, help us! Oh, sweet Jesus. They're..." The final message ended here.

The first ship on the scene was the Spanish freighter, the *San Gabriel.* It was only twelve miles away when it picked up the *Lillie Marlene's* Mayday signal. It was, in fact, the ship the radio operator sighted before he fell silent. As the Spanish steamer pulled alongside, her crew noted that the yacht seemed to be in an undamaged condition and was underway at a slow speed, leaving a narrow wake behind her stern. Suddenly, and unexplicably, the *Lillie Marlene* stopped dead in the water, enabling

the captain of the *San Gabriel* to send out a boarding party. They found a dead ship with a dead crew. The lifeless bodies of the passengers, the film technicians, the ship's officers, and crew, were lying in scattered heaps about the decks and in the cabins below. In the radio room the corpse of the operator lay slumped over the transmitter, the red ON light still blinking on the panel.

The officer leading the boarding crew immediately radioed the captain of the *San Gabriel*. There was terror in his voice as he described what they had found. The victims' bodies had turned green and their faces had been melted away, as if burned by a tremendous heat. A stench pervaded the ship, described as sulfurous in nature. The position of the bodies seemed to indicate that there had been a terrific struggle before they had died. Arms and legs were twisted in unnatural contortions, and the hideously burned faces all seemed to be facing north. Even a small dog, obviously one of the passenger's, bore the same strange injuries.

After a short conference in the wheelhouse, the boarding party signaled the captain of the *San Gabriel* for a towing rope. It was their intent to claim the *Lillie Marlene* as salvage and tow the yacht and her morbid cargo to Honolulu.

Then suddenly, before the *San Gabriel* could come into position, a massive explosion ripped the *Lillie Marlene* from bow to stern. The force from the blast rocked the *San Gabriel* and hurled debris over a quarter of a mile.

Horror-struck, the crew and captain of the *San Gabriel* stood by helplessly as the shattered remains of the *Lillie Marlene* settled and then plunged from sight, taking with it the entire boarding party.

After studying the evidence and listening to eyewitnesses, the Coast Guard Board of Inquiry closed the case with the finding: "The death of the crew

and passengers and the subsequent explosion and
sinking of the yacht, the *Lillie Marlene*, can only
be classified as caused by circumstances or persons
unknown."

Pitt closed the folder and placed it on Hunter's desk.

"What we have there," Hunter said somberly, "is
the only known case of a distress call prior to the
disaster, as well as eyewitness reports as to the condition of the personnel involved."

Pitt said: "It would appear that the *Lillie Marlene*
was attacked by a boarding crew."

Boland shook his head. "The men who boarded
from the *San Gabriel* were cleared. Radio directional
equipment established the Spanish freighter's position
as being twelve miles from the disaster when she
answered the distress call."

"No other ship was sighted?" Pitt asked.

"I know what you're thinking," Denver volunteered.
"But piracy on the high seas went out with the
manufacture of cutlasses."

"Dupree's message also mentioned a mist or fog
bank," Pitt persisted. "Did the *San Gabriel* sight anything resembling a fog?"

"Negative," Hunter answered. "The first Mayday
came in at 2050 hours. That's dusk in this latitude. A
dark horizon would have blotted out any hint of an
isolated fog bank."

"Besides," Denver said, "fog in this part of the
Pacific Ocean in the month of July is as rare as a
blizzard on Waikiki Beach. A small, localized fog bank
is formed when stagnant warm air cools to condensation most often on a still night when it meets with a
cool surface. There are no such conditions around
these parts. The winds are nearly constant throughout

the year and a seventy-two- to eighty-degree water temperature could hardly be called a cool surface."

Pitt shrugged his shoulders. "That settles that."

"What we have there," Hunter said somberly, "is San Gabriel had not arrived when it did, the Lillie Marlene would have exploded and sunk to the bottom anyway. Then it would have been written off as one more mysterious disappearance."

Denver stared at him. "On the other hand, if something not of this world had attacked the Lillie Marlene, they'd hardly have done so with another ship in sight, or allowed time for an inspection by boarders. They must have had a purpose."

Boland threw up his hands. "There he goes again."

"Stick to the facts, Commander." Hunter gave Denver an icy look. "We've no time for science fiction."

The men fell silent; only the muffled sounds of the equipment outside the paneled walls seeped through the quietness. Pitt rubbed his hand tiredly across his eyes, then held his head as if to clear his mind. When he spoke, the words came very slow.

"I think Burdette has touched on an interesting point."

Hunter looked at him. "You're going to buy little green men with pointed ears who have a grudge against seagoing ships?"

"No," Pitt answered. "But I am going to buy the possibility that who or what is behind the disasters, wanted that Spanish freighter to make the discovery for a purpose."

Hunter was interested now. "I'm listening."

"Let's grant bad weather, bad seamanship, and bad luck for a small percentage of missing ships. Then we go one step further and say there's intelligence behind the remaining mysteries."

"Okay, so there's a brain running the show," said Boland. "What did he . . ." He paused and stared at Denver smiling. "Or *it*, have to gain by letting those Spaniards catch him in the middle of a mass murder?"

"Why would he deviate from an established routine?" Pitt replied with another question. "Sailors are notoriously superstitious people. Many of them can't even swim, much less put on a scuba tank and dive under the surface. Their lives are spent crossing the surface. And yet, their innermost fears, their nightmares, are centered around drowning at sea. My guess is that it was a deliberate plot by our unknown villain for the *Lillie Marlene*'s passengers and crew to be found heaped about the decks in ungodly mutilation. Even the dog wasn't spared."

"Sounds like an elaborate plot to scare a few seamen," Boland persisted.

"Not merely scare a few seamen," Pitt continued, "but a whole fleet of seamen. In short, the whole show was staged as a warning."

"A warning for what?" Denver asked.

"A warning to stay the hell out of that particular area of the sea," Pitt answered.

"I've got to admit," Boland said slowly, "that since the *Lillie Marlene* affair, maritime ships have avoided the Vortex section like the plague."

"You've got one problem," Hunter's tone was strangely soft. "The only on-scene witnesses, the boarding crew, were blown up along with the ship."

Pitt grinned knowingly. "Simple. The idea was for the boarders to return to the *San Gabriel* and report to the captain. Our mastermind didn't figure on greed rearing its ugly head. The boarders, as you recall, elected to stay on the ship and requested a tow rope,

probably already spending the salvage money in their minds. They had to be stopped right where the ship sat. If the *Lillie Marlene* had reached port, scientific investigation might have uncovered some damaging evidence. So one good bang and Verhusson's yacht went to the deep six."

"You make a good case," Hunter sighed. "But even if your fertile imagination has stumbled on the truth, we're still left with our primary job finding the *Starbuck*."

"I was coming to that," Pitt said. "The message from the yacht's radio operator and the one from Commander Dupree, they have the same broken sentences: the same pleading tone in their words. The radio operator said: 'Don't blame the captain, he could not have known.' And in the latter part of Commander Dupree's message, he said: 'If I had but known.' A similarity between two men under stress. I don't think so." Pitt paused to let it sink in. "All of which leads to a likely conclusion: Commander Dupree's final message is phony."

"We considered that," Hunter said, "Dupree's message was flown to Washington last night. The Naval Intelligence Forgery Office verified an hour ago the authenticity of Dupree's handwriting."

"Of course," Pitt said matter-of-factly. "Nobody would be stupid enough to forge several paragraphs of script. I suggest you have your experts check for indentations in the paper. Chances are, the words were printed and then indented just enough to match the marking of a ball-point pen."

"It doesn't make sense," said Boland. "Someone would have to have extra copies of Dupree's writing in order to duplicate it."

"They had the logbook, his correspondence, and maybe a diary. Perhaps that's why some of the pages were missing from the message capsule. Certain key words and letters were cut out and pasted together into readable sentences. Then it was photoengraved and printed."

Hunter's expression was thoughtful, his tone neutral. "That would explain the strange wording and the rambling text of Dupree's message. But it doesn't tell us where Dupree and his crew lie."

Pitt raised from his chair and walked over to the wall map. "Did the *Starbuck* send its messages to Pearl Harbor in code?" he asked.

"The code machine hadn't been installed yet," Hunter replied. "And since the sub was operating more or less in our own waters on a test cruise, the Navy saw no great urgency for top secret transmissions."

"Sounds risky," Pitt said, "for one of our nuclear subs to be on the air."

"Strict silence is only maintained when a sub is on patrol or on station. Because the *Starbuck* was a new and untested ship, Dupree was ordered to report his position every two hours only as a precautionary measure in case of a mechanical malfunction. The initial shakedown was scheduled for only five days. By the time the Russians could track the calls and put a ship loaded with electronic spy gear on-the-scene, the *Starbuck* would have been long gone on a return course to Pearl Harbor."

Pitt continued to stare at the map. "These red marks, Admiral. What does it indicate?"

"That's Dupree's position, according to his message."

"And these periodic black symbols, I take it, are the *Starbuck*'s last position reports?"

"Correct."

Pitt continued, his words economical. "The top mark then is the final bonafide message from Dupree."

Hunter simply nodded.

Pitt leaned against Hunter's desk and stared silently at the map for several moments. Finally he straightened and rapped on the area marked as the *Starbuck*'s last position report. "Your search area spreads from this point to where?"

"It extends in a fan-shaped sector three hundred miles northeast," Boland answered, his eyes clouded with puzzlement at Pitt's cross-examination. "If you'd be so good as to tell us what you're after."

"Please bear with me," Pitt said. "Your search operations were massive, over twenty ships and three hundred aircraft. But you found nothing, not even an oil slick. Every scientific detection device was undoubtedly used—magnetometers, sensitive Fathometers, underwater television cameras, the works. Yet your efforts came up dry. Doesn't that strike you as strange?"

Hunter's expression registered uncomprehension. "Why should it? The *Starbuck* could have gone down in an undersea canyon ..."

"Or she might have buried her hull in soft sediment," Denver added. "Finding one little ship in an area that large is as tough as finding a penny in the Salton Sea."

"My friend," Pitt said smiling, "you just spoke the magic words."

Denver looked at Pitt blankly.

"One little ship," Pitt repeated. "In all your searching, you couldn't find one little ship."

"So?" Hunter's tone was icy.

"Don't you see? Your search pattern was supposed to be right in the middle of the Pacific Vortex. Maybe

you didn't hit on the *Starbuck*, but you should have stumbled on to *something*. After all, you had nearly thirty other sunken derelicts to choose from."

"Damn!" Hunter's self-confidence was shaken. "It never occurred to us . . ."

"I see your point," Boland said. "But what does it prove?"

"It proves," Pitt replied, "that you searched the wrong area. It proves that Dupree's message was a clever counterfeit. And it proves that the *Starbuck*'s last radioed positions were an even cleverer case of fraud. In short, gentlemen, the place to find your missing submarine is not to the northeast, but a one-hundred-eighty-degree reverse course to the southwest."

Hunter, Boland, and Denver stared at Pitt in stunned silence, enlightenment spreading across their features.

Denver spoke first. "It fits," he said simply.

Hunter's face began to glow with an enthusiasm that he hadn't shown for months. He gazed long and hard at the wall map for nearly half a minute. Then, he swung abruptly and fastened his gaze on Boland.

"How soon can the *Martha Ann* get underway?"

"Hoist the helicopter on board, finish refueling, make a final check of the detection instruments; I'd say 2100 hours this evening, sir."

Hunter glanced at his watch. "That doesn't leave us much time to plot a search area." He turned to Denver. "This is your realm. I suggest you begin programming a search grid immediately."

"The primary data is already on the tapes, Admiral. It's only a matter of reversing the location input."

Hunter rubbed his eyes. "Okay, gentlemen, it's all yours. I'd give up half these stripes to come with you.

By the way, Mr. Pitt, I hope you won't mind taking an extended ocean voyage?"

Pitt smiled at him. "I have nothing else planned at the moment."

"Good." Hunter rolled a cigarette around in his mouth. "Tell me something; how did an Air Force officer ever become a departmental head of the government's top oceanographic agency?"

"I shot down Admiral Sandecker and his staff over the China Sea."

Hunter stared at Pitt with a strange believing look indeed. *With this man, almost anything is possible,* Admiral Sandecker had told him earlier.

CHAPTER 7

It was one hour after sunset when the AC slipped into a parking stall in the Honolulu dock area. As the front wheels made contact with a wooden tire stop, the engine died and the headlights blinked out. Pitt swung the door open and gazed across the harbor into the inky water.

As the breeze changed direction it carried a heavy odor to his nostrils: the undeniable bouquet of the waterfront. It smelled of oil, gasoline, tar, and smoke, with a tinge of saltwater thrown in. It exhilarated Pitt, carrying the nostalgic sensation of faraway exotic ports.

Pitt pulled himself from the car and glanced about the parking lot in search of any sign of human activity. There was none. Only a seagull, perched on a wooden piling, returned his stare. Pitt reached into the car and pulled the towel-wrapped Mauser from behind the seat. Then he inhaled the harbor night air, tucked the gun under his arm, and began walking along the pier.

If anyone had been loitering around the docks they would hardly have noticed anything unusual about Pitt's appearance. He was dressed in a well-worn khaki shirt over a faded pair of gabardine pants. His feet were encased by a pair of badly scuffed brogans, tied

79

with heavy twine. The cast-off clothing, a gift from the 101st Fleet's Security Officer, was a size too small and bulged at the seams. He felt like a toss-up between a bindle stiff and a skid row derelict. A quart of muscatel in a brown paper bag was all that was missing. Or better yet, a bottle of Grand Marnier Yellow Ribbon: just the right touch of class to go with the rags.

One hundred yards later, Pitt stopped and looked up at the huge black hulk that loomed in the darkness. The only light that beamed down on the weathered and tarred planking came from a few scattered green-shaded lamps that hung awkwardly from the corrugated metal sides of an old warehouse. The eerie glow of the lamps, coupled with the deathly stillness of the evening, only added to the already ghostlike appearance of the monster in the water.

She was an old ship with a straight up-and-down bow and a square, boxlike shape to her superstructure; this was topped by an old-fashioned vertical smokestack that sported a faded blue stripe. Rising from her decks stood a maze of cluttered derricks and masts. At some time in the distant past she had been painted black with the usual red waterline, but now she was grimy, dirty, and rusty. Pitt moved closer until he was standing under her stern. She was large, probably in the neighborhood of twelve thousand tons. He stared up at the dim white lettering just below the fantail. The name was so battered and streaked with rust he could barely make it out in the dim light: MARTHA ANN—SEATTLE.

The gangplank looked like a tunnel leading upward into a forbidding void. Only the muted hum of the generators deep within the hull, and a thin wisp of

smoke curling from the funnel betrayed human presence.

Pitt placed his hand on the coarse railing rope of the gangplank and, leaning forward to compensate for the thirty-degree angle, began the ascent to the *Martha Ann*'s deck. The fading light from the warehouse lamps ceased at the last step of the ramp. Pitt hesitated upon reaching the seemingly deserted deck and peered into the shadows.

"Mr. Pitt?" came a voice from the gloom.

"Yes, I'm Pitt."

"May I see your identification, please?"

"You may, if only I could see who in hell to hand it to."

"Please lay your ID on the deck, sir, and step back."

Pitt grumbled to himself. He was aware that it was normal military procedure to examine identification papers during alerts and emergencies, but why all the fuss to come aboard this old rivet-dangling sea bucket? Setting the Mauser gently on the deck, he pulled out his wallet and groped for his ID. His eyes could not penetrate the blackness so he ran his fingers over a stack of assorted plastic cards until he found one that lacked the telltale raised lettering of a credit card and threw it a few paces in front of his feet. A pencil-thin shaft of light beamed on the card and then touched Pitt's face.

"Sorry to trouble you, sir, but Admiral Hunter ordered strict security all around the ship." A black shadow passed the ID back to Pitt. "If you take the first stairway to your right, you'll find Commander Denver in the chart room."

"Thanks," Pitt grunted. He retrieved the gun and

struggled up the stairway toward the bridge. At the top he found the darkened wheelhouse empty so he walked through the deserted enclosure and cautiously cracked open a door. Here at last he was greeted by a flood of bright light.

"Hello, Dirk," Denver said warmly. He had a cigarette between his fingers and as he waved a greeting to Pitt, the ash fell in a tiny heap on the chart table. He was wearing a black pullover sweater and a pair of soiled denims. "Welcome aboard the U.S. Navy's only floating fossil."

Pitt tossed him an offhand salute. "I didn't expect to find you here, Burdette. I thought you were remaining in Operations with the admiral."

Denver smiled. "I'll get there. But I couldn't resist coming down and wishing you and Paul good hunting."

"We'll need it. If the choice was up to me, I'd take the old-fashioned needle in a haystack any day."

"Do you think this is a strange phenomenon?" Denver asked him.

"Like your boss said, our job is to find and raise the *Starbuck*. Any ghost-catching is strictly a side benefit. Besides, our NUMA scientists and engineers do not make a habit of researching Bermuda triangles or Pacific vortices. We leave that up to imaginative writers with a knack for exaggeration. Any unexplainable discoveries are purely accidental, and afterward, they're quietly filed away."

"Could you give me an example?" Denver asked softly.

Pitt stared vacantly at a half-opened chart on the table.

"There was one instance about nine months ago that smacked of Jules Verne. Two of our oceanographic

ships were conducting subbottom profiling and under-water acoustical tests in the Kurile Trench off Japan when their instruments detected the sound of a vessel traveling at a high rate of speed in very deep water. Both ships immediately heaved to, closing down all engines and turning all instruments to whatever it was that was down there."

"Could an instrument or one of the operators have been mistaken?" Denver murmured.

"Not likely," Pitt answered. "Those researchers were the tops in their respective fields. And, when you consider that two different ships with two sets of pre-cision instruments traced and recorded identical read-ings, you pretty much eliminate any percentage of error. No mistake about it, the thing, the submarine, the sea monster, whatever you wish to call it, was there. And it was moving at one hundred ten miles an hour in a depth of nineteen thousand feet."

Denver slowly shook his head. "Incredible. It's beyond understanding."

"That's only the half of it," Pitt said. "Another ship working over the Cayment Trench off Cuba came up with an identical contact. I've seen both the Cayment and Kurile data. The sonar graphs agree to the milli-meter."

"Was the Navy notified?"

"No way. The Navy doesn't want to hear about weird undersea sightings any more than the Air Force wants to hear about Unidentified Flying Objects. But then, what real proof was there other than a mass of scraggly lines on a few sheets of graph paper?" Pitt leaned back in a chair, propping his feet on the table and bracing the back of his head in his hands. "There was one instance though when we came within a whisker of getting one of the sea's unknown residents

on videotape. A NUMA zoologist was studying and recording fish sounds off the Continental slope near Iceland where he'd dropped a microphone in ten thousand feet of water to pick up noises made by the rarely seen benthos. For several days he recorded the usual clicks and creaking sounds with pretty much the same tones as surface-dwelling fish. He also noted the continuous cracking noise made by shrimps.

"Suddenly, one afternoon, the cracking stopped and he began receiving a tapping sound, as if something was rapping a pencil on the underwater microphone. At first he figured he'd only run onto a fish with a previously unrecorded sound. But it slowly dawned on him that the tapping was in some kind of code. The ship's radio operator was hastily called and he deciphered it as a mathematical formula. Then the noise stopped and a shrieking laughter, eerily distorted by the density of the water, burst from the listening room speakers. Shaking off disbelief, the crew quickly lowered a TV camera. They were about ten seconds too late. The fine bottom silt had been stirred up by a rapid movement, leaving an impenetrable cloud of muck. It took an hour before the bottom cleared. And there, in front of the cameras, was a set of odd-looking indentations in the silt going off into the black void."

"Were they able to make anything out of the formula?" asked Denver.

"Yes, it was a simple equation for finding the water pressure at the depth the microphone was located."

"And the answer?"

"Nearly two and a half tons per square inch."

Silence fell on the chart room, a long, chilling silence. Pitt could hear the water below the ports gently lapping the hull.

"Any coffee around?" Pitt asked.

Denver's mind still roamed the mysterious abyss of the sea. Then with a marked degree of effort, he shrugged it away. "Be assured," he said with a grim smile, "when you take an ocean cruise on the *Martha Ann*, you travel under the finest service in the Pacific." He picked up an old blackened pot and poured the coffee into a battered tin cup. "There you are, sir, and enjoy your trip."

They were sitting at the chart table just beginning to savor the coffee when the door swung open and Boland entered. He wore a soiled T-shirt, faded Levi's, and a pair of brogans in worse condition than Pitt's. The thin shirt showed off Boland's muscular shoulders, and for the first time, Pitt noticed a tattoo on one of his arms. The picture of a knife piercing the skin and oozing blood, adorned his right forearm, and underneath the gruesome illustration in blue lettering, read the words: DEATH BEFORE DISHONOR.

"You two look like you just received Dear John letters," Boland's voice was mocking, yet firm. "What goes?"

"We were just solving the mysteries of the universe," Denver answered. "Here, Paul, have a shot of my world-renowned brew." He pushed a steaming cup toward Boland, spilling a few brown drops on the deck.

Boland took the dripping mug from Denver's hand and looked thoughtfully at Pitt, and when Pitt stared back at him, he slowly cracked a smile, lifted the cup, and sipped at the hot contents.

"Any final orders from the old man?" he asked.

Denver shook his head. "Same as he told you. At the first sign of danger, get the hell out and hotfoot it back to Pearl Harbor."

"That's if we're lucky," Boland said. "None of the

other missing vessels had time for a Mayday signal, much less time to cut ass."

"Then Pitt here is your insurance. And the helicopter."

"It takes time to warm up a helicopter," Boland said doubtfully.

"Not that bird," Pitt said briefly. "I can put her in the air in forty seconds flat." He stood and stretched, his large hands touching the metal ceiling. "One question. That copter can only carry fifteen men. Either the Navy provided us with a crew of midgets, or we're sailing damned shorthanded."

"Under normal standards, we're sailing shorthanded," Denver said. He smiled at Boland and winked. "You couldn't know, Dirk, but the *Martha Ann* is not the decrepit old scow she seems. A large crew is unnecessary because she's equipped with the most advanced and highly automated centralized control system of any ship afloat. She practically runs herself."

"But the scale on the hull. The rust . . ."

"Prettiest fake scenery you ever saw," Denver admitted. "A clever chemical coating that looks like the real thing. Can't tell it from rust under bright sunlight from a foot away."

"Then why the elaborate equipment?" Pitt asked.

"There's more to the *Martha Ann* than meets the eye," Boland said with a hesitant degree of modesty. "You'd never know it to look at her, but she's crammed from keel to topside with salvage equipment."

"A disguised salvage ship?" Pitt said slowly. "That's a new twist."

Denver smiled. "The masquerade comes in handy for the, shall we say, more delicate reclamation projects."

"Admiral Sandecker mentioned a few of your delicate accomplishments," Pitt said. "Now I see how you carried them off."

"No job too large, no job too small," Boland said, laughing. "We could almost raise the *Andrea Doria* if they turned us loose on it."

"Suppose we do find the *Starbuck*, even with your automated gadgetry, you could never bring her to the surface with such a small crew."

"Purely precautionary, my dear Pitt," answered Denver. "Admiral Hunter insisted on a skeleton crew during the search operation. No sense in wasting lives if the *Martha Ann* should meet the same fate as the others. On the other hand, if we get lucky and discover the *Starbuck*, you and your whirlybird then begin a shuttle service between the recovery site and Honolulu by ferrying the salvage crew and any needed parts and equipment."

"A tidy little package," Pitt admitted. "Though I'd sleep better if we had an armed escort."

Denver shook his head. "Can't chance it. The Russians would smell a shady plot the minute they got wind of an old tramp steamer escorted by a Navy missile cruiser. They'd have the *Andrei Vyborg* on our tail by sunup."

Pitt's eyebrows lifted. The "*Andrei Vyborg?*"

"A Russian oceanographic vessel classified by Navy Intelligence as a spy ship. She's shadowed the *Starbuck*'s search operation for the last six months and she's still out there somewhere hovering around poking for the sub." Boland paused for a swallow of coffee. "The 101st Fleet has spent too much time and effort to maintain our cover as a merchantman. We can't afford to have it blown now."

"As you can see," Denver said, "the *Martha Ann* is

completely divorced from the Navy. She's listed under United States registry as a merchant ship. And we intend to keep it that way, nice and discreet."

"Isn't the Navy concerned by the fact that the *Andrei Vyborg* is nosing around alone?"

"She's not alone," Boland said seriously. "We've four ships still combing the northern search area. The Navy never gives up on a search, no matter how hopeless it seems for survivors. Call it Naval tradition if you will, Major, but it's a damn good feeling when you're floating in the sea, clutching a piece of flotsam after your ship has gone down, knowing that nothing is spared to make your rescue . . ."

Boland's lecture was interrupted by a knock on the door. "Come in!" he shouted.

A young boy, no more than nineteen or twenty, stepped through the doorway. He was wearing a white butcher's cap on his head and a pair of blue coveralls. Ignoring Pitt and Denver, he spoke to Boland.

"Excuse me, sir, the chief engineer reports the engine room is in readiness and the bosun's mate has the crew standing by to cast off."

Boland glanced at his watch. "Right. Pass the word to cast off and get underway in ten minutes."

"Yes sir," replied the young seaman. He saluted, turned, and disappeared into the pilothouse.

Boland smiled smugly at Denver. "Not bad. We're forty minutes ahead of schedule."

"The copter tied down and secure?" asked Pitt.

Boland nodded. "She's snug. You can make your final flight checks when it's daylight."

Pitt rose and walked over to the porthole, breathing deeply to cleanse his lungs of the stale smoke from Denver's cigarettes. The harbor air smelled pure in comparison to the stuffy chart room.

"Have you assigned accommodations for Dirk?" Denver asked Boland.

"There's a stateroom next to mine that we keep vacant for VIP's," Boland replied, his lips curled in a sarcastic grin. "In Pitt's case, we'll make an exception."

Pitt fixed a long hypnotic stare devoid of anger or animosity at the smoke curling up from the ashtray. He could shrug off a verbal dig with all the feeling of flipping a mosquito off an arm. Hunter was a clever old fox; placing two men with different temperaments together as a team.

"Well, I guess I'd best shove off," Denver said, breaking the uneasy silence.

"We'll drop you a postcard from time to time," Pitt said.

"You'd better do more than that," Denver shot back, his lips curled in a tight smile, but his eyes hard. "I'm going to reserve the bar at the Reef Hotel for three weeks from today. And woe to the man who doesn't show up." He turned to Boland. "You have the code, Paul. The admiral and I will track you by satellite. When you spot the *Starbuck*, simply radio under maritime transmission that you've stopped all engines to repair a burned shaft bearing. We'll have your exact position in a millisecond."

Denver shook hands with Pitt and Boland. "Little else can be said but good luck!" Before the other two men could answer, Denver abruptly wheeled about and strode from the room.

A few minutes later Denver stood on the dock, leaning against a piling as he watched the crew slip the ship's lines and hoist the gangplank. He idly studied the starboard side of the *Martha Ann* as she moved slowly into the channel toward the mouth of the silent harbor. He stared at the navigation lights until

the gentle throbbing beat of the ship's engines gradually diminished into the darkness. Then he flipped his cigarette into the calm, oily water, shoved his hands in his pockets, and wearily made his way along the dock to the parking lot.

CHAPTER 8

Pitt stood at the rail of the fantail and idly watched the *Martha Ann*'s propellers churn out their wake. The frothing blue and white mass swirled, slowly diminishing a quarter of a mile behind the stern before the sea relentlessly closed over and covered her as though healing a giant scar. The weather was warm and the sky was clear; a solid breeze rushed past from the northeast.

What a crazy group he'd run across in the last two days, he thought despairingly. A devious-minded girl who tried to ram a hypodermic needle into his back, an assassin with tobacco-stained teeth, a bastard of an admiral, a lieutenant commander with a ridiculous tattoo, and a little commander who was apparently the smartest of them all.

But yet, this group wasn't able to haunt the dim reaches of his mind. That was left for another character of the drama, a character who had yet to step on the stage; a giant of a man with golden eyes.

What was his reason for researching the lost island of Kanoli so many years ago? Could he have simply been a scholar trying to unearth a lost civilization, or an occult delving into myths and legends? Or someone with even stranger goals in mind? What was there in the tale of Kanoli that couldn't be found

in half the drivel written about the lost continent of Mu, or in the overabundance of fiction dealing with Atlantis? The mysteries of the Pacific Vortex and the Bermuda Triangle were real enough. There had to be a logical solution to the riddles lying about somewhere, Pitt figured restlessly. A key that was so obvious that it was entirely overlooked.

"Mr. Pitt?"

Pitt's mental gymnastics were broken by the young man in coveralls.

Pitt smiled. "What can I do for you?"

The seaman was about to salute. He appeared flustered at how to act before a civilian, particularly one on a Navy ship.

"Commander Boland requests your presence on the bridge."

"Thank you. I'm on my way."

Pitt swung around and walked across the steel deck past the tarp-covered hatches. Beneath his feet the engines pounded away with a rhythmic beat as the ship ploughed into the calm water, throwing a white salty mist over the railings and onto the superstructure, coating the paint with a glistening layer of dripping wetness.

Pitt climbed the ladder that led to the bridge. Boland was standing in front of the helmsman, gazing through binoculars over the bow at the stark blue horizon. He dropped his glasses a moment, wiping the smudges on the bottom of his T-shirt. Then he returned them to his eyes and again studied the vast emptiness ahead.

"What's up?" Pitt queried. He looked through the window but he could see nothing.

"Thought you'd like to know," Boland said, "we've just entered the new search area." He set the glasses

on the bulkhead shelf, touched a transmitter switch, and spoke sharply in a staccato tone.

"Lieutenant Harper, this is the skipper. Stop all engines. We're heaving to." He looked at Pitt. "Now we go to work."

Boland motioned him down a companion stair that led to an alleyway beneath the bridge. After they had passed several cabin doors, Boland hesitated at one and opened it.

"The heart of the operation," he announced. "Our Flash Gordon Room. Four tons of electronic gimmickry. Please observe the scientific marvels of the 101st at work." He pointed to a long bank of instruments within a large compartment about eight hundred square feet.

"A panel to measure sound velocity and pressure, recording the parameters with time in digital format on magnetic tape. A proton-precision magnetic sensor to pick up any iron on the seafloor. Monitors for the underwater TV cameras." Boland pointed at four monitors embedded in the equipment. "That's why we heaved to, so we can release the sensors and cameras behind the ship on the glide sled and begin scanning."

Pitt studied the screens. The cameras were just being lowered in the water; he could see the swells slap at the lenses as they slipped under the surface and entered the silent void of sun-sparkled, restless liquid. Two of the cameras recorded color, making the blue-green shadows seemingly drift off into infinity.

"The next instrument is an advanced sonar system," Boland continued. "It takes detailed 'sound' pictures of the ocean floor and anything on it. We also have a side-scanning system that takes in half a mile on either side of the hull. Their sensors will also be towed behind the ship."

"A mile-wide detection belt," Pitt said. "That should cut an impressive swath through the search sector."

Pitt noted that Boland made no conscious effort to introduce him to any of the crew manning the equipment. If there was one thing Boland sadly lacked, it was the barest hint of social courtesy. Pitt found himself wondering how Boland ever made lieutenant commander.

"And this little sweetheart over here," Boland said proudly, "is the real brain of the outfit. A Selco-Ramsey 8300 computer system." He nodded at a tall, narrow panel of lights and knobs standing atop a wide-set keyboard. "Latitude-longitude, velocity and heading, complete on-board capability. In short, it hooks into the centralized control system, and from this point in time until we discover the *Starbuck*, this inhuman mass of transistors will run the ship."

"Makes it sanitary," Pitt murmured.

"How's that?"

"Untouched by human hands."

Boland's brow furrowed. "Yeah, you might say that."

Pitt leaned over the keyboard operator's shoulder and studied the printout tapes. "A neat arrangement. The Selco-Ramsey 8300 can be overridden and re-programmed from a master control. In this case, probably the operations bunker back at Pearl Harbor. Makes it handy for Admiral Hunter in the event we go the same way as the people on the *Lillie Marlene*. At the first sign of trouble, he and Denver can override our system, turn the ship around, and bring it back to port. He may lose the crew, but the 101st Fleet gets its super salvage ship home intact. A neat arrangement indeed."

"You know your electronics," Boland said slowly. His face had a strange mixture of suspicion and respect.

"You might say I have a passing acquaintance with most of the equipment you have on board."

"You've seen all this before?"

"On at least three of NUMA's oceanographic research ships. Your capability is a bit more specialized since your primary objective is salvage. But our state-of-the-art is slightly ahead of yours due to the scientific nature of our explorations."

"My apologies," Boland forced a smile. "I've been underestimating your talents." He wheeled, walked across to the detection room officer, spoke a few words to him, and returned. "Come on, I'll buy you a drink."

"Do Navy regulations cover that?" Pitt grinned, somewhat taken by Boland's sudden display of friendliness.

Boland's return grin had a touch of shrewdness to it. "You forget. Technically, this is a civilian ship."

"I'm all for technicalities."

They had just started for the door when the detection room officer announced: "Television cameras and sonar sensors in position, Skipper."

Boland nodded. "Fast work, Lieutenant. We'll get underway immediately..."

"One moment," Pitt interrupted. "Just out of curiosity, what's our depth reading?"

Boland looked at him questioningly and then turned. "Lieutenant?"

The detection room officer was already bent over the sonar sensor, staring intently at the jagged shading that crawled across the readout paper.

"Five thousand, six hundred seventy feet, sir."

"Anything unusual in that?" Boland queried.

"Should be deeper," Pitt answered. "Can we have a look at your ocean floor charts?"

"Here, sir." The lieutenant moved to a large chart table with a frosted glass top and switched on the overhead illuminator. He unrolled a large chart and clipped it to the edge of the table. "North Pacific seafloor. Not very detailed, I'm afraid. Very few depth-sounding expeditions in this part of the world."

Manners suddenly struck Boland. "Dirk Pitt, this is Lieutenant Stanley."

Pitt nodded. "Okay, Stanley, let's see what you've got." He set his elbows on the edge of the table and peered at the strange-looking contours that represented the floor of the Pacific Ocean. "What's our position?"

"Right here, Major." Stanley made a small fix on the chart. "32°10′ N, 151°17′ W."

"That puts us over the Fullerton Fracture Zone," said Pitt slowly.

"Sounds like a football injury." Boland was also hunched over the table.

"No, a fracture zone is a crack in the earth, a seam that allows movement during ocean spreading. There are hundreds of them between here and the California coast."

"I see what you mean by the depth. According to the chart, the seabed should be over fifteen thousand feet deep hereabouts." Stanley underlined the nearest depth reading to their position.

"It's possible that we're near a seamount," Pitt said.

"The bottom is rising on our port side," Boland said quietly. "Two hundred fifty feet in one mile. Nothing strange about that. One of the smaller seamounts might do it."

Pitt shook his head. "Except that none show on the chart."

"Probably hasn't been sounded and marked yet."

"Yet, if the slope is still rising, the summit can't be too far away. It's your ship, Paul, but I think an investigation is in order. The *Starbuck*'s message capsule was sent by persons unknown after she disappeared. It stands to reason that she's resting in a depth that's within reach."

Boland tiredly rubbed his eyes. "Sounds logical, but this can't be the only uncharted seamount in the area. There might be fifty more."

"We can't afford to overlook even one."

Boland looked thoughtful. Then he straightened and faced Stanley. "Lieutenant, program a course toward the high ground. Feed the sensor readings into the computer and place the helm on centralized control. Keep me informed of any sudden changes of depth. I'll be in my cabin." He turned to Pitt. "Now then, how about that drink?"

The TV camera sled and sonar sensors were reeled out on tow lines, the centralized control system was engaged on the computer, and within ten minutes the *Martha Ann* was underway on a slow, wide swing to the east. The helmsman on the bridge stood idly smoking in the doorway of the wheelhouse, the spokes of the wheel slowly turning back and forth as if guided by an invisible hand. The ship pushed through the swells, her crew busy scanning and checking a paneled sea of wavering dials, colored lights, and monitors.

Pitt and Boland remained in the captain's cabin through the midafternoon, the time passing with agonizing slowness as the sonar sensors reported an

ever-rising seafloor. One hour, two, then three. Pitt
kept himself buried in reports and data on the *Starbuck*, while Boland concerned himself with salvage
plans if and when the *Martha Ann* got lucky. Four-
thirty in the afternoon. The idle conversation of the
men on deck and down in the engine room turned
inevitably to women; only the men in the detection
room remained silent, intent on their monitors and
instruments. Stanley's occasional "bottom still rising"
over the intercom, kept a degree of normalcy about
the ship. There was no more tedious routine than
searching for a shipwreck.

Suddenly at five o'clock, Stanley's voice fairly burst
from the speakers. "Bottom up nine hundred feet
in the last half mile!"

Pitt stared at Boland. Without a word, they both
jumped to their feet and hurried to the detection
room. Stanley was bent over the chart table making
notations. "It's unbelievable, Skipper. I've never seen
anything like it. Here we are hundreds of miles from
nowhere, and the seafloor has suddenly risen to only
twelve hundred feet from the surface. And it's still
coming."

"That's one hell of a steep rise," Pitt said.

"Could be part of the Hawaiian Islands slope,"
Boland ventured.

"We're too far north. I doubt if there's any connection. This baby stands all by herself."

"Eleven hundred feet," Stanley said loudly.

"Good Lord! It's got a rising gradient of one foot
in height for every two in length," Pitt said softly.

Boland spoke barely above a whisper. "If it doesn't
level off soon, we'll run aground." He spun around
to face Stanley. "Disengage the computer. Return to
manual."

Five seconds was all it took for Stanley to reply. "Running on manual, sir."

Boland picked up the intercom mike. "Bridge? Boland here. What do you see eight hundred yards dead ahead?"

A metallic voice came back over the speaker. "Nothing, sir. Horizon's clear."

"Any sign of white water?"

"None, Commander."

Pitt looked up at Boland. "Ask him for the color of the sea."

"Bridge. Any change in the color of the sea?"

There was a brief hesitation. "It's turning more of a green, sir, about five hundred yards off the port bow."

"Eight hundred and still rising," Stanley said.

"The plot thickens," Pitt said. "I expected a lighter blue as the summit neared the surface. Green indicates underwater vegetation. Mighty strange for sea plants to grow around here."

"Seaweed doesn't take kindly to coral?" Boland said questioningly.

"That, and the warmer temperatures common to this part of the ocean."

"I've got a solid reading on the magnetometer." This from a blond, curly haired man at a console.

"Where?" Boland demanded.

"Two hundred yards, bearing two hundred eighty degrees."

"Might be paydirt," Boland said elatedly.

"A second reading three hundred yards, bearing three hundred fifteen degrees. Another two contacts. God, they're all around us."

"Sounds like a bonanza," Pitt grinned.

"Stop all engines," Boland yelled into the intercom.

"The bottom contour is jumping off the readout sheet," Stanley said excitedly. "Four hundred fifty feet and she hasn't stopped yet."

Pitt peered at the TV monitors. Nothing showed on the screens yet, and nothing would, with visibility limited to a hundred feet. He took a handkerchief from his hip pocket and wiped his neck and face. He found himself wondering why he was sweating. The detection room was fully air-conditioned. He shoved the now damp handkerchief carelessly back into his pocket and aimed his eyes at the monitors.

The microphone was still in Boland's hand. He lifted it to his lips and Pitt could hear his voice echoing through the ship. "This is Boland. We've made a touchdown on the first pass. All indications are that we're over the graveyard of the Pacific Vortex. I want every man on full alert. We have no picture of the danger here, so we don't want to get caught with our defenses down. As a point of interest, we may well be the only ship on record ever to reach these waters in one piece."

Pitt's eyes never left the monitors. The bottom began showing as the momentum of the *Martha Ann* carried her forward. The diffused brilliance of the water when struck by the sun's rays, broke the surface light into thin beams of yellow shafts which reached downward, displaying an indistinct carpet of colors. A trigger fish was visible now, hanging motionless in the three-dimensional fluid, cautiously eyeing the huge shadow of the hull as it drifted overhead.

Boland placed his hand on the shoulder of the man seated at the magnetometer. "As we pass over the first of the wrecks, sing out a heading for the next one in line." He turned to Stanley. "Signal Lieutenant

Harper in the engine room. Keep it down to bare steerageway."

The atmosphere of the detection room was tense. Two minutes passed; two interminable minutes, while they waited for the dead and buried remains of a long-lost ship to come into view.

The seafloor could be clearly seen on the monitors now. The plant life was strange and lush when it should have been as barren as an underwater lunar landscape. There was no sign of coral, only wide frond kelp and delicately colored seaweed clung to a rocky, uneven bed, constantly changing tint in the tremulous light filtering down from the surface. Pitt was fascinated. It was like looking at a flourishing Oriental garden that had sunk beneath the sea.

A long-haired youngster who manned the sonar spoke with an utter lack of excitement. "Coming up on a wreck, Commander."

"Okay, get ready for a computer scan."

"For the records?" Pitt asked.

"For identification," Boland replied. "The memory banks contain all the known data on the ships that are missing. We'll try and match our data with that in the computer. Hopefully, we can coax the sea into giving up a few secrets."

"Here she comes," Stanley said.

Three pairs of eyes locked themselves on the monitors. It was an eerie sight. The ship, or what was left of it, was covered with a thick layer of seagrowth. Two masts, fore and aft, reached in grotesque and hopeless desperation for the sky. The single funnel was intact with a coating of brown corrosion, and everywhere along the deck there were twisted chunks of nondescript metal. As they watched the screen,

the long greenish body of a moray eel wiggled
furiously through a porthole, its mouth opening and
closing menacingly.

"My God, that sucker was at least ten feet long,"
Boland exclaimed.

"Probably closer to eight, allowing for magnification
of the TV lenses," Pitt said.

"I might be hallucinating," Stanley said, "but I'm sure
I saw the remains of a farm tractor in the hold."

Their attention was interrupted by the hum of the
computer as the printout sheets began folding into
the basket. The instant the machine stopped, Boland
ripped out the paper and began reading aloud.

> Data indicates ship probable Liberian freighter,
> *Oceanic Star*, 5,135 tons, cargo: rubber and farm
> machinery; reported missing June 14, 1949.

The men in the detection room stopped what they
were doing and stared in mute silence at the paper
in Commander Boland's hand. No one spoke. No one
had to.

They had discovered their first victim of the Pacific
Vortex.

Boland was the first to react. He snatched the mike
from its cradle. "Radio room. This is Boland. Open
maritime frequency. Send message code sixteen."

Pitt said: "A little premature concerning the bearing failure, aren't you? We haven't found the *Starbuck*
yet."

"True," Boland admitted briefly. "I'm jumping the
gun but I want Admiral Hunter to know exactly
where we are, just in case."

"Expecting trouble?"

"No sense in taking chances."

"Next contact, bearing two hundred eighty-seven degrees," the sonar operator droned conversationally.

They returned and waited at the monitors until the sloping deck of a steamer came into view, the stern rising high while the bows were lost in the blue green depths. The camera sled passed over a massive round smokestack and they were able to peer down into its black interior. The middle of the ship was laced with valves and piping, and carried no superstructure, but the stern section rose several decks, sprouting an ugly maze of ventilation tubes. Growth had claimed all the metal parts and even the cables trailing off the masts. Exotically hued fish of every variety were swimming among the rigging, as though the skeleton of the dead ship was their own personal playground.

Boland's voice repeated the precise figures on the computer display.

Japanese oil tanker, *Ishiyo Maru*, 8,106 tons, reported missing with all hands, September 14, 1964.

"God," Stanley murmured. "This place is a veritable cemetery. I'm beginning to feel like a damned grave digger."

The roll call of the decayed and lifeless ships was repeated six more times in the next hour. Four merchantmen, a large schooner, and an ocean-going trawler were located and identified. The tenseness in the detection room heightened as each new find was scanned and analyzed. And when the final moment came, the moment they had geared their conscious minds for, it curiously caught them all by surprise.

The sonar operator suddenly pressed his earphones tighter against his ears and fixed an intense, unbeliev-

ing stare at his instrument panel. "I have a contact with a submarine bearing one hundred ninety degrees," he said.

"Certain?" Boland demanded.

"Bet my dear mother's virtue on it. I've read subs before, Commander, and this is a big one."

Boland hit the mike. "Bridge? When I give the word, stop all engines and drop anchor. Fast! Get that?"

"Affirmative, sir," came the rough-edged voice over the speaker.

"What is the depth?" Pitt asked.

Boland nodded. "Depth?" he ordered.

"Ninety feet."

Pitt and Boland stared at one another. "Compounds the mystery, wouldn't you say?" Pitt asked quietly.

"That it does," Boland answered softly. "If Dupree's message was fake, why include the correct depth level?"

"Our mastermind probably reasoned that nobody in their right mind would believe a reading of ninety feet. I'm seeing it with my own two eyes and I still don't believe it."

"She's coming into camera range." Stanley announced. "There . . . there, we have a submarine."

They stared at the image of a massive black shape lying below the slow-moving keel of the *Martha Ann*. To Pitt it was like looking down at a model ship in a bathtub. Her length was at least twice that of the conventional nuclear submarine. Instead of the more familiar hemispherical bows, her fore end was formed with a more pointed design. The usual perfect cigar shape was also missing and had been replaced with a hull that tapered smoothly into a classic swept-back symmetry. Gone too was the great dorsal finlike con-

ning tower of other submarines. In its place sat a smaller rounded hump. Only the control planes on the stern remained the same, as did two bronze propellers tucked neatly under the sleek hull. The submarine looked comfortably serene, like some huge Mesozoic denizen on a late afternoon nap. It was not the way it should have looked, and Pitt could feel his skin start to gooseflesh.

"Away marker," Boland snapped.

"Marker?" Pitt questioned.

"A low frequency electronic beeper," Boland answered. "In case we're forced to leave the area, we have a waterproof transmitter sitting on the seabed giving out periodic signals. That way we can pinpoint the position without a search when we return."

"Our bows have just cleared the wreck, Commander." This from the sonar operator.

Boland bellowed into the intercom mike. "All engines stop. Away anchor." He swung and faced Pitt. "Did you get a look at its number?"

"Nine-eight-nine," Pitt said tersely.

"That's her, the *Starbuck*," Boland said reverently. "I never really thought I'd lay eyes on her."

"Or what's left of her," Stanley added, his face suddenly pale. "Just thinking about those poor bastards entombed down there is enough to make your skin crawl."

"It does give you a queer feeling deep down in your gut," Boland agreed.

"Your gut feeling isn't the only thing that's queer," Pitt said evenly. "Take a closer look."

The *Martha Ann* was pivoting around the anchor now, and her stern, urged by the diminishing momentum, slowly swung on an arc away from the sunken submarine. Boland waited a moment until the TV

cameras were angled to keep the *Starbuck* in viewing range. When the subject centered in the middle of the frame, the lenses locked in place and automatically zoomed in for closer inspection.

"She's lying there in the bottom sand as real and tangible as she can be," Boland murmured slowly as he gazed into the screens. "The bow isn't buried as suggested by Dupree's report. But other than that, I see nothing unusual."

Pitt said: "A Sherlock Holmes you ain't. Nothing unusual you say?"

"No damage is evident on the bows," Boland said slowly. "But she could have been holed beneath the hull which won't show until she's raised. Nothing odd about that."

"It takes a pretty fair explosion to make a hole big enough to sink a ship the size of the *Starbuck* in only ninety feet of water," Pitt said. "At a thousand feet in depth, a hairline crack would do it. But on the surface, she could handle anything less than a large gash. Add to that, an explosion would leave debris scattered around; nothing detonates cleanly without leaving a mess. As you can see, there isn't so much as a rivet lying in the sand. Which brings us to the next startling conclusion. Where in hell did the sand come from? We roamed miles of this seamount and saw nothing except jagged rocks and vegetation. Yet there sits your submarine in the neatest little sand patch you ever saw."

"Could be a coincidence," Boland persisted quietly.

"That Dupree laid his dying submarine on the only soft landing spot within miles? Extremely doubtful. Now we come to the tough one. An observation that can't be so easily explained." Pitt leaned closer to the monitor screens. "The remains of sunken ships are most instructive. To a marine biologist they're the per-

fect laboratory. If the date of the ship's demise is recorded, it's possible for the scientist to establish the growth rate of different types of sealife on the wreck. Please note that the exterior hull of the *Starbuck* is as clean and scrubbed as the day she was launched."

Every man in the detection room turned again from his instruments and peered at the monitors. Boland and Stanley just stood there and peered at Pitt. They didn't have to study the monitors to know he was right.

"It would seem," Pitt said, "at least from outward appearances, that the *Starbuck* sank no more than yesterday."

Boland wearily rubbed a hand across his forehead. "Let's go topside," he said, "and discuss this in the fresh air."

Upon the port wing of the bridge Boland turned and gazed out over the sea. Another two hours and it would be sunset and already the blue of the water was beginning to darken as the sun struck the waves on an oblique angle. He was tired, and his words when he spoke, were low and spaced apart.

"Our orders were to find the *Starbuck*. We've accomplished the first step in our mission. Now comes the job of raising her to the surface. I want you to fly back to Honolulu for the salvage crew."

"I don't think that would be wise," Pitt said quietly. "We're not out of the woods yet. It'll be dark soon. And that was when the *Starbuck* vanished."

"There's no reason for panic. The *Martha Ann* has enough detection equipment to spot danger from any direction, from any distance."

"You carry only hand guns," Pitt came back. "What good is detection if you have no defense? You may have found the graveyard of the Vortex, but you don't

have the vaguest idea of who or what caused the wrecks."

"If the devil and his fleet of ghosts haven't made an appearance by now," Boland persisted, "they're not going to."

"You said it yourself, Paul. You're responsible for this ship and its crew. Once I lift off, you can kiss your last avenue of escape good-bye."

"Okay, I'm listening," Boland said evenly. "What do you have in mind?"

"You've damned well guessed the answer to that," Pitt said impatiently. "We dive on the submarine. Instruments and TV cameras can only tell us so much. A firsthand eyeball inspection is imperative. It'll be dark soon and if there's something rotten in Denmark, we've got to find out damned quick."

Boland casually gazed at the lowering sun. "Not much time."

"Forty-five minutes is all the time we'll need."

"We?"

"Myself and one other man. A former submariner if you've got such an animal."

"My navigation officer, Lieutenant March, served four years in nuclear subs and he's a skilled scuba diver."

"He sounds fine. I'll buy him."

Boland stared at Pitt thoughtfully. "Not good."

"Problem?"

"I'm not too keen on sending you down. Your Admiral Sandecker would have my ass if something happened."

Pitt shrugged. "Not likely."

"You act pretty confident."

"Why not? I'm backed by the most sensitive detec-

tion instruments known to man. Nothing reads on or around the *Starbuck*'s hull. Where's the risk?"

"I'll have Lieutenant March help you with the diving gear," Boland gave in. "We have a diving hatch just above the waterline starboard amidships. March will meet you there. But remember, only a visual survey. After you see whatever there is to see, you get back up." Then he turned and stepped into the pilothouse.

Pitt remained behind on the bridge wing, fighting to keep a grim expression. He felt a touch of guilt, but shook it off. "Poor old Boland," Pitt said softly to himself. "He hasn't the vaguest notion of what I'm up to."

CHAPTER 9

Diving on a sunken ship is both exciting and frightening; it has been compared, by the more superstitious souls, to swimming through the rotting bones of Goliath's corpse. The diver's heart begins to pump at a terrifying pace; his mind becomes numb with unwarranted fear. Perhaps it's the romantic visions of ghostly old bearded captains pacing the wheelhouse deck; or sweating, cursing stokers shoveling coal into fiery ancient boilers; or even tattoo-chested deckhands drunkenly staggering back to the fo'c's'le after a wild night spent in a backwater tropical port.

Pitt had felt all these eerie sensations before on wreck dives. This time it was different. The *Starbuck* looked perfectly natural lying on the bottom. If the underwater world was foreign to a surface ship, it was surely the natural habitat of a submarine. At any second Pitt half expected ballast bubbles to burst from the main vents and the huge bronze propellers to begin turning as the long black shape came to life.

He and March swam slowly along the hull, just inches above the bleak seafloor. March carried a Nikonos underwater camera and began punching the shutter lever, the strobe light flashing like sudden shafts of lightning through an overcast sky. Only the release of air bubbles broke the stillness. Shoals of

brightly colored fish glided around the two creatures
who had invaded the privacy of their backyard.

A black and yellow angel fish approached out of
curiosity. At least forty parrot fish meandered past,
flicking their tails. A brownish shark, about six feet
long with white tips, swam above the men and paid
them no attention. There was such an oversupply of
tasty gourmet morsels, the thought of dining on man
couldn't have been farther from the shark's pea-sized
brain.

Pitt shook off his desire to admire the scenery.
There was too much to accomplish and too little time.
Pitt took a firmer grip on the long, aluminum shaft in
his right hand.

Barf the Magic Dragon, March had called it.
The three-foot cylindrical tube with the needlelike
muzzle reminded Pitt of the tool park cleanup men
use to spear paper trash. It was, in fact, the deadliest
shark killer yet devised. Spear guns, repellents, bang
sticks firing shotgun shells; all worked with varying
degrees of success on man's hated enemy. But none
were as safe and sure as Barf the Magic Dragon.
Pitt had seen commercial models of the shark killer;
they were smaller and packed less punch than the
Navy's version. Basically, it was a gun, and in spite of
its deceptive nonlethal appearance, it would literally
turn a shark inside out. If one of the razor-toothed
monsters came too close, the diver simply jammed the
needled muzzle into the sandpaperlike hide and pulled
a trigger, causing a canister of carbon dioxide to dis-
charge into the shark's body. The resulting explosion
of gas would then blow the vital organs of the bone-
less villain through its gaping mouth while inflating
them like balloons. Even that wouldn't kill the beast.
Only after the gas had forced it to rise to the surface

would it then drown. Sharks have no air bladders or gills like other fish. They cannot float; they must keep on the move every second so they can pass oxygen through their mouths and out their gill-shaped clefts. If a shark doesn't move, it can't breathe.

March clicked the camera shutter, wound forward the film, and clicked one more. Then he motioned Pitt upward. They swam slowly over the level deck, past the closed messenger-buoy hatch, past the ballast vents, and the mooring cleats.

Pitt looked at March's expression through his face mask; fear was welling in the young man's eyes—of what lay on the other side of the pressure hull. March held up his camera and pointed toward the surface; he was running out of film. Pitt shook his head. He took a small rectangular board that was attached to his weight belt and wrote two words on it with a grease pencil: ESCAPE HATCH.

March stared at the message board and pointed a finger at the underwater watch on his wrist. Pitt didn't have to acknowledge; he already knew they were down to their last twenty minutes of air. He held up the board again and gripped March tightly by the arm, digging his fingers into the flesh so the young lieutenant would get the urgency of Pitt's command. March's eyes widened in his face mask. He looked up at the shadow of the *Martha Ann's* hull, knowing they were being watched by the television cameras. He hesitated, killing time, trying to run out the clock.

Pitt wasn't fooled. He dug his fingers into March's arm and squeezed tighter. That did the trick. March nodded in understanding and quickly turned and swam toward the forward bow of the *Starbuck*. Pitt hardly expected the younger man to do otherwise.

Pitt stayed almost on top of March's web-footed fins,

swimming into the stream of bubbles that trailed from the lieutenant's exhaust valve. It took only a few seconds before their shadows crept over the hull and they were hovering again above the deck of the *Starbuck*. A crab rudely interrupted during its promenade across the forward walkway, scurried in a crazy sideways movement until it skidded down the rounded hull and sideslipped to a perfect eight-legged landing on the sand below. If the crab was frightened, so was March. Pitt clearly saw him shudder involuntarily as he stared down at the escape hatch, envisioning the grisly scene below.

OPEN IT, Pitt wrote on his message board. March looked at him, shuddered again, and slowly bent down and knelt over the hatch as he applied pressure to the handwheel. Pitt rapped the muzzle of Barf lightly on the hatch cover, the metallic sound amplified by the water. Spurred into action, March twisted the handwheel until the veins in his neck became taut. It wouldn't budge. He relaxed and looked up at Pitt with questioning eyes tainted with anger. Pitt held up three fingers and pointed at the handwheel, signaling a third try. He moved opposite March and shoved the butt of Barf under the handwheel quadrants as a lever. Then he nodded at March.

Together they twisted. Finally the handwheel gave, but only a bare half inch at first, but since that cracked the seal, it became easier with each succeeding inch until it spun easily and knocked against its stop. March swung the hatch cover open and stared straight down into the air lock. The equal pressure between the lock and the outside was a bad sign. Pitt saw his grand plan beginning to crack, but there was one more card left to play and only one minute left to play it.

Pitt wiped off the lettering on the board and then wrote: CAN YOU OPERATE?

March nodded, shivered inwardly at the ghostly suggestion behind Pitt's question, took his own message board, and replied: NO GOOD WITHOUT POWER.

Pitt simply scribbled: WE TRY!

March, deciding that opposition was useless, hesitated a moment to screw up his courage, and then plunged into the forbidden gloom of the air lock compartment. Pitt waited outside until March could get his bearings from what little light filtered in from above. When he had his hands firmly on the air valves, March nodded and Pitt dropped beside him and tightened down the hatch.

The escape compartment was a tubelike chamber built right into the hull of the submarine. It could hold six men and was designed so that the crew, escaping from their stricken ship, could enter, seal the interior hatch, and then flood the chamber by way of an air-release valve. When the water pressure outside equaled the pressure inside and the remaining air was dumped off, the escaping men merely opened the exterior hatch and rose to the surface. In the case of Pitt and March, they were going to reverse the process by draining away the water and then entering what Pitt hoped would be a dry interior.

Madness was the only way March could describe it, sitting in the total blackness of the chamber, pure madness. It would have been much simpler to open the interior hatch without screwing around in the dark confines of the chamber. Why waste time in the useless exercise of trying to pressurize, when the sub was filled with water? All they were going to find was a murky interior filled with bloated, rotting corpses. They'd both be dead too if they didn't hurry; he ex-

pected to go on his short supply of reserve air any second now. Madness, he thought despairingly again. It seemed impossible, but he imagined himself sweating. Then he turned the valve.

The air hissed softly into the chamber and water began draining away. It must be a dream, March told himself. It couldn't possibly be happening. His body let him know of the drop in pressure and, even though he couldn't see it, he knew his raised hand had passed above the water level. Then he could feel slight waves gently lapping at his face. If the mouthpiece from his regulator hadn't been clenched between his teeth he would have gaped in speechless bewilderment. Fighting off the shock and taking a firm grasp of his senses, he fumbled for the waterproof switch he was certain was in the vicinity of the air-release valve. He skinned his knuckles in hurried groping before his fingers touched the rubber switch. Then he raised it, throwing light into the escape compartment.

March was numbed at what he saw. Pitt stood in front of him, leaning against the bulkhead in relaxed indifference to his surroundings, his face mask already tilted up over his ebony hair, his mouthpiece hanging across his broad chest. He stared back at March through green eyes that seemed to twinkle in the glare while the lips beneath the hardened bronze face twisted at the corners in a grin.

March spit out his mouthpiece. "How could you have known?" he gasped.

"An educated guess," Pitt said casually.

"The lights, the pumping pressure," March said dazedly. "The nuclear reactor must still be operating."

"It would seem so. Shall we have a look?"

To March, Pitt's glacial calm was astounding. "Why

not?" he said. He tried to sound casual but his words
came out like a hoarse croak. The water was completely drained away now and he gazed downward at
the interior hatch of the *Starbuck*.

They removed their air tanks, face masks, and fins
in the certainty that if there was breathable air in the
escape chamber, there had to be breathable air in the
sub itself. March got down on his knees in the inch or
so of water left on the interior hatch, and began
twisting the handwheel. This one gave easily; tiny air
bubbles foamed around the lip of the cover as air
vented from within the sub. He leaned down and
sniffed the escaping air.

"It's okay."

"Crack it some more."

March spun the handwheel until a small rush of air
splashed through the puddle at their feet. Then the
pressure equalized and water gurgled away beneath
the hatch. March felt a despairing apprehension; there
was no mistaking this time the icy sweat that seeped
from his pores. He eased the hatch cautiously up on
its hinges and quickly turned aside. There was no way
that he was going to enter that unholy crypt first. He
needn't have worried. Pitt rapidly slipped past and
dropped down the ladder and disappeared from view.

Pitt found himself in the well-illuminated, cramped,
and empty forward torpedo compartment. Everything
seemed neatly in place as though the owners had
temporarily left to play cards in the ward room or
grab a late afternoon snack in the crew's mess. The
bunks tiered aft of the torpedo storage were tightly
made up; the brass plaques on the circular rear doors
of the tubes shined brightly; the ventilation blower
hummed at normal speed. The only sign of movement

was Pitt's shadowy form making its contorted way
across a bulkhead wall. He stepped back to the escape hatch and looked up.

"Nobody's home. Come on down and bring Barf."

He could have saved his breath. March was already
descending the ladder carrying both Barf and the camera case. He handed Pitt the carbon dioxide gun and
furtively glanced around the compartment. His fear
gave way to astonishment when he saw that Pitt
wasn't fooling about the vacant compartment.

"Where is everybody?"

"Let's find out," Pitt said quietly. He took Barf
from March's hand and nodded at the camera. "That
your security blanket?"

March finally forced a tight smile. "I've got eight
more shots left on the roll. Commander Boland might
like to see what we've discovered. He's not going to
be too happy about our breaking and entering."

"Hell hath no wrath like a commander scorned,"
Pitt said. "I'll take full responsibility."

"They must have seen us enter the escape hatch
from the TV monitors," March said uneasily.

"First things first. I'm counting on you for a personally guided tour."

"I served on an attack sub. The *Starbuck* is an engineering marvel none of us even dreamed about five
years ago. I doubt if I could find the nearest john."

"Nonsense," Pitt said loftily. "If you've seen one
submarine, you've seen them all. Where does this
lead?" He pointed at an aft bulkhead door.

"Probably a companionway running past the missile
tubes to the crew's mess."

"Okay, let's go."

Pitt unlatched the bulkhead door and stepped over
the sill into a compartment with seemingly the same

dimensions as the Carlsbad Caverns. It was vast—at least four decks high, a labyrinth of heat exchanger tubes, drive systems, generators, boilers, and two monstrous turbines. A powerhouse, Pitt thought; one of those gas and electric company powerhouses that burst at the seams with nightmare upon nightmare of piping and machinery. As he stood there amazed at the immensity of the room, March brushed past him and slowly, almost hypnotically ran his hands over the equipment.

"My God," March exclaimed. "They did it. They actually combined the engine room with the reactors and set them in the forward part of the ship."

"I thought nuclear reactors had to be mounted in isolated compartments because of radiation danger."

"They've improved the control, so that a man working in or around a reactor for nearly a year, will receive less radiation than a hospital X-ray technician in a week."

March walked over to a large boilerlike piece of machinery that rose nearly twenty feet high and studied it carefully. He followed the heat exchanger tubes to where they finally merged with the main propulsion turbines.

"The starboard reactor is shut down," he said softly. "But the rods are pulled on the port reactor. That's why the system is providing power."

"How long could it sit unattended like this?" Pitt asked.

"Six months, maybe a year. This is a brand-new system, pretty advanced. Might even go longer."

"Wouldn't you say this is an exceptionally clean engine room?"

"Somebody's kept it up, that's for sure," March said, looking uneasily behind him.

"We'd better push on," Pitt said briefly.

They climbed a ladder to another door and stepped over the sill. They found themselves in the crew's messroom; a large, spacious compartment brightly decorated with long wide tables covered in dark blue vinyl. It looked more like a Holiday Inn Coffee Shop than a dining compartment of a submarine. The grills on the galley stoves were cold and again everything was neat and orderly. No stacked pots and pans, no dirty dishes. Pitt didn't even find so much as a tiny crumb laying about anywhere. He couldn't help but smile as he moved past a thirty-two-inch color TV console and a mammoth stereo. Something didn't jell in the back of his mind. In fact, nothing jelled in this whole crazy, uninhabited vessel. Then he had it— a small piece of the baffling puzzle.

"No paper," Pitt said to no one in particular.

March looked at him. "No what?"

"No sign of paper anywhere," Pitt murmured. "This is where the crew passed time, isn't it? Then why no playing cards, magazines, books? Why no salt and pepper, no sugar . . ." Suddenly he broke off in mid-sentence and walked quickly behind the serving line into the galley. He threw open the doors to the supply lockers and the galley storage compartment. They were completely barren. Only the cooking utensils and dishware remained. He noted with grim satisfaction the specks of corrosion on the dinnerware.

March was regarding him thoughtfully over the serving line counter. "What do you make of it?"

"This compartment's been flooded," Pitt said slowly.

"Impossible," March said simply. "The engine and reactor room . . ."

"Were never touched by water," Pitt finished. "That's obvious. You can't dry out a nuclear reactor like a load of laundry, but you can restore a galley that's been flooded." He carefully closed the storage locker doors, leaving them as he had found them.

They hurried down a long corridor past the officers' ward room, the living compartments, and the captain's stateroom. Pitt made a rapid search of Commander Dupree's quarters but found nothing; even his clothing was gone. Pitt felt as if he were standing in a hospital room where a patient had just died and the orderlies had removed every item of the man's existence.

Swiftly, without speaking, Pitt continued down the corridor and stepped into what he correctly guessed was the main control room. Barf tightly clutched in his hand, he padded silently past rows of electronic equipment. His eyes scanned the panels and stainless steel gauges, the radar scopes, the illuminated charts, and transparent tracking screens. It was difficult for him to believe that he was in a submarine beneath the sea instead of a highly complex command center at the National Space Headquarters. The *Starbuck* was humming softly without human supervision, awaiting the day when a command was given that would awaken and send her surging through the seas once more.

At last Pitt found what he was looking for: the door to the radio room. The equipment waited forlornly, as if somehow expecting the operator to return any second. Pitt sat down and, pulling open the nearest drawer, retrieved a manual on the radio's operation. Good old Navy, he thought; operating instructions are never kept more than spitting distance away. He

leaned forward over the transmitter and arranged the necessary dials and switches. Then he turned to March.

"Find the antenna control and shove it up as high as it'll go."

It took March sixty seconds to discover and activate the topside antenna. Then Pitt gripped the microphone; absorbed in his task in the eerie emptiness of the submarine, the return trip to the surface was completely forgotten for the moment. He set the frequency to maritime transmission, knowing his message would be picked up back in the bunker at Pearl Harbor. This ought to make a few people believe in ghosts, he thought devilishly. Then he pressed the button for TRANSMIT.

"Hello, hello, *Martha Ann*. This is *Starbuck*. I repeat, *Starbuck*. Do you read me? Over."

Boland had not been idle. Pitt had no sooner pulled the *Starbuck*'s escape hatch closed when Boland ordered two of his best men to prepare for diving. They were to carry extra air tanks to replace the ones carried by Pitt and March, which, he figured, must surely be on reserve air by now. He pounded his fist helplessly on the chart table. They had been in that sub too long; they must be trapped in the escape compartment. Goddamn Pitt, he thought, Goddamn him to hell for pulling such a stupid stunt.

He grabbed the intercom mike. "You men on the dive platform. You've got less than five minutes to get them out of there. So move your ass."

He jammed the microphone back in its cradle and turned to the TV monitors. His eyes locked on the viewing screens with a cold, impassive stare. "How long?"

Stanley glanced at his watch for the fiftieth time. "If they don't exert themselves, I give them another three minutes."

As they watched the divers hit the water and swim furiously toward the submarine, footsteps sounded in the passageway outside; the boatswain burst into the detection room.

"We've got them!" he yelled. "We've got the *Starbuck* on the radio!"

"What are you talking about?" Boland snapped.

"We're in voice contact with the *Starbuck*," the boatswain said more slowly.

The radio man thought the boatswain had hardly left for the detection room before Boland was leaning over his shoulder. He looked up.

"Believe it or not, sir, Major Pitt is calling us from inside the submarine."

"Tie me in and throw him on the speaker," Boland said. He couldn't mask the excitement in his voice— perhaps Pitt could do the impossible after all.

"*Starbuck*," Boland transmitted, "this is *Martha Ann*. Over."

Boland stared at the speaker as though he half expected Pitt to walk through it.

"*Martha Ann*, this is *Starbuck*. Over."

"Is that you, Pitt? Over."

"In the flesh."

"What is your condition?"

"We're fit. March sends his love." Pitt paused to increase his volume. "The *Starbuck* is not flooded. I repeat, the *Starbuck* is not flooded. If we had another ten men down here, we could sail her home."

"The crew?"

"No trace. It's as though they never existed."

Boland didn't answer immediately. He tried to di-

gest the enormity of Pitt's words, vainly picturing in
his mind a deserted and ghostly ship sitting unattended and ignored. He was conscious of nothing
around him; he didn't even notice half of the crew
of the *Martha Ann* standing in the passageway in
stunned silence. First came the creeping wave of
numbed disbelief, and then slowly, the agonizing,
intolerable realization that it was true.

"Please repeat!"

"The vessel is totally deserted. At least from the forward torpedo room to the main control room amidships. We haven't searched the aft compartments yet.
Somebody was kind enough to keep the electric bill
paid up. We have power from the port reactor."

Boland's knees felt unsteady. He hesitated, clearing
his throat, and said: "You and March have done your
bit for the cause. Make your way to the escape hatch
and return to the *Martha Ann*. I'll have men with extra air tanks waiting for your ascent. Is Lieutenant
March standing by?"

"Negative. He went aft to check for flooded compartments and to make sure the Hyperion Missiles are
still snug in their cradles."

"I guess you know you're broadcasting to every receiver within a thousand miles on this frequency."

"Who'd believe a broadcast from a submarine that's
been sunk for six months?"

"Our friends in the USSR, for one." Boland paused
to wipe his forehead with a handkerchief. "I suggest
we call it a day. Soon as March returns, head back
topside. The admiral may call for a full report. And,
just so you don't get your signals crossed again, that's
an order!"

He could almost see the grin on Pitt's face.

"Okay, Father. Set up the bar. We'll be there in . . ."

Pitt's voice died in mid-sentence. The only sound that emitted from the speaker was the muted rasp that came between transmissions. Boland brought the mike to his lips again, his eyes narrowing from a growing, inner fear.

"I don't read you, *Starbuck*. Please repeat."

Still the muted rasp from the speaker.

"Come in, Pitt. Dammit, why don't you acknowledge?"

Silence was his only reply.

CHAPTER 10

Pitt sat there without moving, gaping speechlessly at the wild-eyed, heavily bearded apparition that stood in the doorway of the radio room. He sat there while he absorbed the shock, waiting for the repulsive and foul-smelling thing to dissolve back into the hallucination where it belonged. He blinked, hoping his mind would erase the image, but the thing simply blinked back.

Then the mouth moved and a hoarse voice whispered, "Who are you? You're not one of them."

"What do you mean?" Pitt said quietly, controlling his voice.

"They'll kill you if they knew you used the radio." The voice sounded remote and distant.

"They?"

Pitt's hand crept down to Barf and closed over the handgrip. The thing in the doorway took no notice.

"You don't belong here," the apparition went on vacantly. "You're not dressed like the others."

The man himself was clothed in dirty rags that resembled a naval noncom's dungarees, but there was no indication of rank. The eyes were dull and the body thin and wasted. Pitt decided to try a long shot.

"Are you Commander Dupree?"

"Dupree?" the man echoed. "No, Farris, Seaman First Class Farris."

"Where are the others, Farris? Commander Dupree, the officers, your shipmates?"

"I don't know. They said they would kill them if I touched the radio."

"Is anyone else on board?"

"They keep two guards at all times."

"Where?"

"They could be anywhere."

"Oh, my God!" Pitt gasped, his body suddenly taut. "March!" He leaped to his feet and pulled Farris into the radio operator's chair. "Wait here. Do you understand me, Farris? Don't move."

Farris nodded dully. "Yes, sir."

Barf held in front of him, Pitt moved swiftly from compartment to compartment, stopping every few seconds to listen. There was no sign of Lieutenant March, and the only sound came from the humming of the duct fans. He stepped into what he immediately recognized as the sick bay. There was an operating table, cabinets filled with neatly labeled bottles, surgical instruments, an X-ray machine, and even a dentist's chair. There was also a crumpled shape lying between the beds that jutted from the far bulkhead. Pitt bent down, although he knew who the inert form had to be.

March was lying on his side, his arms and legs twisted in rubbery grotesqueness, his body fluid circling the body in a congealing pool. Two small round holes bled on a direct line from his chest to the back of his spine; he lay on the cold steel deck, the eyes open, staring unseeing at the blood that had emptied from his veins. Moved by an instinct as old

as man, Pitt gently reached down and closed March's eyes.

As a shadow crept horizontally across the deck and then vertically up the bulkhead, Pitt snapped his body in a half arc and rammed the point of Barf into the stomach of the man standing behind him and pulled the trigger. The black outline against the white paint also betrayed the blurred shape of either a gun or a club in one of the intruder's hands, and, if Pitt had wasted a fraction of a second, he'd have been as dead as March. As it was, he barely had time to see that his assailant was a tall, hairy man, wearing only a brief green cloth around his loins. The face was intelligent, almost handsome, with blue eyes and a burled mass of blond hair. The features Pitt soon forgot. It was the next agonized moment in time that he carried to his grave.

The carbon dioxide hissed as it unleashed its immense pressure into pliant, human flesh. The man's body instantly bloated in a distorted monstrosity of ugliness, the stomach protruding together with the small balloonlike pieces of skin that formed between the ribs. The abject look of horror on the face was wiped out in half a second as his grayish-green innards shot from his nose and ears in a fine spray coating the deck for six feet in each direction, and the mouth contorted to twice its size as a great mass of bloody tissue and pieces of internal organs vomited forth in a cascade of red, slimy matter over the inflated torso in unison with the eyeballs which popped out of both sockets and hung swaying over the puffed cheeks. The arms went straight out to the sides and the hideously deformed figure fell backwards to the deck, slowly deflating to its previous size as the carbon dioxide escaped from the body's orifaces.

Pitt, the bile rising in his throat, turned from the sickening sight, leaned down, and picked up March, carefully laying him on one of the beds. He covered the young lieutenant with a blanket. Pitt's eyes were sad and bitter. He knelt beside the still form as if to say: I shouldn't have let you die. Dammit to hell, March. I shouldn't have let you die.

Pitt stood up, his legs unsteady. The game had changed drastically now. The Vortex had scored close to home.

He turned again to the deformed body on the deck and realized that he was staring at his first tangible evidence. This was no supernatural being from outer space. This was a two-armed, two-legged human being that bled like everyone else.

Pitt didn't wait to see more. If there was another one of them lurking nearby, Pitt knew he wouldn't get another chance at killing them from the inside out. The gas canister held only one shot.

Pitt felt helpless, but suddenly it came to him; the weapon he'd seen in the shadow on the wall, the weapon that had killed March. In two steps, he had found it under the surgical table. He hadn't noticed it before because it was shaped more like a small glove with the index finger pointing, than a standard pistol. The grip was the five-finger type in which each finger had its own special rest and support. The hand fit the stock as though it had been poured in. Only a short two-inch barrel protruding above the thumb indicated a firing chamber. There was no trigger in the usual sense, but a small button set so that the tip of the finger rested on its sleeve, ready to fire with only an ounce or two of pressure.

Pitt didn't wait to test it. Quickly he reached the

radio room, grabbed a protesting Farris by the arm, and raced toward the escape hatch.

They almost made it. Ten more steps across the engine and reactor room and they would have reached the torpedo room door. Pitt braked suddenly, his feet digging in, driving backward against the force of Farris's forward motion behind him as he came face-to-face with a massive mountain of a man wearing only brief green shorts and holding the same type of odd weapon that Pitt clutched in his hand.

Pitt lucked out—surprise was on his side. He had expected and feared an untimely confrontation. The other man clearly had not. There was no "who are you?" or "what are you doing here?" Only the pressure of Pitt's fingers on the button and an almost inaudible serpentlike hiss as his weapon spoke first.

The projectile from Pitt's gun—he still wasn't sure what it was that spat out of the tiny barrel—hit the man high on the forehead at point-blank range. The stranger jerked back violently against the turbine, then fell forward, head and chest striking heavily on the deck. Then, even before the man uttered his last gasp, Pitt had stepped around him and was shoving Farris through the doorway into the torpedo room.

Farris stumbled and fell, sprawling on the deck, taking Pitt down with him, but not before Pitt had smashed his leg just below the knee on the door sill and dropped the weapon. The sharp pain felt as though his leg had been suddenly hacked off. But it was not the pain that paralyzed him as he struggled to rise from the deck, but rather a numbing fear, the realization that he'd blundered by dashing headlong into the forward torpedo room. He groped frantically for the strange gun, knowing it was too late, knowing

that either of the two men standing in the compartment could kill him with ridiculous ease.

"Pitt?" said the smaller of the two men.

Pitt was certain that his ears and his mind were
deceiving him. Then he found himself gazing into the
face of the *Martha Ann*'s helmsman.

Pitt blurted: "You followed us?"

"Commander Boland thought you and March must
be about out of air," answered the helmsman. "So he
sent us down with auxiliary tanks. We came in through
the escape compartment. We never expected to find
it dry."

Pitt's numbed senses were forging back now. "We
haven't much time. Can you flood this compartment?"

The helmsman stared at him. The other man, Pitt
recognized as one of the deckhands, merely looked
blank. "You want to flood . . ."

"Yes, dammit. I want to fix it so no one will be
able to raise this ship for at least a month."

"I can't do it . . ." the helmsman said hesitantly.

"There's no time to waste," Pitt said softly. "March is
already dead, and we will be too if we don't hurry."

"Lieutenant March dead? I don't understand. Why
flood . . ."

"It doesn't matter," Pitt said, staring directly into
the helmsman's eyes. "I'll take full responsibility."
Even before the words were out, the same empty,
worthless phrase he'd given to March haunted him.

The other seaman pointed at Farris, sitting on the
deck, staring straight ahead at nothing in particular.
"Who's he?"

"A survivor of the *Starbuck*'s crew," Pitt answered.
"We've got to get him topside. He needs medical attention in the worst way."

If the seaman was surprised at meeting someone

who should have been dead for months, he didn't show it. Instead, he simply nodded at Pitt's gashed and bleeding leg. "Looks like you could use some of that yourself."

The leg had lost all feeling. Pitt was thankful there was no telltale lump that betrayed a fracture. "I'll survive." He turned back to the helmsman. "Flood this compartment!"

"You win," the helmsman said mechanically. "But only under protest . . ."

"Protest it is," Pitt said impatiently. "Can you do it?"

"No matter what we did, a good salvage crew could blow her out inside of two days. The escape hatch in this compartment is the only way anyone could get in from the outside, so that's some help as long as the sub's power supply can't be reached. Best solution would be to jam the emergency valves closed to prevent blowing and jam the torpedo tubes open to keep the sea coming in. Then disconnect the extraction pumps in case whoever tries to clear the compartment plugs in an outside power source. Probably take them a day and a half to figure out what we've done, and then three or four hours to put everything back in order and pump out and pressurize the compartment."

"Then I suggest you start by securing the door to the engine room."

"There is another way to add a few extra hours," the helmsman said slowly.

"Which is?"

"Shut down the reactors."

"No," Pitt said firmly. "When we're ready, we won't be in a position to afford the luxury of reactor start-up time."

The helmsman looked at Pitt without expression. "God help us if you screw up." He turned to the other seaman. "Disconnect the pumps and throw open the inner torpedo tube doors. I'll handle the vents and the exterior tube doors from the outside." He faced Pitt. "Okay, Pitt, the evil deed is about to be done. But if you're wrong, we'll be the oldest men in Uncle Sam's Navy before we're through paying for this."

Pitt grinned. "With a little luck, you may even get a medal."

The helmsman offered a sour expression. "I doubt that, sir. I doubt that very much."

Boland knew how to pick his men. The two salvage men went about their business as calmly and efficiently as if they were mechanics in the pits at the Indianapolis Speedway on Memorial Day. Everything went off smoothly. The helmsman went out through the escape hatch to open the outer torpedo tube doors and jam the exhaust vents, and it seemed to Pitt that he had barely wrapped his leg with a torn piece of blanket from an empty bunk when the helmsman was giving the prearranged all-finished tapping signal on the hatch. Then Pitt hauled Farris up into the escape tube while the other seaman began opening the valves to let the sea into the lower compartment. When the incoming water had reached equal pressure with only an air bubble two feet from the ceiling, he dove down and unclamped the torpedo tube doors. He was amusingly surprised to see a blue parrot fish swim nonchalantly out of the tube and into the compartment.

Pitt had to force Farris to don the air tank and regulator, and he slipped the face mask over the uncomprehending eyes.

"I'll see that he makes it, sir." The seaman had squeezed next to Farris and held him in a vicelike grip around the waist.

Pitt, grateful to be rid of the responsibility, merely nodded a *thanks* and donned his own diving gear, substituting a fresh air tank for the one he'd drained on the descent. Then the seaman tapped on the hatch with the butt end of a knife and let the helmsman have the honor of cracking the cover from the outside.

In theory, they could have all ridden to the surface in the air bubble as it escaped from the submarine, but theory doesn't always allow for the unexpected, like Pitt's air valve getting hung up on the lip of the escape hatch and being left behind. For a minute he was poised there, watching helplessly as the others shot to the surface, never once noticing that Pitt had missed their bubblelike elevator.

Pushing his weight downward until the valve came free was relatively easy, but when he swam out into the open sea, another unexpected threat came his way: a Sphyrna Levini, eighteen feet of hammerhead shark. For a moment Pitt thought the great gray two-thousand-pound bulk, one of the few species of sharks known to attack humans, was going to ignore him and pass overhead. But then in an unerased moment in time, he watched the broad, flattened head turn and approach, its mouth a mass of razor-sharp teeth curved into a vicious expression.

Pitt's Barf was lying useless, back on the submarine; his only weapon, and a pitifully inadequate one at that, was the small, glove-shaped gun that had killed March. As the shark was homing in on the blood clouded around his leg, Pitt stared spellbound at the shark as it swam effortlessly toward him, curving

slightly in a circle staring at him from one great eye on the end of the hammer.

It cut its arc even smaller, narrowing the gap until it brushed by him only a few inches away; Pitt lashed out with his left hand and rammed his fist against the monster's gills. What a useless, almost comical gesture, he thought, but the unexpected contact surprised the shark, and Pitt felt the pressure of water as the shark spun and swam away. But then it made a U-turn and came back. Pitt kept facing it, kept kicking his fins frantically. He stole a look at the surface, no more than thirty feet away, but he wasn't going to make it; the man-eater was on its second pass and Pitt was down to his last ace.

Pitt held out the gun and carefully aimed; the shark had but to open its mouth and Pitt's hand would be clenched between its teeth. As the creature moved in, Pitt squeezed the button trigger and shot it squarely in the cold, tranquil left eye.

The shark rolled by and thrashed wildly, the rush of water whirling Pitt in a mad backward somersault as though he were being caught by a breaking surf. With all his strength he recovered and broke for the surface, keeping a wary eye on the shark, glancing skyward so he wouldn't ram his head into the keel of the *Martha Ann*. A shadow fell across him; he peered up to see the helmsman twenty feet above, motioning Pitt in his direction. Pitt didn't need an engraved invitation. He made the distance in ten seconds. Then he turned and waited for the next attack. The great board-headed murder machine had halted and staring menacingly out of its good right eye, its powerful fins barely propelling the massive body through the water. Suddenly it spun about and unpredictably swam off

at incredible speed, disappearing in the dark blue of the water.

Exhausted and shaken, Pitt gratefully let himself be pulled up onto the diving platform where helping hands removed his diving gear. He was totally exhausted. Then he looked up and found Boland standing, grimly staring down at him.

"Where's March?" Boland's tone was edged with ice.

"Dead," Pitt replied simply.

"These things happen," he said, and walked away.

Pitt stared at the drink in his hand. His face was devoid of expression but his eyes were tired and red. The brilliant tropical sunset threw its final rays of the day through a porthole and sparkled off the ice floating in the Scotch. Pitt rolled the glass over his forehead, mingling the condensation with his perspiration. He had finished giving Boland the whole story. And now, when he should have relaxed, he somehow sensed that the terrible events of the past hour were only the beginning of something even more sinister.

"You're not to blame yourself for March's murder," Boland said earnestly. "If you had become trapped in the escape chamber, and if he'd drowned, then it would have been on your hands. But God only knows there was no way you could have foreseen a pair of killers roaming the *Starbuck*!"

"Come off it, Paul," Pitt said wearily. "I forced that boy to enter the sub. If I hadn't been so eager to prove a point he'd be alive now."

"Okay. A life has been lost, but the staggering importance of what you found more than offsets a single life. If it cost me every man in this crew to return the

Starbuck safely to the security of Pearl Harbor, I wouldn't hesitate to sacrifice them all, and that includes you and me."

"I appreciate what you're trying to do, Paul," said Pitt.

Boland smiled. "I'm a nice guy because of your influence with admirals. Beyond that, I think you're a pretty shrewd operator. I believe your insane act of flooding the forward torpedo compartment has a Machiavellian scheme behind it. Got an explanation?"

"Simple," Pitt said briefly. "I sabotaged the *Starbuck* to keep her on the bottom for a few days."

"Go on," Boland said. There was no smile now.

"To begin with, there were two armed men down there, and Seaman Farris, who was starved and mistreated. The *Starbuck* was his prison. He couldn't escape because there was no place to go. Even the guards came on in shifts. From where, I can't guess, but they didn't live on the sub."

"How can you say for sure?"

"The epicurean in me. I checked the galleys in the crew's mess and the officer's wardroom. There wasn't a hint of groceries. The guards had to eat. Even Farris couldn't last six months without food. Either there's a McDonald's in the neighborhood we don't know about, or those guys go home for lunch. I strongly suspect the latter. Whoever they are and wherever they come from, they're lurking around down there right now, waiting for an opportune moment to grab the *Martha Ann*. If we disappear like the rest, the Navy Department can kiss off the *Starbuck* for good. That's why I flooded the torpedo compartment. If our mystery pals get wise to the *Martha Ann's* real intent, it stands to reason they'd move the *Starbuck* the hell

out of the area before the Navy steamed over the horizon."

"We could airlift a crew here inside of three hours."

"Too late. We've been on borrowed time ever since we anchored. Whatever happened to those other ships will probably happen to us."

Boland looked skeptical. "The whole idea sounds pretty fantastic. According to radar, there isn't another vessel within five hundred miles, and sonar reports the area clear of any submarines. Where in God's name can they come from?"

"If I knew the answer to that one," Pitt said irritably, "I'd demand a raise in pay . . . and get it."

"Unless you can come up with a tighter case than that," Boland responded, "we'll remain anchored here till morning. Then at dawn we'll begin raising the *Starbuck*."

"Wishful thinking," Pitt said. "By dawn the *Martha Ann* will be lying beside the *Starbuck*."

"You forget," Boland persisted quietly, "I can radio Pearl Harbor and have air support overhead before dark."

"Can you?" Pitt asked.

Boland thought he had an unnecessarily positive look in his penetrating green eyes, but with Pitt it was hard to be sure. Pitt's expression showed exactly what Dirk Pitt wanted it to show and no more.

"Has Admiral Hunter acknowledged your calls?"

"We've only sent on maritime frequency, the same as you from the submarine."

"Doesn't it strike you as odd that Hunter hasn't sent a communication concerning the discovery of the *Starbuck*? You said it yourself. My call from the submarine was heard by every transmitter within a thousand miles. How come none broke in to say

'screw you,' or 'how's the weather?' Why haven't
Hunter or Gunn requested details? Chances are you'll
find nothing got through, even that phony bit about
the burned propeller shaft bearing."

Pitt struck home this time. Boland raised an eyebrow and then calmly touched one of several intercom
switches and said: "This is Commander Boland. Open
communication to Pearl on Code Overland Six. Let
me know as soon as they acknowledge."

"Code Overland Six, yes sir," replied the rough voice
from the speaker.

"What makes you think we didn't get through?"
Boland asked.

"Except for the *Lillie Marlene*, no one else ever got
off a message. Not even the *Starbuck*. It stands to reason that our unknown friends aren't about to let the
world know what we've found."

"If you're correct, then they must be jamming our
transmissions."

"You bet your life they're jamming," Pitt said seriously. "That explains why no signals ever came from
the missing ships. They sent them out all right, but
nothing was received at the maritime stations on Oahu.
It also explains the fake position report from Dupree
before the *Starbuck* supposedly vanished. Our unknown friends have a high-power radio transmitter
stashed somewhere. Probably on one of the Hawaiian
Islands. They'd need a land base to support an antenna tall enough to overpower signals from ships at
sea."

"Commander Boland?" a voice rasped from the
speaker.

"Boland here. Let's have it."

"Nothing, just nothing, sir. They acknowledge all
right, but not on Code Overland Six. I've repeated

the call four times. All they do is send back a request
for a message. Can't figure it, Commander. The calls
on the maritime channel came in letter perfect. Somebody is trying to get cute."

Boland flicked off the intercom. Nobody said anything. It didn't seem important that we were in contact, Pitt thought. All that mattered was that we were
in contact with the wrong party.

"Not good," said Boland, his expression grim.

"That answers one question. But what really happened to the *Starbuck's* crew six months ago? And,
if she's sitting down there all prim and proper, why
hasn't she been put in operation?"

"We can scratch the Russians or any other foreign
power," said Boland. "No way they could have kept
this a secret this long."

"Crazy as it sounds," said Pitt, "I don't think the
capture of the *Starbuck* was a conspiracy, or a pre-
conceived act."

"You're right. It sounds crazy," Boland said evenly.
"It's not exactly the easiest trick in the world to un-
intentionally put the grab on a nuclear submarine in
mid-ocean."

"Somebody mastered it," Pitt retorted. "March and
I found nothing to indicate the slightest damage inside or out of the hull."

"It won't wash. An army couldn't have gained entrance inside the sub. The array of sophisticated
detection gear must have given off a warning. The
Starbuck has automatic alarms that will wake up the
dead when activated by open ventilators or hatches.
Nothing but fish could have come within spitting
distance."

"Still, even modern submarines aren't prepared to
repel boarders."

Before Boland could reply, he was interrupted by the intercom speaker. "Skipper?"

"Go ahead."

"Could you please come to the bridge, sir. There's something you ought to see up here."

"Give me a clue."

"Well . . . sir . . . it's kind of crazy . . ."

"Come man," Boland snapped, "spit it out!"

The voice from the bridge hesitated. "Fog, Commander. Fog is coming up out of the water and covering the surface like an old Frankenstein flick. I've never seen anything like it. It's unreal."

"I'll be right there." Boland stared grimly at Pitt. "What do you make of it?"

"I'd say," Pitt murmured softly, "we've had it."

CHAPTER 11

The fog was a thick white quilt rising over the water, swirling in coils from the light breeze, opaque and oppressive in its clammy wetness. The men on the bridge strained their eyes, peering vainly into the billowing mist; they feared something beyond that can't be seen or touched or understood. Already a shroud of moisture was crawling over the ship, and the visible light became an eerie mixture of orange and gray from the light refraction of the setting sun.

Boland rubbed the sweating beads from his forehead, took a reassuring glance through the wheelhouse windows, and said: "It looks common enough; density is somewhat high."

"There's nothing common about that fog except the color," Pitt said. Visibility barely took in the bows of the *Martha Ann*. "The high temperature, time of day, and a three-knot breeze hardly make for normal fog conditions." He leaned past Boland and studied the radar, watching closely for nearly a minute, checking his wristwatch every so often while making a series of mental calculations. "It shows no signs of movement or dissipation; the wind hasn't budged its mass. I doubt whether old Mother Nature could come up with a freak like this."

They went out on the port bridge wing, two shaded

silhouettes against the peculiar light of the mist. The
ship rolled a scant degree or two under the gentle
Pacific swells. It was as though time had ceased to
exist. Pitt sniffed the air. He couldn't place it at first,
but then he became conscious of what he was trying
to connect; a distant memory.

"Eucalyptus!"

"What did you say?" Boland asked.

"Eucalyptus," Pitt said. "Don't you smell it?"

Boland's eyes narrowed questioningly. "I smell
something but I don't recognize it."

"Where are you from and where did you grow up?"
Pitt asked.

Boland looked at him, mesmerized by Pitt's urgency.
"Minnesota. Why?"

"God, I haven't smelled this in years," Pitt said.
"Eucalyptus trees are common around Southern California. They have a distinct aroma and yield an oil
used for inhalation purposes."

"That doesn't make sense."

"I agree, but there's no denying the fact that this
fog reeks of eucalyptus."

Boland flexed his fingers, speaking to Pitt without
facing him. "What do you suggest?"

"In simple English, I suggest we get the hell out of
here."

"My thoughts, exactly." He stepped back into the
wheelhouse and leaned over the intercom. "Engine
room? How soon can we be underway?"

"Say when, Commander," the voice down in the
bowels of the ship echoed metallically.

"Now!" Boland said. He turned to a young officer
on watch. "Up anchor, Lieutenant."

"Up anchor," the boyish watch officer affirmed.

"Detection room? This is Commander Boland. Any readings?"

"Stanley here, sir. All quiet. Nothing except a school of fish about a hundred yards off the starboard beam."

"Ask him how many and how large," Pitt said, his face set.

Boland nodded silently and issued the request to the detection room.

"By rough count, over two hundred of them swimming at three fathoms."

"Size, man. Size!" Boland snapped.

"Somewhere between five and seven feet in length."

Pitt's eyes shifted from the speaker to Boland. "Those aren't fish. They're men."

It took a moment for Pitt's words to hit. "Men?" Boland said flatly, as if trying to memorize it. "How can they attack from the surface? The *Martha Ann* has twenty feet of freeboard."

"They'll do it; you can be sure of that."

"The hell they will," Boland said harshly. He pounded his fist on the binnacle, snatched a microphone and Pitt could hear his voice echoing throughout the ship. "Lieutenant Riley; issue sidearms to the entire crew. We may have uninvited visitors."

"It'll take more than a few sidearms to turn back a horde that size," Pitt said. "If they make it over the railings, there will be little fifteen men can do against two hundred."

"We'll stop them," Boland said resolutely.

"You better be prepared to ditch the ship if the worst happens."

"No," Boland said calmly. "This decrepit-looking old gutbucket may not look like much, but she still belongs to the United States Navy. I'm not going to

give her up without making somebody pay. Tell
Admiral Hunter what happened here. Tell him ..."

"Tell him yourself. I'm not lifting that helicopter
off this ship without you and your crew."

Boland's lips arched into a grim smile. "Good luck!"

"I'll see you on the flight pad," was all Pitt said.
Then he turned and passed through the door.

The pilot's seat was damp and sticky as Pitt climbed
onto its vinyl padding. He went through his preflight
checklist as the mist tightened around the ship. The
atmosphere was heavy and all light was muted.
Nothing could be seen outside the ship; the sea was
gone, the sky was gone, and only a tiny world of two
hundred square feet was recognizable from the cockpit windows.

He engaged the auxiliary power unit and pushed
the starter switch. The APU struggled and moaned in
protest as its electrical output shoved the copter's
turbine into even faster revolutions until the exhaust
temperature gauge and the whine from the exhaust
pad notified him of a smooth start. Then the rotor
gears meshed and the giant blades began slowly
beating the misty air with their peculiar swishing
sound.

When the needles of the gauges on the instrument
panel settled in their normal operating positions, Pitt
reached over to the copilot's seat and picked up the
towel-encased Mauser. He laid the gun in his lap and
quickly unwrapped it, making certain the shoulder
stock was attached securely. Then he shoved the fifty-
shot clip into the receiver, climbed from the cockpit,
and peered into the ghostly light. Nothing could be
distinguished. The landing skid offered him some

protection as he crouched on his heels and aimed the gun into the gloom.

Ninety seconds was all Pitt had to wait before two spectral forms materialized over the railing at the stern and drifted menacingly toward the vibrating helicopter. Pitt waited until he was certain they were not members of the *Martha Ann*'s crew. Then the Mauser spat.

The pair of seminude figures fell silently as their now familiar projectile guns dropped from their hands and clattered to the steel plates of the deck. Pitt swung around and scanned a full three-hundred-sixty-degree circle before he briefly inspected the fallen men. They lay twisted and limp beside each other, their life oozing from their torn chests. The green-colored, almost nonexistent attire around their hips, and the weapons they'd carried, were identical to those he'd seen on the men he'd killed on the *Starbuck*. The only difference his eyes could detect, a difference he hadn't had time to notice before, was a small plastic box that seemed to be adhered to each man's chest under their armpits.

Before he could study the corpses in more detail, his gaze was diverted by another figure that slowly rose over the handrail. Pitt pointed the gun and fanned the trigger with one gentle kiss of the finger. A short blast shattered the sound of the copter's whirling blades for the second time, and the indistinct form suddenly vanished backward into the mist. Cautiously Pitt crept over to the handrail. He was almost on top of what he was searching for when his hand brushed against it. It was a grappling hook, its six curved prongs covered under a thick sheathing of foam rubber, its length disappearing into the unseen water below.

It was now easy for him to see how these strange
men from the sea, under concealment of the fog, had
silently dispatched almost a hundred ships and
thousands of their crewmen to the bottom of this
godforsaken piece of the Pacific Ocean.

Pitt's thoughts were interrupted by the heavy
thunder of the .45 automatics, punctuated by the
sharper crack of the .30-caliber carbines. Screams from
wounded men reverberated the mist. Pitt felt remote
and oddly detached from the fight that was growing
in intensity.

A stray bullet whined past the helicopter and
dropped far out into the water. "Damn you!" Pitt
shouted. One bullet into a vital part would destroy
the copter.

Three shapes that became men stumbled onto the
flight pad, with glazed eyes and sweat trailing down
their faces. "C'mon, don't lag," Pitt boomed. "Get a
move on!" Pitt didn't turn as he spoke; he kept his
eyes peeled into the gloom. Nearly a full minute
passed before another figure ran onto the flight pad.
The young sailor's panicky headlong dash was so rapid
that he slipped on the wet deck and would have
skidded between the railing bars and over the side
but for Pitt's strong grasp on a flailing arm.

"Take it easy!" Pitt admonished. "It's a long swim
home."

"I'm sorry, sir," the seaman blurted. "You can't see
the bastards; they're on you before you have a chance."

Pitt pushed the young seaman under the haven of
the helicopter as four more men appeared out of the
gray film. One was the helmsman with Farris in tow.
The sole survivor of the *Starbuck* was mentally dis-
connected from the battle going on around him. He

looked straight through Pitt, his eyes wide and dull with abstract unconcern.

"Set him in the copilot's seat and strap him in tight," Pitt ordered the helmsman. Then he turned his attention toward the forward part of the ship. He cupped his left ear and listened, picking up heavy footsteps several feet beyond the unpenetrable haze.

"Pitt, you there?" a voice yelled.

"Keep coming," Pitt shouted back. "No sudden moves!"

"No problem there," said the voice. "I'm lugging a wounded man."

Out of the fog came Lieutenant Harper, the engineering officer who weighed almost two hundred fifty pounds. Over his shoulder he carried a boy who could not have been more than nineteen years of age. The boy's face was ashen, and a thick stream of blood ran down the length of his right leg, splattering in dark, maroon-colored drops to the deck. Pitt reached out and grasped a huge bicep, pulling the massive body attached to it onto the flight pad.

"How many more behind you?"

"We're the last."

"Commander Boland?"

"A whole gang of those naked bastards jumped him and Lieutenant Stanley just aft of the bridge." Harper's voice was apologetic. "I'm afraid they got 'em both."

"Get the kid into the copter and see what can be done to stop the bleeding," Pitt ordered. "And have the men form a firing line with what weapons you have left. I'm going to make one last check for wounded."

"Watch your step, sir. You're the only pilot we got."

Pitt didn't wait to answer. He jumped off the pad and lunged blindly across the deck, his feet slipping on the wet plates, his breath coming in short deep pants. Shapes loomed up in the mist and Pitt opened up with the Mauser and cut them apart. Three men from the sea went down like wheat beneath a scythe. Pitt kept his finger on the trigger, spraying a path in front of him. His foot caught on a rope and he fell sprawling on the deck, the raised rivets marking a neat pattern of bruises in his chest. He lay there a moment, his injured leg throbbing in sledgehammer blows of pain. It was quiet, far too quiet; no shouting voices or gun flashes arose from the fog.

He crept along the deck, keeping to the gunwales, using the lifeboats for cover. The Mauser, he was certain, was down to its last few shells. He stuck his hand in something slimy wet. Without looking, he knew what it was. It trailed off into the gloomy void so he followed it. The stain became a trickle in some places and enlarged to a pool in others. It ended at the still, dead form of Lieutenant Stanley, the detection room officer.

Pitt felt nothing but pure anger, yet his mind was sharp and decisive. His face tightened in a mask of frustration at his impotency to do anything for Stanley. He forced himself to push on, driven by some subconscious urge that told him Boland wasn't dead yet. And then he stopped, listening. A muffled moan came from somewhere directly in front of him.

Pitt almost came upon him before his vision did. Boland was crawling on his stomach, pulling his body across the deck, while a four-foot shaft from a fish spear protruded from his shoulder. His head was bowed and his fists were clenched; the T-shirt that covered his chest and shoulders was drenched in red.

He looked up at Pitt dazedly, his face distorted with pain. "You came back?"

"I lost my head," Pitt said with a tight grin. "Brace yourself; that spear has to come out." He shoved the Mauser into his belt and then gently dragged Boland to a more comfortable position against a bulkhead, keeping his eyes peeled for any more killers. He grasped the spear shaft in both hands. "Ready on the count of three."

"Make it quick, you sadist," Boland said, his eyes filled with pain.

Pitt increased his grip and said: "One." He placed his foot on Boland's chest. "Two." Pitt put his muscles into play and yanked hard. The blood-red spear slid free from Boland's shoulder.

Boland lurched forward and groaned. Then he fell back against the bulkhead and stared up at Pitt through glazed eyes. "You son of a bitch," he mumbled. "You didn't say three." Then his eyes rolled upward and he passed into unconsciousness.

Pitt cast the dripping spear over the side and picked up Boland's limp body, hoisting it over his shoulder. He crouched low and ran as fast as the weight of his load and his stiffening leg would allow, using the cargo hatches and loading derricks as cover. Twice he had to freeze when he heard indistinct sounds coming from the fog. Weakly, dizzily, he pushed himself on, with the knowledge that eleven men would die if he didn't get the helicopter off the *Martha Ann*'s deck. At last, his breath coming in fiery pants, he tottered onto the edge of the flight pad.

"Pitt coming through," he gasped as loud as his tortured lungs would allow.

The strong arms of Lieutenant Harper lifted Boland from Pitt's shoulder and carried the unconscious com-

mander to the helicopter. Pitt pulled the Mauser from his belt and pointed the muzzle in the direction of the bows, firing till the last shell casing completed its arc and dropped to the deck. Then he climbed into the cockpit and threw himself in the pilot's seat, certain that he had beat the odds.

Pitt didn't bother to clasp his safety belt; he eased the throttle from idle, manuevering the helicopter cautiously upward as the rotor blades increased their humming and the landing skids lifted slowly from the flight pad. The copter rose several feet into the fog before Pitt dipped it forward and deserted the *Martha Ann*.

Once clear of the ship, Pitt kept his eyes on the TURN AND BANK indicator until the little ball held steady within the center of its dial. Where's the sky? he shouted in his mind. Where? Where?

Suddenly it was there. The helicopter shot into the evening moonlight. The beating rotor blades rose higher as Pitt gained altitude, and lazily, like a homing gooney bird, the lumbering craft leveled its aluminum beak and began chasing its mooncast shadow toward the distant green palms of Hawaii.

CHAPTER 12

Henry Fujima was the last of a dying breed, a fourth generation Japanese-Hawaiian, whose father, his father before him, and his father before him, had all been fishermen. For forty years during good weather, Henry doggedly pursued the elusive tuna in his hand-built sampan. The sampan fleets that Hawaii had known for so many years, were gone now. Increasing competition from the international fisheries and from irregular catches, had taken their toll of the fleet until only Henry was left to cast his solitary bamboo pole over the upper skin of the great Pacific.

He stood on the rear platform of his solid little craft, his bare feet planted stiffly against the wood, stained through the years from the oil of thousands of dead fish. He cast his line in the early morning marching swells, his mind wandering back to the old days when he fished with his father. He longingly recalled the charcoal smell of the hibachis and the laughter as the saki bottles were passed from sampan to sampan when the fleet met and tied up together for the night. He closed his eyes, seeing the long dead faces, hearing the voices that spoke no more. When he opened them again, they were drawn to a smudge on the horizon.

He watched it grow and magnify into a ship, a rusty old tramp that surged through the sea. Henry had

never seen a large merchantman cut through the waves so quickly. Judging from the white froth that burst nearly to the hawseholes, the ship's speed was close to twenty-five knots. Then he froze.

The ship was holding her course and Henry was directly in her track. He tied his shirt to the fishing pole and frantically waved it back and forth. In terror he watched the bow grow over him like a monster about to swallow a fly. He screamed, but no one appeared over the high bulwarks; the bridge was empty. He stood in helpless bewilderment as the great corroded ship tore into his sampan, shattering the tired little boat into a spray of wooden splinters.

Henry struggled underwater, the barnacled plates slicing his arms as they slid past. The propellers thrashed by and only his desperate struggles kept him from being sucked into their murderous rotating blades. Reaching the surface, he was fighting to catch his breath between the swirling, chopping waves from the ship's wake. At last he managed to keep his head above the surface, slowly treading water and rubbing the salty sting from his eyes, the blood flowing from his torn arms.

It was after ten in the morning when Pitt finally let himself into his apartment. He was tired and his eyes smarted when he closed them. He limped slightly, his leg had been rebandaged, and other than a trace of stiffness, he felt nothing. All he wanted more than anything in the world was to fall into bed and forget the past twenty-four hours.

He had ignored orders to land the crew of the *Martha Ann* at either Pearl Harbor or on the heliport at Hickam Field. Instead he had set the helicopter down neatly on the lawn not more than two hundred

feet from the emergency receiving entrance of Tripler Military Hospital, that great concrete edifice perched on a hill overlooking the south coast of Oahu. He had stood by until Boland and the young wounded seaman were quickly wheeled on their way to the operating tables before he allowed a helpful Army doctor to stitch up the gash in his leg. Then he unobtrusively slipped out a side exit, hailed a cab, and peacefully dozed during the ride to Waikiki Beach.

He couldn't have been asleep in the familiar comfort of his own bed more than half an hour when someone began pounding on the door. At first it seemed like a distant echo in the back of his head and he tried to tune it out. Then he struggled out of bed and weaved across the suite to the door and opened it.

There is a strange sort of beauty in a woman caught in the throes of fear, as though a long hidden animalistic instinct makes her fervently alive. She wore a short muumuu emblazoned with red and yellow flowers that barely covered her hips. Her chestnut eyes gazed up at him, wide, dark, and afraid.

Pitt stood there for a moment before he stepped back and motioned her in. Adrian Hunter swept by him into the apartment, turned, and threw herself into Pitt's arms. She was shuddering and her breath came in choking sobs.

Pitt held her. "Adrian, for God's sake."

"They killed him," she sobbed.

Pitt pushed her back at arm's length and stared into her puffed and wet eyes. "What are you talking about?"

The words tumbled out of her. "I was lying there in bed with ... with a friend. They came through the terrace window, three of them, so quietly we didn't know they were even in the room until it was too late.

He tried to fight with them but they carried funny little guns that made no sound. They shot him. God, they shot him a dozen times. His blood was everywhere. It was horrible."

She trembled; Pitt steered her to the couch and held her tightly.

"I screamed and ran into the closet and locked the door," she continued. "They laughed; they stood there and laughed. They thought I was trapped in the closet but it's a two-way closet. It opens up into the guest bedroom. I grabbed a dress off a hook and escaped through the guest room window. I didn't want to go to the police. I was afraid. I tried to call Daddy, but his office said he couldn't be reached. By that time I was in a panic. I had no place else to go, no one to turn to, so I came here."

She brushed at her eyes with her hand. She stood silhouetted against the light and Pitt could see she wore nothing beneath the muumuu. "It's a nightmare," she whispered. "A dirty, wretched nightmare. Why did they do such a thing? Why?"

"First things first," he said gently. "Get in the bathroom and fix your face. Your eye makeup's halfway down your chin. Then you're going to tell me who it was *they* killed."

She pushed herself away. "I can't."

"Get wise," he snapped. "There's a dead body decorating your apartment. How long do you think you can keep it a secret?"

"I . . . I don't know."

"It'll take the Honolulu police all of twenty minutes to put a make on him anyway. Why the martyr act? Is he a local celebrity with a wife and ten kids or what?"

"Worse. He's a friend of my father's." Her eyes were pleading.

"The name," he demanded.

"Captain Orl Cinana," she murmured slowly. "He's Daddy's fleet officer."

Pitt had enough sense to stay expressionless. It was worse than he thought. He pointed toward the bathroom and simply said: "Go!"

Obediently she padded to the bathroom, turned, and gave him a funny helpless smile and then closed the door. As soon as he could hear the sound of water splashing in the sink, Pitt reached for the telephone. He had better luck than Adrian. Five seconds after he told the 101st Fleet's operator his name, Admiral Hunter was exploding on the line.

"What in hell's the idea of not reporting to me?" Hunter charged.

"I was spun out, Admiral," Pitt answered. "I would have been no use to you until I cleaned up and grabbed a couple of hours' sleep. Which, thanks to your daughter, makes it impossible."

When Hunter spoke again, it was in another voice. "My daughter? Adrian? She's with you?"

"She's got a dead body in her apartment. She couldn't reach you so she came here."

Hunter paused for all of two seconds. Then he came back stronger than ever. "Give me the details."

"From what little I can get out of her, it seems our friends from the Vortex walked in off the terrace and gunned the guy down. Adrian escaped through a double closet."

"Is she hurt?"

"No."

"I suppose the police know about this."

"Fortunately, she didn't call them. As far as I know, the victim is still bloodying up her carpet."

"Thank God for that. I'll get our security people over there right away." Pitt heard Hunter shout muffled commands over the other side of the line. He could easily visualize everyone within shouting distance jumping like frightened rabbits. He came back. "Did she identify the victim?"

Pitt took a deep breath. "Captain Orl Cinana."

Hunter had class. Pitt couldn't take that away from him. The shocked silence ended in a fraction of a moment. "How soon can you and Adrian get out here?"

"At least half an hour. My car's still parked at the Honolulu dock. We'll have to take a cab."

"Better you stay where you are. It seems these killers are everywhere. I'll have a guard detail sent immediately."

"Okay, we'll sit tight."

"One more thing. How long have you known my daughter?"

"Pure coincidence, sir. We both happened to be at the same party a few hours after I brought you the *Starbuck*'s capsule." He made a serious effort to sound extremely casual. "She heard me mention your name and she introduced herself." Pitt knew what Hunter was thinking so he second-guessed him. "I suppose during the course of the conversation I must have mentioned that I was staying at the Moana Towers. She must have remembered in her panic and came here."

"I don't know how Adrian screws her life up so," he said. "She's really a very decent girl."

Pitt paused. How do you tell a father his daughter is a sex maniac who's either drunk or stoned eighteen hours out of twenty-four?

"We'll start for Pearl as soon as the guards get here," was all Pitt could think of to say. Then he hung up and poured himself a shot of Scotch. It tasted like a drain cleanser.

They came ten minutes later, not to escort them to Admiral Hunter's headquarters at Pearl Harbor, but to abduct Adrian and murder Pitt. His attention was divided between Adrian curled up on the couch dozing peacefully like a baby, and the front door. Pitt felt the skin on the back of his neck tighten till it seemed it would pull apart. He had no time to grab the phone.

They had dropped from the roof on ropes, five of them, silently entering the room from the balcony in Pitt's bedroom, their familiar compact pistols pointed not at Pitt's heart, but at Adrian's uncaring, unconscious brain.

"You move; she dies," said the man in the middle, a giant of a man with blazing golden eyes.

Pitt, in those first few seconds of shock, was conscious only of his total absence of emotion, as if his complete lack of anticipation had somehow deprived him of any facility to think. But then came the slow bitter realization that this massive man standing before him had been manipulating his waking destiny for over a week. It was the man with the deep yellow eyes who had haunted his dreams and nightmares, the man who had discovered the secret of Kanoli from the archives of the Bishop Museum so many years ago.

The huge man stepped closer. He looked too young for a man who must have been nearing his seventies. The aging process had not wrinkled his skin nor withered his muscles. He was dressed casually like a beach bather with swimming trunks and a hotel towel thrown carelessly over one shoulder, while the other men with him wore street clothes. His face was

long and gaunt, and was framed by a heavy layer of
unkempt silver hair.

The giant walked over and, gazing down from his
hypnotic yellow eyes six feet, eight inches above the
ground, he smiled with the friendliness of a barracuda.

"Dirk Pitt of the National Underwater Marine
Agency." The voice was quiet and deep, but there
was nothing evil or menacing about it. "This is an
honor. I have followed your exploits over the years
with some interest and occasional amusement."

"I'm flattered you found me entertaining."

"Spoken like a brave man. I'd have expected nothing
less." The giant nodded to his men. They pinned Pitt
helplessly to a chair before he could begin to realize
what was happening.

"My apologies for the inconvenience, Mr. Pitt. A
dirty game, unpleasant as dirty games go, but
essential. It is unfortunate that I had to draw you
into my strategy. I had intended on utilizing your
services purely as a messenger. I could not have foreseen your ultimate involvement."

"A neatly staged event," Pitt said slowly. "How long
did you follow me around, waiting for an opportunity
to fox me into discovering the Starbuck's message
capsule? Why me? A ten-year-old boy could have
picked up the capsule on the beach and carried it to
Admiral Hunter."

"Impact, Major. Impact and believability. You have
influential friends and relatives in Washington, and
your record with NUMA is quite respectable. I knew
there would be doubts about the accuracy of the
message so I counted on your reputation to give the
discovery impact and believability." He smiled faintly
and ran his hand through the wavy mass of gray hair.
"But it proved to be a most regrettable choice. As it

turned out, you were the one who convinced Admiral Hunter that Commander Dupree's message was counterfeit."

"A pity," Pitt said sarcastically. He decided to throw out a probe. "Your informant didn't miss much."

"Yes, he was quite diligent at times."

There was a long moment's silence. Pitt turned and looked at Adrian. She was still serenely curled on the couch. Lucky her, Pitt thought; she's sleeping through the whole ugly scene. He pushed his attention back to the giant. "I don't believe you've given me the courtesy of your name."

"It does not matter. My name is of no further consequence to you."

"If you're going to kill me, I think it only fair to know who's responsible."

The huge man stood there hesitating, then he nodded heavily. "Delphi," he said simply.

"That's all?"

"Delphi will suffice."

"You don't look Greek." Pitt's hands were firmly tied behind the chair now; two of the men stood guard with their weapons still aimed at Adrian. The other two finished with Pitt and moved back. Except for Delphi, they all looked ordinary; medium height and weight, tanned skin, dressed in casual slacks and aloha shirts. Their faces were expressionless; they accepted Delphi's unspoken authority mutely and unquestioningly. There was no doubt in Pitt's mind that they would kill on command.

"You've built a ruthless and efficient organization. You've concocted one of the great mysteries of the age. Thousands of seamen lie dead from your hands. And for what?"

"I'm sorry, Mr. Pitt. This isn't a play where the

arch villain tells all before he does away with the hero. No theatrics, no prolonged climaxes, no suspenseful divulgence of unnecessary secrets. It's a waste of time to explain my motives to anyone with less intellectual understanding than a Lavella or a Roblemann."

"How do you mean to do it?"

"An accident. Since you love the water, you shall die from the water, drowned in your own bathtub."

"Won't that appear ridiculous?"

"Not really. I intend to make it convincing. The police will simply assume you were shaving with your electric razor while taking a bath. Admittedly a stupid thing to do. The razor slipped from your hand and into the water. The resulting voltage was sufficient to render you unconscious; your head slips beneath the water and you drown. The investigators will report it as an accidental death, and why not? Your name will be printed in the obituary columns of the newspapers, and in time, Dirk Pitt will become a distant memory among his relatives."

"Frankly, I'm astounded I'm worth all the effort."

"A fitting end for the man who came unnervingly close to destroying an undertaking that has been brilliantly designed and executed for over thirty years."

"Spare me the ego," Pitt growled. "What about Adrian? It might look funny if we both drowned while shaving in the tub."

"Ease your mind. Miss Hunter is not destined to be harmed. I'm taking her as a hostage. Admiral Hunter will think twice before he continues his quest for the Pacific Vortex."

"That won't stop Hunter for more than two minutes.

Duty takes priority to family in his book. You're wasting your time. Let her go."

"I'm also a man of discipline," said Delphi. "I never deviate once I've drafted my plans. My goals are elementary. I simply wish to be free from the destructive designs of the Communist countries and the imperialistic impulses of the United States. Between them they will destroy civilization. I intend to survive."

Time, Pitt thought. He had to keep the giant talking. Another few minutes and Hunter's men would be at the door. Talk was his only weapon.

"You're insane," Pitt said coldly. "You've gotten away with mass murder for decades in the name of survival. Spare me the old trite phrases about communism and imperialism. You're nothing but an anachronism, Delphi. Your kind went out of style along with Karl Marx, slicked-down hair, and buggy whips. You've been buried half a century and don't know it."

Delphi's studied calm cracked slightly at the edges; a taut flush touched the wide cheekbones, but he immediately gained control again.

"Philosophical detachment is for the ignorant, Major. In a few minutes your irritating harassment will be mine no longer." He nodded. One of the guards went into the bathroom to turn on the water in the bathtub. Pitt tried moving his hands. Although his wrists were wrapped many times, they were loose enough so as not to leave telltale bruises on the skin.

Then, suddenly, Pitt thought his senses were deceiving him; the sweet, fragrant smell of plumeria began to envelope him. It was impossible, yet he knew she was there. Summer was in the room.

Delphi silently pointed to Adrian, and the man who

had tied Pitt pulled a small case from his pocket, inserted a needle into a hypodermic, and then lifted the
the hem of Adrian's short muumuu, unceremoniously
jabbing the needle into one well-rounded buttock's
cheek. She stirred slightly, sighed, frowned, and then
within seconds went into a sleep bordering on a coma.
Quickly, Delphi's assistant placed the hypodermic
case back in his pocket and lifted Adrian up in his
arms, waiting expectantly for new orders from his
master.

"I'm afraid this is good-bye," said Delphi.

"You're leaving before the main event?"

"There is little to see that interests me further."

"You'll never get her out of the building."

"We have a car waiting in the basement garage,"
Delphi said smugly. He stepped over to the door,
opened it a crack, and peered into the hall. As Delphi
was halfway through the doorway, Pitt yelled out.

"One final question, Delphi."

The giant hesitated, turned and glared at Pitt.

"The girl who called herself Summer, who is she?"

Delphi grinned evilly. "Summer is my daughter."
He waved a salute. "Good-bye, Major."

Pitt desperately tried one last parting shot. "Give
my regards to the gang on Kanoli."

Delphi's eyes hardened. Some unformulated doubt
seemed to cloud his mind for a moment, then it
quickly dispersed as he stared at Pitt.

"Good-bye," he said, and then he passed into the
hallway like a shadow.

Pitt had failed to delay Delphi and to prevent
Adrian's abduction. He sat there, agonized, as the
man in the bathroom came out, nodded, and then
returned. The other guard set down his gun in a chair

and approached Pitt, his round, ordinary features masking any dark hint of sadistic traits.

Pitt saw the blow coming, but was too late to duck. He could only bow his head. The guard's fist connected solidly on the top of Pitt's cranium, smashing him out of the chair to the floor against the balcony curtain.

Blackness tightened its hold on his brain but Pitt shook it off and pushed himself groggily to his feet. He dimly perceived the guard kneeling on the carpet, holding a deformed wrist in one hand, and heard him whining like a wounded animal. The bastard broke his wrist, Pitt concluded. A grim smile touched Pitt's face as he realized the pain from the growing knot on his head was nothing compared to a fractured bone.

Pitt stood without moving. Then a hand from behind the curtains touched his arm. He felt a back and forth motion as the cord that bound his arms and wrists was cut. The aroma of plumeria swept over him like a warm and releasing wave. In an instant the bonds were gone and a small double-edged knife was carefully slipped into the palm of his right hand. He didn't dare turn to her, to pull away the curtains that concealed her. Instead he grasped the knife tightly and wiggled his hands to be sure he could call upon them without any numbness or restricting stiffness.

The guard stopped his low wail and began crawling across the carpet toward Pitt. His partner in the bathroom went about his business, not aware of anything above the gush of the bathtub faucet. Then the guard eased the broken limb into his lap, reached toward the chair with his good hand, and grabbed his gun, swinging the muzzle in a short arc and aiming at

Pitt's chest, his pain and hate wiping away all thought of obeying Delphi's orders for an accidental death.

Sweat drained from every pore on Pitt's body. The guard was too far away to make any kind of a move; the projectile from the gun would ventilate his torso before he could even leap half the distance between them. The guard sat for an agonizingly long time, merely staring at Pitt. Then he began inching closer, pushing one knee in front, then the other, half a foot at a time, narrowing the gap to five feet. Still too far.

Pitt was going through the tortures of the damned. Three feet; Pitt needed three feet between them before he could strike with any hope of drawing blood first. An arm's length. It would take an arm's length, he told himself as he gauged the required distance.

The guard crept closer. He kept the gun pointed at Pitt's chest, letting it wander from time to time to the forehead. Once a smirk crossed his face as he leveled it in the direction of Pitt's genitals.

Patience, Pitt told himself over and over. Patience. The two most important words in the English language, he repeated in his mind, were *patience* and *hope*. He just might be able to bring it off; the guard had almost moved into range now. Pitt waited tensely a few seconds longer for insurance. If he rushed the moment, he might not be able to shove the gun far enough away from his body before it discharged, and he had no doubt that the guard's reflexes would squeeze the little firing button at the slightest contact. His only chance of success lay in surprise. He still held his freed hands behind his back, lulling the guard into the security of an easy kill. This had to be it. He let his jaw fall lower and lower and forced his eyes wide in mock terror.

Then Pitt lunged. He knocked the gun upward with

his left arm, ignoring the hiss of the projectile as it passed a scant inch over his shoulder, while in nearly the same motion, he swung his right hand in a short sweeping arc, the sharp blade of the knife slashing the guard's throat to the windpipe. A hideous rasping sound came from the gash in the guard's throat as blood spurted over his chest, over the carpet, over Pitt's arms. The guard's eyes looked on Pitt in glazed shock before they rolled up beneath the lids, and then his body gave a convulsive heave as he slowly collapsed.

Pitt sat transfixed for an instant at the sight of the dead guard. Then he retrieved the gun from the floor and stepped softly toward the bathroom. He could hear the whirring of the electric razor as the other guard readied the instrument for Pitt's execution. The tub was full and waiting. Pitt kept his eyes on the bathoom door as he quietly advanced along the wall.

Suddenly the doorbell chimes echoed through the apartment. Pitt, jolted by the unexpected sound, jerked up and froze as the guard charged from the bathroom, stopping in mute shock at the ghastly sight of his dead comrade laying on the floor. Then he turned and stared blankly at Pitt.

"Drop the gun and freeze," Pitt said sharply.

Delphi's executioner stood still and squinted at the small automatic in Pitt's hand. The door chimes sounded again. The man leaped sideways and, as he brought up his gun to fire. Pitt shot his assailant in the heart.

The guard remained standing, gaping at Pitt through stunned and vacant eyes. His hands fell limp; the projectile gun dropped softly to the carpet as he slowly sank to his knees before toppling sideways and ending in a fetal position on the floor.

Pitt remained immobile, listening to the frantic pounding on the front door, his eyes taking in the debris of death at his feet. The four walls of the room seemed to close in on him. Something was missing. His mind refused to cooperate; the last few minutes had left him confused and numb. Someone else should have been there...

Summer!

He threw back the curtains that bordered the balcony, finding nothing but the wall behind them. Frantically he searched the room, calling her name. She did not answer. The balcony, he thought. She must have followed Delphi and his men from the roof. It was empty, but a rope was tied to the railing that led to the terrace of the apartment below. She had escaped the same way as before.

Then his eyes caught a small flower laying in one of the lounge chairs. It was a delicate plumeria blossom; its exquisite white bloom flushed yellow on the inside. He held it up, studying it as one might study a rare butterfly. Delphi's daughter, he thought to himself. How was it possible?

He was still standing there on the balcony with the flower in one hand and the gun in the other, gazing out over the brilliant blue rippling ocean when Hunter's security men broke through the door.

CHAPTER 13

"Mr. Pitt . . ." The attractive young WAVE spoke hesitantly. "The admiral's expecting you. Oh, by the way," she said, lowering her eyes, "we're all proud to have you in the 101st for what you did on the *Martha Ann*."

"How's the admiral taking his daughter's kidnapping?" He hadn't meant to sound so brusque.

"He's a tough old bird," she answered simply.

"Is he in his office?"

"No, sir. They're all waiting in the conference room." She rose and came from behind her desk. "This way, please."

He followed her down a corridor, where she stopped at a door on the right, knocked, held it open, announced him, and closed it quietly behind him when he had passed through.

There were four men in the room. Two he knew, two he did not. Admiral Hunter came forward to shake Pitt's hand. He looked older, far older, far more weary than when Pitt had last seen him, only four days previously.

"Thank God you're safe," Hunter said warmly, surprising Pitt with a tone of intense sincerity. "How's your leg?"

"Okay," Pitt said briefly. He looked into the old man's eyes. "I'm sorry about Captain Cinana . . . and

Adrian. It was my fault. If only I'd been more alert."

"Nonsense!" he said with a tight grin. "You got two of those bastards. It must have been quite a fight."

Before Pitt could answer, Denver came up and thumped him on the back. "Good to see you. You look as rotten as ever."

"Dog tired, maybe. Thirty minutes sleep out of twenty-four hours beats the hell out of my girlish complexion."

"Sorry about that," said Hunter. "But we're running out of time. Unless we can raise the *Starbuck* damned quick, we can write her off for good." The harsh edge of strain showed unmistakably in the lines around Hunter's eyes. "For what little time that is available, we have you to thank. Flooding the forward torpedo compartment was an act of genius."

Pitt grinned. "The *Martha Ann*'s helmsman was dead sure we'd both wind up paying for damages out of our wages."

Hunter allowed the bare hint of a smile to tug at the corner of his lips. "Come and sit down; but first let me introduce you to Dr. Elmer Chrysler, Chief of Research for Tripler Hospital."

Pitt shook hands with a short little man who had a bony handgrip like a pair of pliers. The head was completely shaven and the ears held a giant pair of horned-rimmed glasses. The brown eyes in back of the lenses were beady, but the smile was large and genuine.

"And Dr. Raymond York, Head of the Marine Geology Department for the Eton School of Oceanography." York didn't look like a geologist; he looked more like a burly truck driver or longshoreman. He was big, just touching six feet, and wide in the shoulders. He flashed a set of perfectly spaced teeth.

As they were introduced, Pitt's hand was crushed by five of the largest and meatiest fingers he'd ever seen.

Hunter motioned Pitt to a chair and then said: "We're anxious to have your account of the *Martha Ann*'s loss and the fight in your hotel room."

Pitt relaxed and tried to force his tired mind into categorizing the events in their proper perspective. He knew they were all watching him closely, listening to every detail he could dredge up from memory.

Denver nodded. "Take your time and forgive us if we butt in every now and then with a question."

Pitt began softly. "I suppose it all started when we discovered the rise on the seafloor, a rise not charted on our underwater topographical maps."

Then Pitt told them everything. The two scientists took notes while Denver watched over a tape recorder. Occasionally one of the men seated around the conference table would interrupt and ask a question which Pitt would answer as best he could. His only omission concerned Summer; he lied, saying he had palmed a knife before Delphi's men had bound him.

Hunter pulled the cellophane from a pack of cigarettes and wadded it in an ashtray. "What about this Delphi character? So far, Major Pitt's verbal contact with this fellow is the only communication we've had with anyone connected, if indeed he is, to the Vortex."

Dr. Chrysler leaned across the table. "Could you describe this man in detail?"

"Approximately six feet eight inches in height," Pitt replied. "Well proportioned for his size; I'm not versed at guessing weight for someone that tall. Rugged, lined face, graying hair, and, of course, his most striking feature, yellow eyes."

Chrysler's brow furrowed. "Yellow?"

"Yes, almost gold."

"That's not possible," Chrysler said. "An albino might have pink eyes with a slight orange tint to them. And certain types of diseases might alter the color to a pale sort of grayish-yellow. But a bright gold? Not likely. The iris of the eye simply does not contain the right pigments for such a hue."

Dr. York took a pipe from his pocket and idly twisted it in his hand. "Most strange that you should describe a giant of a man with yellow eyes. There really was such a person."

"The Oracle of Psychic Unity," Chrysler said softly. "Of course, Dr. Frederick Moran."

"I don't recall the name," said Hunter.

"Frederick Moran was one of the century's great classical anthropologists. He advocated the theory that the human mind would be the crucial factor in man's eventual extinction."

York nodded. "A brilliant but egocentric man. Disappeared at sea nearly thirty years ago."

"The Delphi Oracle," Pitt said to no one in particular.

Denver caught the connection immediately. "Of course. Delphi comes from the oracle of ancient Greece."

"It's not possible," Chrysler said. "The man's dead."

"Is he?" Pitt questioned. "Maybe he found his Kanoli."

"Sounds like a Hawaiian Shangri-la," said Hunter.

"Perhaps it is," Pitt said. He related briefly his conversation with George Papaaloa at the Bishop Museum.

"I still find it hard to believe that a man of Dr. Moran's stature," said York, "could simply drop from

sight for three decades and suddenly reappear as a murderer and kidnapper."

"Did this Delphi say anything else that might tie him to Dr. Moran?" Chrysler asked.

Pitt smiled. "He implied that my intelligence fell far short of Lavella and Roblemann, whoever they might be."

Chrysler and York stared at each other.

"Most strange," York repeated. "Lavella was a physicist who specialized in hydrology."

"And Roblemann was a renown surgeon." Chrysler's eyes suddenly widened and locked on Pitt. "Before Roblemann died, he was experimenting on a mechanical gill system so that humans would be able to absorb oxygen from water."

Chrysler paused and walked over to a water cooler in one corner of the room. He filled a paper cup, creating deep, gurgling sounds from inside the glass bottle, and then returned to the table, downing the cup's contents before continuing.

"As we all probably know, the primary function of any respiratory system is to obtain oxygen needs for the body and to cast off carbon dioxide. In animals and humans, the lungs hang loosely in the chest and must be inflated and deflated by means of the diaphragm and air pressure. Once the air is in the lungs, it is absorbed into the lining and then into the bloodstream. On the other hand, fish obtain their oxygen and expel the carbon dioxide through soft vascula tissues containing many tiny filaments. The device Roblemann supposedly created was a combination gill-lung that was surgically attached to the chest with connecting lines for the transportation of oxygen."

"It sounds incredible," said Hunter.

"Incredible, yes," said Pitt. "But it explains why none of the men who boarded the *Martha Ann* carried diving gear."

"Such a mechanism," Chrysler added, "would hardly allow a human to remain underwater much more than half an hour."

Denver shook his head in wonderment. "Maybe half an hour doesn't seem like much, but it still beats the hell out of lugging the bulky equipment in use today."

"Do you gentlemen know what became of Lavella and Roblemann?" asked Hunter.

Chrysler shrugged.

"They died years ago."

Hunter picked up a phone. "Data Section? This is Admiral Hunter. I want details on the deaths of two scientists named Lavella and Roblemann. Pipe it through the minute it's in your hands. Well, that's a start. Dr. York, what do you make of the marine geology in the Vortex area?"

York opened a briefcase and laid several charts in front of him on the table. "After questioning the survivors from the *Martha Ann*'s instrument detection room, Commander Boland at the hospital, and listening to Pitt's remarks, I'm forced to only one conclusion. The Vortex is nothing more than a previously undiscovered seamount."

"How is it possible that it was never found before now?" Denver queried.

"It's not at all unusual," said York, "when you consider that mountain peaks on land were being discovered right up until the late 1940s, and we have yet to map in any detail, ninety-eight percent of the ocean's floors."

"Aren't most seamounts the remains of underwater volcanos?" Pitt probed.

York filled his pipe bowl from a tobacco pouch. "A seamount may be defined as an isolated elevation that rises from the seafloor, circular in dimension, with fairly steep slopes and a comparatively small summit area. But in answer to your question, most seamounts are of volcanic origin. However, until a scientific investigation proves otherwise, I might suggest a different approach." He paused to tamp and light his pipe. "If we suppose the myth of Kanoli is true, and the island and its people did indeed sink beneath the sea during a cataclysmic disaster, then I might consider the theory that it was uplifted in the beginning and sank in the end by faulting rather than by vulcanism."

"In other words, an earthquake," said Denver.

"More or less," York returned. "A fault is a fracture in the earth's crust. As you can see by the charts, this particular seamount sits on the Fullerton Fracture Zone. It's quite possible that heavy activity could build a rise of several hundred feet, pushing it above the sea's surface during the span of a thousand years and then suddenly drop it back in a matter of days." He was facing the window, his eyes turned inward, envisioning the step-by-step process of destruction. "Mr. Pitt's report on the seabed rise and the cooler water temperature around the mount, also tends to support our fault theory. Cold, deep-bottom water often upwells thousands of feet to the surface from extensive fractures along the seafloor, and this in turn explains the absence of coral; coral will not thrive in water temperatures of less than seventy degrees."

Hunter stared thoughtfully a moment at the charts before speaking: "Since the people who boarded the *Martha Ann* had to come from somewhere, could they have come from the seamount itself?"

"I don't understand," York replied.

"Nothing showed on the *Martha Ann's* radar. That eliminates another ship in the area. Except for the sunken wrecks, no other vessel was detected on sonar which eliminates a submarine. That leaves two choices. They either came from a man-made underwater living chamber, or from within the seamount itself."

"I'd have to strike out the underwater chamber," Pitt said. "We were attacked by a force of nearly two hundred men. It would take an immense facility to house that number underwater."

"Then we're left with the seamount," said Hunter.

Chrysler rested his chin on his hands and looked across the table at Pitt. "I believe you said, Major, that you smelled eucalyptus when the fog surrounded the ship."

"Yes, sir, that's correct."

"Odd, most odd," Chrysler murmured. He turned to Hunter. "As astounding as it might sound, Admiral, your suggestion of the seamount isn't too farfetched at that."

"How so?"

"Eucalyptus oil has been used for a number of years in Australia for purifying the air in mines. It is also known to lower the humidity within a closed area.

The phone buzzed; Hunter picked it up, saying nothing, only listening. When he replaced the receiver in the cradle, he wore a satisfied expression. "Drs. Lavella and Roblemann were lost at sea on board a research vessel named the *Explorer.* It was under charter to a Pisces Metals Company for an expedition to study deep-sea geology for a positive mining operation. The *Explorer* was last seen steaming north of Hawaii about..."

"Thirty years ago," Denver finished. He looked up from a sheaf of papers in his hands. "The *Explorer* was the first ship to disappear in the Vortex."

"A dime to a doughnut, Frederick Moran went down on the same ship," said Pitt.

"Most likely the leader of the expedition," Chrysler said flatly.

"The puzzle is taking shape," York muttered. "Yes, by God, it figures." He leaned back in his chair and looked up as if contemplating the ceiling. "Many of the islands where Pacific natives lived were honey-combed with caverns. They were used primarily for religious reasons. Burial caves, temples, idol rooms, and such. Now if the Vortex seamount was a volcano and disappeared in a shattering explosion, obviously nothing of the native civilization would be left. But if the island dropped beneath the surface due to a movement of the Fullerton Fracture, the likelihood is excellent that many of the caves survived."

"What's your point?" Hunter asked impatiently.

"Dr. Lavella's field was hydrology. And hydrology, gentlemen, is the science dealing with the behavior of water in circulation on the land, in the air, and underground. In short, Dr. Lavella would have been one of the few people in the Western World who could have designed a system for pumping dry a net-work of caverns under the sea."

Hunter's tired eyes gazed at York steadily, but the doctor made no further comment. Hunter rapped his knuckles against the table and rose to his feet.

"Dr. York, Dr. Chrysler, you've been a great help. The Navy is in your debt... Now, if you'll please excuse us ..."

The two civilians shook hands, bid their good-byes,

and left. Pitt rose and walked slowly over to the big map on the other end of the long room.

Denver slouched in his chair. "Now, at least, we know who we're up against."

"I wonder," Pitt said quietly, staring at the red circle in the middle of the map. "I wonder if we'll truly ever know."

It was four hours later when Pitt released his hold on a comforting sleep and drifted awake. He waited a moment and then focused his eyes on two upright brown bars directly in front of his face. His foggy mind cleared in an instant as he recognized a pair of shapely, tanned feminine legs. He stretched out his hand and ran the back of a finger up one of the nylon-clad calves.

"Stop that!" the girl yelped. She was cute, and her face had a soft surprised expression. The figure was lush and was tightly enclosed in the chic uniform of a naval officer.

"Sorry, I must have been dreaming," Pitt said, smiling.

Her face flushed with embarrassment as she unconsciously smoothed her skirt and demurely stared at the floor. "I didn't mean to wake you. I thought you were already up and I brought some coffee." Her eyes smiled nicely. "I can see now that you don't need it."

Pitt followed her snappy swivel action as she walked from the room. Then he sat up on the leather couch, stretching his arms as he glanced around the admiral's paneled study.

It was obvious that Hunter was busy. The desk and floor were littered with charts and papers, and a huge

ornate ashtray was filled to the hilt with cigarette butts. Pitt groped in his pockets for his cigarettes but couldn't find them. He resigned himself to their loss and reached for the coffee. It was hot, but the acid taste restored his dulled senses to near normal. At that moment Hunter walked briskly into the room.

"My apologies for not allowing you more shut-eye, but we've made a couple of breakthroughs."

"I take it you've found Delphi's transmitter."

Hunter's eyebrows raised a notch. "You're pretty perceptive for a man who just woke from a sound sleep."

Pitt shrugged. "A logical guess."

"It took a recon plane all of two hours to spot it," Hunter said. "A three-hundred-foot antenna mast doesn't exactly lend itself to concealment."

"Where is it located?"

"On a remote corner of the island of Maui, situated in an old abandoned Army installation built during World War Two for coast defense artillery. We checked through old records. The property was sold off years ago to an outfit called . . ."

"The Pisces Metal Company," Pitt interrupted.

Hunter scowled good-naturedly. "Another logical guess?"

Pitt nodded.

Hunter gave him a wolfish grin. "Did you know the *Martha Ann* will be docking in Honolulu about this time tomorrow?"

Pitt was properly surprised. "How is that possible?"

"Minutes after you airlifted the crew off the flight pad," Hunter answered, "we programmed the computers to bring the ship back to Hawaii."

"Smash a few instruments; cut a few wires," said

Pitt. "Surely Delphi's men could have stopped the engines or knocked the steering equipment out of control."

"You might think so," Hunter replied. "But the *Martha Ann*'s override command system was designed with that very probability in mind. We work under the constant threat of capture and impoundment by a foreign government at odds, shall we say, with the 101st Fleet's rather clandestine salvage operations. The engine room and navigational controls are automatically sealed off by electronic command with steel doors which would take at least ten hours to cut through. By that time, the ship is safely back in international waters and ready to raise wrecks another day."

"Is she running without crew?"

"No, we airlifted a crew at first light," Hunter said. "Damned good thing too. The helicopter arrived just in time to see the *Martha Ann* run down a fishing boat. They managed to pull the skipper out of the drink only minutes before the sharks would have gotten him. It was a damn near thing."

"Now that the *Martha Ann* is on her way home, what about the *Starbuck*?"

"We write her off," Hunter answered tonelessly. "Orders from the Pentagon. The Joint Chiefs have firmed their decision; better to mangle the *Starbuck* as soon as possible so her missiles can't be launched and then raise her later."

"How do you intend to 'mangle' her?"

"At 0500 hours tomorrow morning the frigate *Monitor* will launch a Hyperion Missile on the position where you found the *Starbuck*. The concussion from the warhead's detonation, combined with the water pressure, will collapse and inundate any air pockets

inside the seamount, as well as destroy the submarine."

"An overkill," Pitt muttered.

"I agree. I presented my case for going back with a crack team of Navy Seals and recapturing the sub, but was voted down. Better safe than sorry, so sayeth the big brass on the Potomac. They're afraid that if Delphi has computed the launching sequence, he could conceivably level thirty cities anywhere around the world."

"An extremely complicated procedure. He'd have to reprogram their guidance controls to strike targets outside of Russia."

"Doesn't matter where he might send the warheads. The Joint Chiefs are afraid he's learned how to do it."

"I disagree. If Delphi has been sitting on the thirty nuclear missiles for six months without letting anyone know about them or if he was threatening to use them, it's obvious that he hasn't figured out the launch systems."

"You're probably right, but it won't change anything. I have my orders and I intend to obey them."

Pitt gave Hunter a long stare. "Are your superiors aware of Adrian's abduction?"

Hunter shook his head slowly. "I'll not confuse the issue with a personal problem."

"If she and Delphi are still on the island and can be tracked down before tomorrow morning..."

"I know your train of thought. Capture Delphi and the crisis is over. A good script, but it won't play. Unfortunately they're both at the seamount."

"You can't know that for certain."

"My people sifted through all the licensed private aircraft in the islands. They discovered a jet seaplane registered to our old friend, the Pisces Metal Company. A team of security men surrounded the dock

where it was kept, but they were too late. Witnesses said that two hours before a giant man and a dark-haired woman climbed on board and took off. We then picked it up on satellite recon and tracked it to the *Starbuck*'s position."

"Then we must assume Adrian is with him at the seamount."

Hunter nodded without answering.

Pitt pulled up a chair opposite Hunter's desk. "Erasing the *Starbuck* and the seascape around her is a grave mistake. We don't know anything about Delphi and his setup. He may have other bases scattered around the globe. Is he a front for a foreign government? What if the crew of the submarine are still alive out there? There are too many unanswered questions at stake to let the whole thing be blown away. Give me one bona fide reason why we should sit around like zombies while a bunch of conference table intellectuals seven thousand miles away dictate our actions from a few scraps out of a data processor. I say we ought to . . ."

"That will do!" Hunter's voice was authoritative. "I do what I'm told, and so will you."

"No, I won't!" Pitt's tone was quiet. "I refuse to stand idle while a terrible mistake is being committed."

A subordinate had never refused to obey Hunter in his thirty years in the Navy. He was at a loss as how to react. "I can have you locked up till you cool off," was his only retort.

"You can damn well try," Pitt said coldly. "I'm right and you have no sound argument. If we eliminate Moran or Delphi, or whatever he calls himself, and another ship disappears, we'll always wonder. And if more vanish over the next few years, we'll have to

start from scratch. There'd be nothing to go on but a nagging doubt that we failed."

Hunter gazed at Pitt. Twenty years ago it would have been Hunter on the other side of the table, staking his life on a conviction, ready to gamble away a service career on something he believed in. Giving up a ship, in this case, the *Starbuck*, ran counter to the traditions he had served since his first day at the Naval Academy. Yet, he had never disobeyed an order in his life, and there were times he wished he had. There might be a chance, an almost hopeless, impossible chance. Something that Admiral Sandecker had said about Pitt came back to him. "With this man, almost anything is possible."

He made his decision. "Okay," he said, "you bought yourself a show. There'll be hell to pay in Washington; but we'll worry about that later. Whatever plan you've got, it had better be good."

Pitt relaxed. "Simply put; we put a trained submarine crew inside the *Starbuck* and order a squad of marines to shut down Delphi's transmitter before 0500 hours tomorrow."

"Easier said than attempted," muttered Hunter. "We've less than fifteen hours."

For several moments Pitt was silent. When he spoke, he sounded cold and grim.

"There's a solution. It'll cost the taxpayers a few bucks. But it has a better than fifty-fifty chance at succeeding."

Hunter stirred uneasily as Pitt explained his plan. He reluctantly gave his permission, thinking that either the plan was insane, or that Pitt hadn't told him all of it. He guessed the latter.

CHAPTER 14

The ancient Douglas C–54 aircraft sat poised on the runway, aiming its bow down the black asphalt between the bordering rows of colored marker lights. The wings and fuselage quivered in symphony with the four vibrating engines as their prop wash hurled dust and debris under the horizontal stabilizer into the night. Then the plane began to move forward, gathering speed with agonizing slowness as the runway lights reflected off the shiny aluminum surface and flickered across the windows. Finally it lifted off the concrete and swept elegantly over the lights of Honolulu, making a wide left bank over Diamond Head and heading north into the tradewinds. Soon Pitt's hand eased the four-throttle arms back and cocked an ear to the roaring engines as he checked the RPM and torque gauges, satisfied that the shuddering and noisy relic would get him where he wanted to go.

"I've been meaning to ask you, Ace. Have you ever ditched an airplane in the drink?" This from a short, barrel-chested man in the copilot's seat.

"Not lately," Pitt replied.

The dark, curly-haired little man threw his arms in the air and faked a pained facial expression. "Oh, Lord, why did I let myself get conned into this insane comedy?" He turned and offered Pitt a crooked smile.

"I guess I'm just so good-natured at heart that everybody takes advantage of me."

"Don't hand me that crap," Pitt blurted. "I've known you since kindergarten—no one's ever taken advantage of you."

Al Giordino slouched down in his seat and brushed a straggling lock of black hair from one eye. "Is that so? What about the time I worked for months selling violets on street corners so I could take that gorgeous little blond cheerleader to the high school prom?"

"Well, what about it?"

"God, what gall... well, what about it?" he mimicked. "You bastard. When we got to the dance you told her I had the clap ... she wouldn't have anything to do with me for the rest of the evening."

"Ah yes, now I remember," chuckled Pitt. "She even insisted I take her home." He tilted his head back and closed his eyes, reminiscing. "What a soft, cuddly little creature she was. It's too bad you two didn't hit it off."

Giordino's face registered blank astonishment. "Talk about cavalier treatment."

Pitt and Giordino were close friends; they were classmates in both high school and college. Giordino held his hands aloft and stretched. He was short, no more than five feet four in height, his skin dark and swarthy, and his Italian ancestry clearly evident in his black curly hair. Complete opposites in appearance, Pitt and Giordino were ideally suited to one another; one of the primary reasons why Pitt had insisted that Giordino become his Assistant Special Projects Director. Their escapades, much to the chagrin of Admiral Sandecker, were already legend throughout the oceanographic agency.

"Won't Hickam Field's commanding officer be a

mite irritated when he finds out we broke his private airplane?" asked Giordino.

"He can't wait. As soon as this old museum-piece lands in the drink, the good general will put in a requisition for a new jet transport."

Giordino sighed wistfully. "Ah, to own your own airplane. I'd like an antique B-17 Flying Fortress with a king-sized bed and a wet bar stocked with booze."

"And you can paint out the Air Force insignia on the wings and replace it with a pair of bunnies."

"Not bad," Giordino said. "Just for that, I might even let you borrow it now and then, for a small fee, of course."

Pitt gave up. He looked out the side cockpit window at the sea below and spotted the lights of a merchantman headed in a northeasterly direction toward San Francisco. He could discern no whitecaps; the black ocean seemed smooth and unbroken. A calm sea is best for impact, he reflected, but it also makes it difficult to judge height.

"How much further to your mysterious playground?" asked Giordino.

"Another five hundred miles," Pitt replied.

"At the rate you're pushing this old whale, we should be there in less than two hours." Giordino propped his feet on the instrument panel. "We're already at twelve thousand feet. When do you want to start your descent?"

"In about an hour and forty minutes," Pitt answered. "I want to take the last leg on the deck. I'm not taking any chances on detection until we set this baby right on the front porch."

Giordino let out a low whistle. "Sounds like we'll have to pick a winner on the first pass."

"We won't get a second chance."

Giordino leaned over and tapped a wide dial in the middle of the instrument panel. "We might do it so long as that underwater position marker keeps beeping away."

Pitt glanced at the homing device and adjusted his course until the needle behind the circular glass settled between the proper markings.

"The signal should become stronger the closer we get."

"Just get us within five hundred yards," Giordino said hopefully. "And Selma Snoop will take us the rest of the way." He nodded toward a small blue watertight box, a battery-operated radio direction finder tightly strapped to the arm of his seat.

"You sure Selma is checked out?" Pitt said.

"She works," Giordino said patiently. "Like I said, put us down within five hundred yards of the beeper and I'll put us down on the *Starbuck.*"

Pitt smiled. In spite of his indolent attitude, Giordino was a perfectionist who rose to every occasion with a style that always amazed Pitt. He motioned silently to Giordino and lifted his hands from the control column. Giordino nodded, and took over command of the aircraft as Pitt unreeled from the cramped pilot's seat, left the cockpit, and moved aft into the passenger section of the fuselage.

Seated in the plush comfort of the general's private transport were twenty men—probably, Pitt mused, twenty of the most resigned men on the face of the earth. They were resigned to death; there was no other way to describe it. True, they volunteered, but the prospect of adventure had overridden their desire for a long and fruitful life. Each man was incased in a black rubber wet suit with the zipper pulled

open to allow cool air to evaporate the sweat oozing from his skin. Behind them, lashed to cargo rings on the floor, rested an assortment of equipment and variously shaped bundles. And toward the rear of the fuselage was a row of air tanks, firmly secured and shielded to prevent them from hurtling across the compartment during the touchdown.

The nearest diver, a blond man with Scandinavian features, gazed up at Pitt's arrival. "Madness, sheer madness."

Lieutenant Commander Samuel Crowhaven was definitely a very unhappy man. "A promising career in the submarine service and I have to throw it away by smashing into the ocean in the middle of the night."

"No great danger. It's really no different than driving a car into a garage," Pitt said soothingly. "I wouldn't worry too much . . ."

Crowhaven was genuinely surprised. "Like driving a car into a . . . you've got to be kidding."

"Easing this bird down on the water is my responsibility, Commander. If I were you, I'd worry about what comes next."

"I'm an engineering officer on a submarine," Crowhaven said morosely. "I'm not cut out to play commando."

"I promise not to murder you and your men on landing," Pitt said quietly. "And Giordino will get you to the *Starbuck*. After that, it's your show."

"Are you sure she's dry?"

"Except for the forward torpedo compartment, she was dry when I left her."

"If nothing's been touched, I can have the torpedo room pumped clean and the sub underway inside of four hours."

"The schedule allows for four and a half. That only leaves you a safety margin of thirty minutes."

"Not much time."

"It's all you've got."

Crowhaven shook his head sorrowfully. "Suicidal, that's what it is."

"You realize, of course, that you may have to fight your way into the sub."

"As I've said, I'm no commando. That's why I invited those steely eyed killers from the SEAL's."

Pitt looked at the five men Crowhaven jerked his thumb at. Members of the Navy's select security force. There was no denying that they were a hard-looking lot. They sat off by themselves, constantly checking and rechecking their equipment and weapons— big, silent, purposeful-looking men, highly trained for fighting on land or underwater. Pitt turned back to Crowhaven.

"And the others?"

"Submariners," Crowhaven said proudly. "Not many to operate a submarine the size of the *Starbuck*, but if anyone can bring it back to Pearl Harbor, they can. Providing one of the reactors is doing its thing. If we have to start cold, we'll never get her clear in time."

"You'll have a reactor," Pitt said confidently. He put up a calm front. In truth, there was no way of knowing whether the sub was still there, or if the port reactor was still pounding its atoms. Wait and hope: the phrase crossed his mind again. There was little else he could do except face the obstacles when the time came. "But if you have problems, get your men out of there by 0430."

"I'm no hero," Crowhaven said dolefully.

Pitt patted him on the shoulder, turned, and walked back to the cockpit.

* * *

Admiral Hunter glanced at his watch for the twentieth time in the last hour. He mashed out the cigarette he'd been nervously puffing, rose from his chair, and crossed the busy operations room to peer at the huge map covering the wall. Behind him Denver was slouched in a stiff-backed chair, his feet balanced on the back of another chair. Denver didn't fool Hunter for a moment with his display of indifference. When the message came on the progress of the aircraft, he jerked upright almost instantly.

"Big Daddy, this is the Kid. Do you read? Over." Pitt's voice crackled through the amplifier mounted over the radio set.

Hunter and Denver were both leaning over the operator before he acknowledged.

"Big Daddy here, Kid. Go ahead. Over."

"Prepare crew for pit stop. Am going for the checkered flag. Over." It was Pitt's signal that he was descending to wave top level and beginning his final dash prior to ditching the plane in the water over the seamount.

The operator answered in the microphone. "Trophy awaits winner. Over."

"See you in the winner's circle, Big Dad . . ."

The voice over the speaker stopped in midword.

Hunter snatched the microphone. "Come in, Kid. This is Big Daddy. Over."

There was a pause. Then the voice came in stronger with a slight change in tone. "Sorry, Big Daddy, for the delay. What are your instructions? Over."

"Instructions?" asked Hunter slowly. "You request instructions?"

"Yes, please comply."

As if in a trance, Hunter set the microphone down and switched off the transmission switch.

"Dear God, they're onto us," he said mechanically.

Denver couldn't hide his shock. "That wasn't Pitt's voice," he said incredulously. "Delphi's transmitter must have invaded the frequency."

Hunter slowly sunk into a chair. "I should have never gone along on this insane scheme. Now there's no way Crowhaven can communicate with us once he's entered the *Starbuck*."

"He could transmit in code through the communications computers," Denver offered.

"Have you forgotten?" Hunter said impatiently. "The communications computers weren't installed in time for the *Starbuck*'s sea trials. The radio can only be operated on standard frequencies. Until the marines move in on Delphi's transmitter, he'll be monitoring every open frequency on the air. Even if Delphi isn't wise to our exact plans as of this moment, he'll know he's been had the instant Crowhaven begins sending..."

"And attack the *Starbuck* or blow it to pieces," Denver finished.

Hunter's voice dropped until it was barely distinguishable. "God help them," he murmured. "He's the only one who can now."

Pitt ripped off his earphones and hurled them on the cockpit floor. "The bastard's cut us off," he snapped. "If Delphi guesses what we're about, he'll lay a trap sure as hell."

"A wonderful feeling knowing that I've got friends like you," Giordino said with a sarcastic smile.

"You *are* lucky." There was no answering smile on Pitt's face. "Chances are, Admiral Hunter is praying we'll abort the mission."

"No way," Giordino said seriously. "You people

overestimated this big yellow-eyed clown. Bet you a case of good booze we get in and out before it dawns on him that he's been hit by the two greatest submarine thieves in the Pacific."

"If you say so."

"Face it," Giordino said loftily. "Nobody in their right mind would voluntarily ditch an aircraft in the sea during the dead of night—except you, that is. This Delphi guy probably thinks we're only on a reconnaissance flight. He won't suspect anything before daylight."

"I like your optimism."

"Mom always said I had a way with words."

"What about our passengers?"

"Nobody begged them to come. They're probably back there writing their obituaries anyway. Why disappoint them?"

"Okay, we'll go for it." Pitt reached around the control column and tapped the altimeter. The small white needles lay idly on the bottom pegs. He turned on the landing lights and watched the water hurtle under the fuselage as the air speed indicator quivered at two hundred seventy knots. Then he pulled on a second set of earphones and listened intently for a few moments. "The signals from the underwater marker are nearing their peak," he said. "We had best run over the final landing check."

Giordino sighed lazily, unbuckled his seat belt, moved back to the engineer's panel, and passed the checklist to Pitt. "Read it back to me."

Pitt read off the numbered items on the printed card while Giordino acknowledged.

"Spark advance selector switches?"

"Twenty percent normal," Giordino answered.

"Mixture levels?"

"Check."

Pitt droned on through the tedious but necessary routine while diverting a cautious eye every few seconds on the sea a bare fifty feet below. Finally he reached the last item on the card.

"Center wing tank line valve and boost switches?"

"Closed and off."

"That's it," Pitt said, flipping the check card over his shoulder onto the cabin floor. "Nobody will need that again."

Giordino bent over the controls and pointed. "The stars near the horizon straight ahead ... they're fading out."

Pitt nodded. "The fog bank."

An ominous smudge soon appeared against the black horizon line. Pitt gradually closed the throttles until the air speed indicator read one hundred twenty knots.

"This is the magic moment," Pitt said quietly. He glanced briefly into Giordino's dark eyes—his friend's face, though unsmiling, was calm and unworried.

"Give me one-hundred-degree flaps," Pitt said. "Then get back in the main cabin with the others and act like a bored streetcar conductor."

"I'll entertain them with a series of my best yawns." Giordino leaned over the copilot's seat and held the ON position of the flaps switch until it registered one hundred degrees. "So long, pal. See you after the bash." He gave Pitt's arm a gentle squeeze, then he turned, and left the cockpit cabin.

There was a crosswind; Pitt crabbed the C-54 to compensate for the drift. As the plane settled a few feet lower, he could clearly make out the height of the swells in the brilliance from the landing lights.

He silently wished he could have layed her on the surface with no beams showing, but that would have been impossible. Not yet, not yet, he said over and over in his mind. Three more miles. It would take split second timing to ease the plane down short of the marker and the fog and still have momentum left to carry it well into the target area. The air speed was dropping past one hundred five knots.

"Easy, baby; don't stall on me just yet."

Pitt concentrated on keeping the wings level—if one of the tips dug into a wave crest, the plane would be transformed into a giant cartwheel. He gently nudged the plane lower, dropping behind the rows of waves, attempting to land on the downward side of one, using its slope to slacken the impact. The propellers were throwing up huge billows of spray behind the engine nacelles, and the fog was beginning to enshroud the cockpit windshield when the first impact came.

It was like a clap of thunder, only louder. A round, red auxiliary fire extinguisher broke loose from its mounting and sailed over Pitt's shoulder, crashing into the instrument panel. Pitt was just recovering from the shock when the plane bounced over the water like a skipping stone and smacked its aluminum belly for the second time. Then the nose dug into the backside of a swell and the C–54 stopped abruptly in the middle of a great splash.

Pitt stared dazedly through the dripping windshield at the mist. He did it. He had brought her down in one piece. The plane was gently rising up and down with the swells. It would float, maybe for a few minutes, maybe for days, depending on how badly the underbelly was ruptured. He exhaled a tremendous

sigh and relaxed, noting with satisfaction that the
batteries had survived the impact and were keeping
the interior of the cabin bathed in a soft light. He
flicked off the ignition switches and the landing lights
to conserve the battery cells, tore off his seat belt,
and hurried through the door to the main cabin.

He found a far more confident group of men this
time. Crowhaven was the first to slap his back. The
rest whistled and applauded; all, that is, except for
the five SEAL's. They were already efficiently going
about their business removing the escape hatch and
checking each man's equipment.

"Good show, Dirk." Giordino grinned broadly. "I
couldn't have done better myself."

"Coming from you, that's a blue-ribbon compliment." Pitt quickly donned his diving gear, slipping
on an air tank and adjusting a face mask.

"How long will she float?" asked Crowhaven.

"I checked the lower deck," said Giordino as he
examined the air tanks on Pitt's back. "There's only
minor seepage."

"Shouldn't we chop a hole in her so she'll sink?"
Crowhaven persisted.

"Not a wise move," Pitt answered. "When Delphi
discovers an abandoned aircraft floating around with
no crew, he'll think we took to the life rafts. That's why
I left all the rescue equipment back at Hickam. It
would never do for him to find the life rafts safe and
sound and unopened. Hopefully, he'll be searching for
us on the surface while we're below."

"There must be an easier way to make admiral,"
Crowhaven said acidly.

Pitt went on. "When you get the sub underway,
communicate with Admiral Hunter on twelve hundred
fifty kilocycles."

Crowhaven's eyes narrowed. "You're putting me on. That's a commercial frequency. I could get my tail in a sling with the Federal Communications Commission if I transmitted over twelve hundred fifty."

"Very likely," Pitt agreed wearily. "But Delphi's got a monitoring system that won't quit. He's already invaded our preplanned frequency. Twelve-fifty is your only chance of getting through. We'll worry about where the chips fall if we're lucky enough to enjoy the next sunrise."

Pitt pulled on his fins and checked his breathing regulator. Then he leaned out the open hatch and peered into the blackness. The swells were washing across the leading edge of the wings as the plane took on a slight nose downward attitude. He turned to Giordino.

"Ready with your magic box?"

Giordino held up the signal detector.

"Shall we?"

"Yes, let's."

"Go find us a submarine," Pitt said, nodding out the hatch.

Giordino sat with his back facing the water for a moment while he adjusted his mouthpiece. Then he threw a jaunty wave to Pitt and disappeared backward into the sea.

Silently, one by one, five SEAL's and Crowhaven followed by his men, splashed into the darkness outside the aircraft. Each went through the door grim-faced. Pitt glanced below him and observed the under-water dive lights blinking on and wavering into the distance as each man aimed his beam on the man ahead and began swimming downward into the depths.

Pitt was the last to leave. He took one last look

around the interior of the aircraft, and, like a man
leaving the house for a weekend vacation, he dutifully
opened the cover to the cabin circuit box and switched
off the lights.

CHAPTER 15

The dark, tepid Pacific water closed over Pitt's head; he momentarily allowed his body to go limp in the weightless dimension of the sea. The circular beam from his dive light illuminated the diver twenty feet below, who was looking over his shoulder to see if Pitt was trailing his kicking fins. It suddenly occurred to Pitt that being last man in line might be dangerous. The suffocating blackness plunged him into a profound sense of anxiety; he was certain that every type of predator imaginable was sneaking into position for a quick bite of his legs. Every few seconds he spun around, flashing the light in all directions, but met no monsters of the night. The only odd-looking creature in his field of vision was his fellow human swimming unconcerned below.

Pitt's apprehension eased somewhat when the bottom loomed up through his face mask—for all he knew he might have been swimming upside down. The rocks took on morbid shapes with ghostlike faces, but they seemed like old friends when he reached down and touched their coarse, solid features. A nervous squid, the first sign of sealife, dashed across his narrow angle of sight and vanished. Then the rock formations tapered away and the seafloor became sandy; Pitt's adrenaline surged through his body as a huge black

shape rose up under the swaying concert of light beams.

The *Starbuck* lay just as he'd left her, looking like a great spectral monster in the blackness. Kicking his fins, Pitt swam past the Navy men to the head of the line and, grasping Giordino by the arm, peered into his friend's face mask. The face inside was softly distorted by the dive light but Giordino's eyes were bright and, in spite of the mouthpiece, his grin was clear and distinct as he gave a "thumbs up" sign.

Pitt wrote some words on his message board, motioned to Crowhaven, and held it up.

THIS IS WHERE WE GET OFF. SHE'S ALL YOURS.

Crowhaven nodded, his blond hair drifting in loose strands. He quickly began distributing his men: four submariners and one SEAL were to enter through the flooded forward torpedo compartment and close the vents and valves left open by the *Martha Ann*'s divers. The rest of the men were to drop through the aft escape chamber into the dry section of the submarine and make their way to the control room.

The submariners' fear had left them now. The time had come for them to rely on their own skills and experience. The men forward entered in one group, but the crew aft had to divide into three shifts due to the chamber's compact interior. Pitt closed the hatch after the last five men dropped into the sub and waited until he felt the surge from the exhaust vents as the water was expelled from inside the escape compartment. Then he pounded the butt of his knife against the hull three times. Almost immediately three muffled knocks came from inside, signaling *no problems so far*. Pitt swam along the narrow top deck to the bow where he repeated his poundings. The reply came back much

slower this time with more of a muted sound due to the acoustics of the flooded torpedo room.

Pitt wrote again on the board.

ENTRANCE AROUND SOMEWHERE. 18 MINUTES.

Giordino understood. Eighteen minutes of air; that's all the time they would have to search for the entrance to the seamount. Pitt tapped him on the shoulder and darted off to the right. Giordino followed Pitt's slithering form as they silently glided over the eerie seascape, bound together by the fragile glow of their lights. They didn't bother memorizing landmarks; instead they placed their trust in the compass strapped to Pitt's left wrist as the only means of rediscovering the *Starbuck* before their air ran out.

Their first encounter was with another victim of the Vortex, slowly materializing in the twin shafts of their lights. The plates on the side of the hull were smooth and clean, and there was no sign of weed growth; it was a fresh wreck. Pitt was at a loss; he had studied the list of missing ships and except for the *Starbuck*, no new disappearance had been reported in the last six months. How could a ship this size vanish without being reported overdue in port?

She was sitting upright as though she were still floating on the surface, refusing to concede her fate. They swam past the deserted decks and saw that she had once been a trawler, a large one. A pity, Pitt thought. She was certainly a fine ship. The bulwarks gleamed and the superstructure fairly bristled with the latest design in electronic scanners and antennae.

So far, there was no sign of Delphi's men, but just to be on the safe side, Pitt gestured for Giordino to stand watch while he searched the bridge. Giordino waved a hand in acknowledgment, stationing himself

at a bulkhead below the starboard bridge wing where he switched off his light and instantly melted into the black depths.

Pitt snaked through the open door of the wheel-house and into its ominous, cryptlike interior. He shined his light about, rooted to the spot by the strange surroundings. His eye caught an ugly transparent snake that wiggled across the ceiling and dissolved into an open vent, then another long reptilian form that slithered into a ceiling corner and then slowly meandered into the vent. The snakes were streams of his own exhaust bubbles that had risen to the top of the cabin before discovering an escape route to the surface.

Pitt didn't know what he expected to discover in the ship, but what he found gave him nightmares for many years to come. The charts, folding back and forth from the current, lay on the table, still firm to the touch as though they had been immersed just the day before. The spokes of the wheel were thrown out in a pathetic circle of despair, as if knowing that no hands would ever grip their contour again. The brass on the binnacle gleamed in the faint light and the compass needle still faithfully pointed toward some forgotten course, while the arrows on the tele-graph were settled forever on the ALL STOP position. Pitt bent closer; something was out of kilter. The letters beneath the signal lever weren't printed in English. He studied them intently for a moment and then swam back to the binnacle, aiming his light at the nameplate screwed flush above the compass open-ing. His knowledge of the Russian language con-sisted of less than twenty words, but he could make out enough of the backward alphabet to decipher the ship's name: ANDREI VYBORG.

So the Russian spy trawler had found the *Starbuck*, Pitt reflected. Only to die and rest beside her, courtesy of Delphi and his pirates. Pitt didn't have time to reflect further. Just then something touched him on the back of his shoulder. Pitt spun around, beaming his light into the face of a man.

It was a face that was frighteningly unnatural and twisted with an ungodly expression. The white blur of teeth shone through a mouth that was agape, and he stared unblinkingly out of one eye; the other eye was hidden by a small crab that had eaten itself halfway into the socket. The man swayed and motioned like a drunken scarecrow, his arms lifting and falling as if beckoning under the silent, unrelenting force of the current. The terrifying wraith hovered four feet from the deck and moved against Pitt who was rooted to the spot, frozen immobile at the sight.

Pitt savagely shoved the dead body away, watching it float toward the inner doorway of the wheelhouse where it dissolved into the curtain of black beyond.

There was nothing more to be seen or accomplished on the Soviet trawler. It was time to get the hell out; there were only a few minutes left before he and Giordino would be on their reserve air.

Giordino was still standing his vigil under the bridge wing when he heard the sound waves off in the distance. He swam up to the wheelhouse and motioned for Pitt, who was just exiting, to douse his light.

Pitt complied; they both crouched below the port window, listening to the approaching whirr of an electric motor several seconds before the dim glow of a light came into view.

At first it looked like a strange, primeval creature, but as it neared, they could see that it was an underwater craft designed like a porpoise with a horizontal

fluke on the tail for control. Two figures sat astride the sleek mini-sub, the man in the front saddle steering, while his partner navigated from behind. A small propeller churned the water behind the rear stabilizer and pushed the two men through the depths at a pace of about five knots. The craft and its passengers were headed directly toward the bridge of the *Andrei Vyborg*.

Pitt and Giordino pressed their bodies against the bulkhead beneath the window. It was too late to contain their breathing; they could do nothing but watch helplessly as their bubbles floated upward into the path of the sub. In a synchronized movement, they each unsheathed their knives and waited for the inevitable confrontation—the twin streams from their exhaust air were bound to give their presence away.

The sub veered around the forward mast and approached the wheelhouse. It was so close now that Pitt could distinctly make out the small breathing units attached to the crew's chests. His grip on the knife tightened; he braced his body to spring through the doorway, hoping to get in the first thrust, knowing his small blade was no match for the projectile guns.

The moment of suspense ended. At the last possible instant, the sub's bow tilted sharply upward, passing through the bubbles and disappearing over the bridge. The sound of the motor slowly diminished. Almost immediately its light was lost to sight and seconds later the last beat of the propeller died away.

Giordino switched on his light and Pitt could see him shrug his shoulders in a questioning, baffled gesture. Then it slowly dawned on Pitt. The *Andrei Vyborg* had not yet belched all of her air pockets. Everywhere along the hull and superstructure small trails of air and oil mingled and rose in lazy spurts to

the ocean's surface. Delphi's men had simply ignored all signs of bubbles, knowing that a sunken ship takes months, sometimes years, to expel its trapped air.

Pitt tapped his watch and pointed in the direction of the retreating mini-sub. Giordino nodded and together they swam over the ship's railing, dropped down to the seafloor, taking advantage of its grotesquely shaped rocks and vegetation for cover. As the dark hulk of the *Andrei Vyborg* receded behind them, Pitt threw her a last look over his shoulder. The Americans now knew the location of her grave, but the Russians, he was certain, would never be told where to find her.

Pitt's depth gauge readings began rising. He led Giordino up a slope on the seamount. The water was cold, far colder than it should have been for this part of the Pacific. Their eyes strained the length of their light's rays, searching the bottom for signs of activity, but evidence that would betray the geometrical straight lines of human manufacture failed to materialize. There had to be an opening, Pitt thought. The mini-sub must have come from somewhere.

They were past their time limit now. There was no chance of making it back to the safety of the *Starbuck*. They had no choice but to keep going until the air in the main tanks was nearly exhausted and then head for the surface in the impossible hope they might somehow be picked up before the concussion from the *Monitor*'s missile crushed their bodies to pulp.

Suddenly Pitt noticed a change in the water temperature. It had become warmer, perhaps by as much as five degrees. At the same moment, a powerful current rolled across the slope, sweeping the sand into small swirling clouds, stretching the weed growth on

a wavering horizontal plane. The sudden surge of the
current thrust its invisible mass against the two men,
thrusting them over the seafloor like Ping-Pong balls
in a hurricane. The vicious flow swept both men
through a thrashing forest of seaweed, the fronds
flaying their faces, leaving red lash marks across
their cheeks and foreheads.

Pitt somersaulted and collided with a huge out-
cropping of rock that was coated with a thick blanket
of marine growth. The green slime rubbed off in
his hands and the sharp edges from a colony of shell
creatures sliced into his rubber wet suit. He was
pinned against the rocks for an instant, and then the
unpredictable whim of the current jerked him back
into its path. He felt something grasp his leg. It was
Giordino's arm, circled around Pitt's thigh just under
the crotch, holding on with all the force of a hydraulic
vise.

Pitt looked into Giordino's face mask and he could
have sworn he saw one brown eye wink. The added
weight of their combined bodies was already reduc-
ing the drag from the current, and more important,
Giordino's grip would keep them from becoming
separated during their swirling journey through the
tempest of exploding sand and seaweed.

Pitt became aware of a dull clanking noise. An odd
tolling sound coming from his airtanks smashing
against the rocks. He tumbled on his back for a
fleeting moment and shined his light upward, briefly
watching the surface shimmer back in the reflection.
He reached out as if to touch it and then realized
that his mind was wandering. He jerked his senses
back to the moment just in time to throw up his arm
and shield his face before ramming a massive barnacle-
coated boulder.

What rescued him in those first jarring seconds was the quarter-inch rubber thickness of his wet suit. But it wasn't enough to save him completely. The barbed growth cut past the rubber and nylon inner lining; Pitt was stabbed with pain as the water around his arm burst into a cloud of his blood. His face mask was ripped away and the swirling sand invaded his eyes and nostrils, scouring the delicate membranes. He tried to exhale through his nose to clear the sand, but only succeeded in adding to the irritation. His eyes stung from the combined attack of sand and saltwater; the sudden closure of the lids threw his brain into spinning blackness.

Then his head slammed into a low rock and a sky-rocket soared and burst into a brilliant rainbow of color, sputtered out, and all was still.

Giordino felt Pitt's body go limp and collapse; the dive light dropped from an open hand and fell to the bottom. Giordino shone his own light into Pitt's face, perceiving the loss of consciousness. He satisfied himself that Pitt's mouthpiece was still secured between the teeth and then tightened his stubby arms around Pitt's leg and continued hanging on.

A stretch of sandy gravel passed under Giordino; he lashed out with his feet, desperately attempting to drag them as a brake. Both his fins were torn away and the skin flayed from his feet and ankles. He clenched his teeth on the mouthpiece of his airhose until the rubber split, and dug his bleeding feet deeper into the sand. It was a move born of desperation, and it failed. His feet merely gouged two grooves in the yielding sea bottom before losing their hold and breaking loose.

Suddenly, like a cat who tires of a mouse, the treacherous undercurrent spun them out of its main-

stream and released them. Giordino quickly reached out and grabbed a handful of seagrass, pulling his unconscious burden toward a small, craterlike pocket on the bottom. Then he relaxed and drifted downward in the calm water, letting Pitt sink gently beside him.

It was quiet in the operations bunker at Pearl Harbor. The typewriters were mute; the computers sat silent and inoperative, their tape reels staring like great round unlidded eyes. Half the staff was grouped around the radio center, the men thoughtfully smoking and saying nothing, the women nervously pouring coffee, looking pale and drawn. The tenseness in the atmosphere lay heavily and drained everyone's energies. Hunter and Denver sat on either side of the radio operator, looking at each other through tired, bloodshot eyes.

Denver pulled a small plastic vial from his breast pocket and idly toyed with it, rolling it back and forth on the table. Hunter studied him for a moment and then raised his eyebrows questioningly.

"What's that thing?"

Denver held it up. "Pitt gave it to me to have analyzed. It was originally in a hypodermic syringe."

"Pitt gave it to you?" Hunter persisted. "What's in it?"

"DG–10," Denver said briefly. "One of the deadliest poisons around. Extremely difficult to detect. The body has all the appearances of a heart seizure."

"What was he doing with it?"

Denver shrugged. "I don't know. He was very sly about it. Said we'd know in the end."

Hunter's eyes were remote, unseeing. "An enigma, that man's a don't-give-a-damn enigma..."

"Telephone, Admiral."

Hunter was interrupted by an officer who held out a receiver.

"Who is it?"

The officer looked lost for a moment, then hesitantly said: "It's Aloha Willie, the late night disc jockey on radio station POPO."

Hunter's mouth dropped. "What is this, mister? I don't want to talk to any damned disc jockey. How did he get on our private lines anyway?"

The officer looked extremely ill-at-ease. "He said it was urgent, sir. His contest riddle is: the Blackbird has come home to nest. He said you'd win a prize if you knew the answer."

"What nonsense is this?" Hunter fairly exploded. "You tell that nut to..." Suddenly Hunter's lips froze and his eyes widened. "My God, *Crowhaven*."

He snatched the receiver and talked rapidly with the voice on the other end of the line. Then he thrust the receiver back at the stunned officer and turned to Denver.

"Crowhaven is sending over the frequency of a Honolulu radio station."

Denver's expression was one of abject bewilderment. "I don't understand."

"It's brilliant. Positively brilliant," Hunter said excitedly. "Delphi would never think to monitor the frequency of a commercial broadcast station, especially a rock 'n' roll program. Nobody but a handful of kids would be tuned in at this time of the morning." He leaned over the radio operator. "Set your frequency to 1250."

At first the concrete walls were greeted by a loud blast of music which assaulted the eardrums of everyone in the bunker. Then, before the confused staff

crowded around the radio fully absorbed the shock, a high-pitched voice that spit words like a machine gun broke through the speaker.

"Hi-ho there, you early morning birdwatchers. This is Aloha Willie with the top forty tunes rockin' your way across the tropical airwaves with some really great sounds for you disc hounds. Time now, three-fifty. Okay, are you ready, group? Glue your ears to the transistors and listen now as we play the flip side of the latest comedy record by Big Daddy and His Gang. Take it away Big Daddy."

The radio operator in the bunker pushed the transmit button and cut in on the program. "Big Daddy calling Our Gang. Come in please. Over."

"This is Our Gang, Big Daddy. Do you read? Over."

Denver leaped to his feet. "That's Crowhaven. He's done it! He's calling from inside the *Starbuck!*"

"We read you, Our Gang. Over."

"Here is the final score. Visitors: one run, one hit, three errors. Home Team: no runs, three hits, four errors."

Hunter gazed emptily at the speaker. "The code for casualties. Crowhaven had taken control of the submarine but it cost him one dead and three)

"We acknowledge the score, Our Gang," droned the radio man. "Our congratulations to the visiting team for their win. When can they leave the ball-park?"

The reply came back without hesitation. "The showers are steaming and the locker room should be)

< wounded."

emptied in another hour. Will load bus and leave stadium by 0400."

Denver rapped the table with his fist and a big

smile widened across his cherubic face. "The reactors are generating steam to the turbines and they'll have the forward torpedo compartment pumped dry in an hour. Thank God, they're ahead of schedule."

Hunter reached over and took the microphone from the operator.

"Our Gang, this *is* Big Daddy. Where is the Kid?"

"The Kid and his sidekick went over the hill in search of a lost gold mine. No word since then. Assume they became lost in the desert and ran out of water."

Hunter silently set down the microphone. There was no need to translate. The message was all too clear.

"We'll bring you up-to-date on the sports at 0500," Crowhaven's voice continued. "Our Gang, out."

Aloha Willie cut back in without missing a beat.

"There you have it, group. Now for number twelve on the charts: Avery Anson Pants singing 'The Great Bikini Ripoff' . . ."

The radio operator switched off the speaker. "That's it, sir, until 0500."

Admiral Hunter moved slowly away and sank in a chair. He stared dully at the wall.

"A high price to pay," Hunter said softly.

"Pitt should have stayed with Crowhaven," Denver said bitterly. "He should have never gone off in search of your daughter . . ." Denver caught himself too late.

Hunter looked up. "I did not give Pitt permission to look for Adrian."

"I know, sir," Denver shrugged helplessly. "I tried to discourage him, but he insisted on making the attempt. He does what he wants to do."

"Did what he wanted to do," Hunter said hopelessly, his voice trailing off softly.

* * *

"Welcome back to the land of the walking dead."

Pitt slowly focused his eyes and looked up into the ever-grinning face of Giordino.

"Who's walking?" Pitt muttered. He wished he were unconscious again, wished the burning ache in his gashed arm and the throb from his bruised head belonged to someone else. He didn't move; he just lay there and soaked up the sea of pain.

"For a while there I thought you'd need a casket," Giordino said casually.

He held out his hand and Giordino pulled him to a sitting position. Pitt blinked his eyes to remove the sand and saltwater. "Where in hell are we?"

"An underwater cave," Giordino answered. "I found it right after you blacked out and we escaped from that god-awful current."

Pitt looked around the small chamber, lit dimly by Giordino's dented dive light. It was about twenty feet wide and thirty feet long, and the ceiling was between five and ten feet high. Three quarters of the floor was water while the remainder consisted of the rocky shelf that he and Giordino rested on. The walls of the semi-flooded gallery were smooth and covered by a score of tiny crabs that scooted about the ledge like frightened ants.

"I wonder how deep we are," Pitt murmured.

"My depth gauge read eighty feet outside the entrance."

Pitt longed for a cigarette. He dragged his sore body across the shelf to one wall and leaned against it, staring in dumb fascination at the blood that splotched his black rubber wet suit.

"A pity I don't have a camera," said Giordino. "You'd make a great human interest story."

"Looks worse than it really is," Pitt lied. He nodded at Giordino's feet. "I'm sorry I can't say the same about your bug-crushers."

"Yeah, I don't think any of my piggies will be going to market for a while." Giordino coughed up mucus and spat it in the water. "Now what?"

"We can't go back outside," Pitt said thoughtfully. "With all this blood, we'd draw every shark within ten miles." He paused, glanced at his watch, and then stared at the water. "We've got nearly two hours before the *Monitor* cuts loose. What say we spend it looking around?"

Giordino's expression was devoid of enthusiasm. "We're hardly in prime condition to go exploring caves."

"You know how easily I get bored sitting around."

Giordino wearily shook his head. "The things I do for a friend." He took careful aim at a crab, spat, and missed. "I guess anything beats an evening with these guys."

"What's the status of our equipment?"

"I'd hoped you wouldn't ask," Giordino said. "All in about the same shape I'm in. Except for our air tanks, which are, if you'll pardon the expression, on their last gasp, we have exactly one face mask, forty feet of nylon line, one flipper, and this light which has just about had it."

"Forget the air tanks. I'll try a free dive first."

Pitt slipped the fin on a foot and took the nylon cord, wrapping one end around his waist. "You rest easy and hold on to the other end of the line. When you feel three jerks, get out of there fast. Two jerks, pull like hell. One jerk, follow me in."

"It'll be lonesome here," Giordino sighed. "Just me and the crabs."

Pitt grinned. "You won't be lonely long."

Pitt picked up the light and sat on the edge of the shelf. He inhaled and exhaled several times, hyperventilating to purge the carbon dioxide from his system. Finally, satisfied that his lungs could hold no more, he slid into the gloomy water and stroked toward the bottom of the cavern.

Pitt was an excellent diver. He could stay underwater, holding his breath, for nearly two minutes. His muscles ached and the bloody cuts in his skin smarted from the saltwater, but he plunged downward with one hand touching the smooth surface of the wall, while the other gripped and aimed the light. The wall sloped on a broken angle for fifteen feet and then leveled out into a confining shaft. Pitt came to a mound of fallen rock that nearly blocked his forward progress, but he managed to snake over the obstacle and found that the walls began expanding away from his line of vision. He pulled his body through into the new chamber and made a gliding ascent, slowly waving the one flipper.

In a matter of seconds, he popped into sweet air and a gallery that was flooded by a soft yellow glow. It was a golden world, a world of yellow where even the shadows were cast in matching hues. The roof was at least twenty feet high and glistened with a mass of tiny stalactites which trickled water in small splashing drops throughout the interior.

Pitt breast-stroked through the gold-tinted water to a rock-carved grand stairway which stretched into a long curving tunnel with odd-looking triangular-grooved notches imbedded in the steps. Two effigies of

square-bearded men with fishtails instead of legs, crouched in a sphinxlike fashion on each side of the landing. The statues were deeply eroded from the dripping water and appeared to be extremely old.

He hoisted his buttocks onto the bottom step of the landing and removed his mask, blinking his eyes to adjust to the eerie strangeness of the light. The tightness of the wetsuit began to irritate his arm. Tenderly, favoring the gashes on his arm, he managed to slip it from his body. When he unwrapped the nylon cord from around his waist he noticed a scant three feet of slack. He gave the cord one sharp tug and as soon as it became taut, he hauled it in hand over hand until Giordino's curly head popped to the surface.

"I've gone to a yellow hell," Giordino sputtered. He pushed the hair out of his eyes and extended his hand to Pitt.

"Welcome to Delphi's House of Horrors." He grabbed Giordino's hand and hauled him from the water onto the step.

Giordino nodded toward the sculptures. "The local reception committee?" He rubbed a hand over one of the squared-off beards, stroking the stony surface. "Any idea what causes the weird light?"

"It seems to emanate from the rocks."

"That it does," Giordino agreed. "Take a look at my hand." He held up his palm and the skin emitted a faint glow. "I can't give you a chemical analysis of the mineral content, but I'm reasonably certain it contains a healthy dose of phosphorescence."

"I've never known it to be quite this bright," Pitt said.

Giordino sniffed the air. "I smell eucalyptus."

"Eucalyptus oil. They use it to lower the humidity and keep the air from getting stale."

Giordino began peeling off his own wet suit, gently easing it over his injured feet. They were, Pitt discerned in the strange light, torn nearly to the bone and were soon surrounded in a spreading pool of blood. But, he thought, he could still walk easily enough.

"I'm going to scout the stairway. Why don't you hang around and enjoy the sights?"

"No chance," Giordino smiled gamely. "I think it wiser if we stuck together. I'll keep up. Just mind the road ahead."

Pitt squinted at Giordino's bleeding body and then looked down at his own. We're certainly a sorry-looking invasion force, he thought; they were both hurt badly.

"Okay, tough guy, but don't play silent hero." Pitt knew his words were useless. Giordino would follow until he passed out. Without waiting for a comment, he turned and began walking up the stairway.

They climbed with agonizing slowness amid the unreal surroundings into a winding tunnel. The only sounds came from their labored breathing and the constant splatter of water trickling from the ceiling. The tunnel gradually narrowed until it was slightly over five feet high and three feet wide. The steps suddenly shortened until they became a smooth ramp.

Pitt kept his back pressed against the damp surface of the wall, and stooped to keep from hitting his head, while inching his way through the passage. The batteries of the dive light were almost dead, and the beam they projected through the lens barely cast

more illumination than the phosphorescence. Every thirty feet he paused and waited for Giordino to hobble painfully within arm's length. Pitt noted that each time he halted, Giordino took a little longer to catch up. It was becoming increasingly apparent to him that Giordino couldn't last much longer.

"Next time, find a cave with escalators," Giordino panted. It took him three breaths to get the words out through clenched teeth.

"A little workout never hurt anybody," Pitt said. He had to keep Giordino going now. If they didn't find a way to the surface above the seamount, they would die a lonely death, crushed under thousands of tons of rocks and water.

Pitt pushed on. The dive light was down to a faint glow and he simply, uncaringly, let it slip from his hand to the rock floor. He hesitated a moment, staring unconcernedly at the light as it rolled down the tunnel in the direction he had climbed. He vacantly wondered what Giordino would think when it came rattling by.

Pitt's gooseflesh rose in unison with a sudden cold air current that danced across his skin. There had to be a vent or an opening ahead. Soon a gentle, textured blue film met his eyes. The blue seemed to waver and alternate in tones that cast soft, animate shadows on the passage walls. Pitt moved closer. The thing swirled with a movement that was familiar. Why can't I recognize it, he dazedly wondered. His brain was fogging—fatigue rushed through his veins and deadened all his thought processes. He stopped and waited for Giordino, but Giordino did not come.

Pitt couldn't combat his feelings of isolation and oppression. For the second time in the last hour he found himself forcing back the black veil that circled

his vision. He reached out with his hand and lightly touched the shimmering blue light. His fingers met with a soft, smooth substance.

"A curtain," he mumbled to no one. "A lousy curtain."

He parted the folds and stumbled into a fairyland of gleaming black statuary and blue velvet-covered walls. The huge room was decorated with delicately sculptured fish in ebony stone imbedded in a deep indigo carpet. The carpet was unlike anything Pitt had ever seen. It encased his feet to the ankles. He looked up and saw that the entire fantastic setting was reflected in a gigantic mirror which spanned the ceiling from wall to wall. In the center of the room, elevated by four carved leaping sailfish, was a clam shell-shaped bed adorned by the body of a naked girl lying on a sparkling satin spread, her white skin contrasting vividly with the blue and black motif of the chamber.

She lay on her back with one knee drawn up and one hand palmed around a small white breast as though caressing it. Her face was enticingly hidden by long, sleek hair that glinted in the light as it trailed across the pillow. The rise and fall of her breathing distinctly showed that her stomach was hard and firm.

Pitt leaned unsteadily over the bed and brushed the hair away from her face. His touch awakened her and she moaned softly. Her eyes slowly opened and locked on Pitt, gazing unseeing for a moment until her sleep-dulled brain registered the sight of the bloody specter standing over her bed. Then her lovely face snapped into shock and her large, inviting lips opened for a scream that was never uttered.

"Hello, Summer," Pitt muttered with a crooked smile. "I was in the neighborhood and thought I'd drop in."

Then the door in Pitt's skull slammed shut and he pitched backward onto the waiting carpet.

CHAPTER 16

Pitt lost count of the number of times he struggled up from the dark mist, only to slip off the top rung of consciousness and fall back into the black void. People, voices, and scenes barreled through his mind in a disjointed swirl of kaleidoscopic confusion. He tried to slow down the blur of images, but the crazy vision persisted; when he opened his eyes to erase the nightmare from his mind, he saw the nightmare itself: the bestial yellow eyes of Delphi.

"Good morning, Mr. Pitt," Delphi said drily. The tone was courteous, but the hatred was manifest in the icy lines of the face. "I regret your injuries, but you can hardly sue for damages, can you?"

"You neglected to post NO TRESPASSING signs." Pitt's voice came through his ears like the halting speech of a senile man.

"An oversight. But then no one invited you to blunder into our power turbine's exhaust current."

"Power turbine?"

"Yes." Delphi seemed to relish Pitt's questioning look. "There are over four miles of tunnels here in my sanctuary, and as you've noticed, it can be rather cold. Therefore, we require an extensive heating and electrical supply as only steam turbines can produce."

"All the comforts of home," Pitt mumbled, still try-

ing to clear his head. "I take it they're responsible
for the surface fog."

"Yes, the vented heat from their power plants coming in contact with the cooler water causes a mist-
like condensation. Presto: instant fog bank!"

Pitt pushed himself upright to a sitting position.
He tried to read the hands on his watch but the dial
was a blur.

"How long have I been out?"

"You were discovered in my daughter's sleeping
quarters precisely forty minutes ago." Delphi stared
speculatively at Pitt's bruised and scarred body, be-
traying no degree of emotion or concern.

"A nasty habit of mine," Pitt said, smiling. "Always
showing up in ladies' bedrooms at inconvenient times."

Delphi maintained his bland expression. The silver-
haired giant sat on a white, sculptured stone couch
lined with red satin cushions while Pitt noted wryly
that he was delegated to the cold, marble-smooth
floor.

He ignored Delphi for a moment and took in the
surroundings. It looked like one of those futuristic
displays at world expositions. The room was of comfortable proportions, about twenty-five square feet,
with walls decorated with original oil paintings of
seascapes grouped in neat but casual array. Incan-
descent lighting came from rounded brass fixtures
beamed at a white ceiling.

Toward the far wall was a broad walnut desk with
a red leather top, handsome matching desk furniture,
and a modern and expensive intercom. But the unique
innovation that set the room apart from anything that
might even slightly resemble it, was the large transparent portal into the sea. It was an arch nearly ten
feet wide, and eight feet high; through the thick,

clear crystal Pitt could see a garden of spiral- and mushroom-shaped rocks that were outlined by underwater lights. An eight-foot moray eel slithered along the lower edge of the portal and cast a stony eye at the occupants of the room. Delphi did not notice the eel; the golden eyes beneath his half-closed lids were still aimed at Pitt.

Pitt's gaze wandered back to Delphi.

"You don't seem talkative this morning." Delphi smiled. "Perhaps you're concerned with the fate of your friend?"

"Friend? I don't know what you're talking about."

"The man with the injured feet. You left him in an abandoned passageway."

"Litter is everywhere these days."

"It's stupid of you to continue your display of ignorance. My men have discovered your aircraft."

"Another bad habit. I double-park."

Delphi ignored the remark. "You have exactly thirty seconds to tell me what you're doing here."

"Okay, I'll tell all," Pitt said randomly. "I chartered a plane to fly to Las Vegas on the special casino tour and we got lost. That's all there is to it, I swear."

"Very witty," Delphi said wearily. "Later you'll be begging for mercy."

"I've always wondered how I'd bear up under torture."

"Not you, Pitt. I wouldn't consider causing you the slightest discomfort. There are several more refined methods of getting at the truth." Delphi rose from the couch and bent over the intercom. "Bring me the other." He straightened and offered Pitt a rigidly fixed and lifeless smile. "Make yourself comfortable. I promise the wait will be short."

Pitt rose awkwardly to his feet. He should have

been reeling from dizziness and exhaustion. Yet, unaccountably, the adrenaline began to pump and his mind ran sharp.

He stole a glance at his watch. It read 0410. Fifty minutes until the marines attacked the transmitter on Maui. Fifty minutes until the *Monitor* blew the seamount into gravel. There was little chance of getting out alive now. The sacrifice would be worth it, he thought grimly, if only Crowhaven got the *Starbuck* underway. He closed his eyes and tried to imagine the *Starbuck* cutting a course through the ocean back to Hawaii, but somehow the picture wouldn't come.

Crowhaven could not remember when he had seen so much blood. The deck of the control room was coated with it, while several places along the electrical panels were splattered wildly in the manner of a Jackson Pollock abstract painting.

Things had gone smoothly at first. Too smoothly. The entry into the aft storage compartment had gone off without opposition; they'd even had time to remove their diving gear and take a short breather. But when the advance party of SEAL's crept into the *Starbuck's* control room, hell broke loose.

For Crowhaven, the next four minutes were the most frightening of his life. Four minutes of ear-splitting thunder spouting from the automatic weapons in the hands of the SEAL's, four minutes of groans and cries that amplified and echoed around the steel-walled interior of the sunken submarine.

Delphi's men were firing their strange silent guns until cut down by no less than six to eight solid hits from the SEAL's rapid fire weapons. He wondered how it was possible for anyone to stand up to such punish-

ment unless they had gone mad. Three men were killed outright and the other four had died since his message to Hunter. Nothing could have saved them.

As for his side, one SEAL was dead; one of those bastards lying on the deck had struck him through the left temple, and three more were wounded seriously. Gritting their teeth against the pain, they were secure in the knowledge that he, Crowhaven the Wizard, was going to raise this big steel deathtrap and get them proper medical treatment faster than a speeding bullet.

But he was already fourteen minutes behind schedule. He was sorry he'd put his foot in his mouth by promising Admiral Hunter to have the *Starbuck* underway by 0400. It was the suction—six months of lying on the bottom of the ocean had built up a staggering suction around the hull. All the ballast vents had been blown; but it hadn't been enough to break away from the clutching grip of the seafloor. He began to wonder bleakly if they were going to meet the same fate as the *Starbuck*'s original crew.

His second in command, a scowling chief petty officer, approached.

"There's nothing left to dump, Commander. Main ballast tanks are empty, and all diesel fuel and freshwater tanks have been blown. She still won't budge, sir."

Crowhaven kicked the chart table like an unruly child.

"No, by God, she's going to move if I have to tear the guts out of her." He stared at the chief with a withering gaze. "Full astern!"

The chief's eyes widened. "*Sir?*"

"I ordered *full astern*, dammit!"

"Begging the commander's pardon, that'll beat the

hell out of the screws, sir. They're half stuck in the seabed now. And there's a good chance we'd shear a shaft."

"It beats the hell out of dying," Crowhaven said curtly. "We'll kick this mother out of here as though she were a mule in a swamp. No more arguments, Chief. Give me *full astern* for five seconds and then jam her *full ahead* for five seconds. Keep repeating the process until we bust her into scrap or she breaks free."

The chief shrugged in defeat and hurried off to the engine room.

After the turbines were engaged, it took only half a minute before the first dire report came into the control room.

"Engine room, Commander," the chief's voice carried through the speaker. "She can't take much more. We've already bent the screw blades, twisting them into the sand. They're out of balance and vibrating like crazy."

"Keep at it," Crowhaven snapped over the microphone. He didn't have to be told; he could feel the deck shuddering beneath his feet as the giant propellers pounded themselves against the bottom.

Crowhaven stepped over to a young red-haired, freckle-faced man standing in front of several deck to ceiling control panels, intently studying the massive banks of gauges and colored lights. His face was pale and he was mumbling softly to himself; Crowhaven guessed he was praying. He put his hand on the technician's shoulder and said: "Next time we come up on *full astern,* blow all the forward torpedo tubes."

"Think that will help, sir?" The voice was imploring.

"It's only a drop in the bucket pressure wise, but I'm willing to snatch at any straw."

The chief's voice came through from the engine room again. "The starboard shaft just went, Commander. Broke clean through aft of the seal. Took two bearings with it."

"Maintain procedure," Crowhaven came back.

"But sir," the chief's voice was pleading, desperate. "What if the port shaft goes? Even if we break free to the surface, how do we make headway?"

"We row," Crowhaven said curtly. "I repeat, maintain procedure!"

If both propeller shafts were going to shear, they were going to shear. But until the port shaft went with the starboard, he'd rip it to pieces while he still had a chance at saving the *Starbuck* and his crew. God, he wondered, how could so much go so wrong at the very last minute?

Lieutenant Robert M. Buckmaster, U.S.M.C., unleashed a short burst from his automatic rifle at a concrete bunker and wondered the same thing. The best-laid plans of mice and men, he thought. The operation should have been simple: take the transmitter, his orders said. A group of Navy men were still hidden in the tropical underbrush waiting for word of the capture so they could commandeer the equipment and send the coded messages that Buckmaster didn't understand. Marine lieutenants were seldom privy to classified information, he mused. It's okay to get killed, but it's not okay to know why.

The old Army installation on the northwest tip of Maui had looked deserted and innocent enough, but the instant his squad began infiltrating the perimeter,

they'd run into more detection and warning gear than surrounded the gold depository at Fort Knox. Electrified wire, light beams which activated ear-blasting sirens, and bright flood lamps drenching the entire installation in a blinding, naked glare. Nothing in his briefing had prepared him for this, he thought angrily. Sloppy planning; no detailed warning of the obstacles. Lieutenant or not, he was personally going to read the riot act to his commanding officers for causing this mess.

From windows, doorways, and rooftops that had seemed empty only moments earlier, the defenders opened up with a heavy burst of automatic weapons fire, halting Buckmaster's commando force in their tracks. The marines answered back and their aim had been deadly; bodies were beginning to pile up around the bunkerlike openings. At the height of the battle, a burly, grizzled-looking sergeant ran through the shadows cast by the flood lamps, and threw himself down on the ground next to Buckmaster.

"I pulled one of their guns off a dead body," he shouted above the din. "It's a Russian ZZK Kaleshrev."

"Russian?" Buckmaster echoed incredulously.

"Yes, sir." The sergeant held up the automatic weapon in front of Buckmaster's eyes. "It's the newest light arm in the Soviet arsenal. Beat's the hell out of me how these guys got hold of them."

"Save it for the Intelligence Section." Buckmaster turned his attention back to the transmitter buildings as the noise of firing increased in the darkness.

"Corporal Danzig and his squad are pinned down behind a retaining wall." The sergeant broke off to fire a series of short bursts to draw some of the defenders' attention. "I'd give up retirement for a ninety-millimeter tank buster," he yelled between bursts.

"This was supposed to be a surprise assault, remember? They told us we wouldn't need any heavy armament."

Suddenly there was a tremendous explosion; a huge cloud of dust billowed up and chunks of concrete fell over the area like hail. The shock of the concussion made Buckmaster gasp; then he slowly rose to his feet and stared at the shambles of the transmitter buildings.

"Radio!" he shouted. "Dammit, where's the radio man?"

A marine with a blackened face clad in black and green camouflage fatigues, raced from the shadows. "Here, Lieutenant."

Lieutenant Buckmaster took the offered receiver, dreading what he had to say.

"Big Daddy . . . Big Daddy. This is Mad Chopper. Over."

"This is Big Daddy, Mad Chopper. Go ahead. Over." The voice in the receiver sounded as though it were coming from the bottom of a well.

"The gang down the block blew the deal right in our faces. I repeat, blew the deal right in our faces. We won't tune in the news tonight."

"Big Daddy understands, Mad Chopper. He sends his regrets. Over and out."

Buckmaster jammed the receiver back in its cradle. He was mad and he didn't care if they knew it all the way back to the Pentagon. Something had gone terribly wrong here tonight. The whole atmosphere had an ominous stink about it. He vaguely wondered, as his men began regrouping, whether he would ever know who had gotten the short end of the stick.

CHAPTER 17

The door opened and two men dragged Giordino into the room, dropping him roughly onto the floor. Pitt caught his breath. Al was in pitiful shape; his mangled feet hadn't been treated; there wasn't the least sign of disinfectant or bandages on them. Blood from a gash above his left eye had hardened, gluing his eye half shut, leaving an appalling malevolent expression that burned with the fires of unadulterated defiance.

"Well now, Major Pitt," Delphi said reproachfully. "Nothing to say to your boyhood friend? No? Perhaps you have forgotten his name? Does Albert Giordino ring a bell?"

"You know his name?"

"Of course. Does that surprise you?"

"Not really," Pitt said easily. "I imagine Orl Cinana supplied you with a complete rundown on Giordino and myself."

For one long moment the towering hulk behind the desk didn't get it. Then Pitt's words began to sink in and Delphi lifted an interrogatory eyebrow.

"*Captain Cinana?*" His voice was rock-steady, but Pitt detected a very slight touch of doubt. "You're fishing in the wrong current. You have nothing to . . ."

"Cut the theatrics," Pitt sharply interrupted. "Cinana may have collected his captain's pay from the

231

United States Navy, but he played ball on your team. A nice setup: an informer sitting on the top level of your opposition. You knew what the 101st Fleet's operational plans were before they were set down on paper. How did you recruit Cinana, Delphi? Money? Or was it blackmail? Judging from your track record, I'd say blackmail."

"You're very observant."

"Not really. An easy scent to pick up. The good captain had outlived his usefulness as a stool pigeon. He couldn't live with the role of traitor any longer. Cinana began cracking; he was on the verge of a nervous breakdown. Add his little illicit affair with Adrian Hunter, and poor Cinana had to be eliminated before he spilled your organization. But you bungled his murder, Delphi. You bungled it beyond comprehension."

Delphi looked at Pitt in bleak suspicion. "You're guessing."

"No guesswork," Pitt said. "It was a chance meeting between us in the Royal Hawaiian Hotel Bar that fouled your plan. Cinana was waiting for Adrian Hunter when I wandered in the door. He, of course, had no idea I was another one of Adrian's playmates, but he couldn't run the risk of an embarrassing introduction—a rendezvous with an admiral's daughter twenty years his junior, in a dark corner of a bar, might conjure up any number of nasty visions—so he ducked out before she showed up. Then when Summer stepped on stage for the assassination, she mistook me for Cinana. And why not? I fit the description. Neither Cinana nor I had worn our uniforms that night, and to top it off, I was conveniently drinking with Miss Hunter. There was no doubt in Summer's mind. She took care of Adrian and then lured me onto

the beach where she tried to pump me full of poison. It was only after she found herself in my apartment, that it began to dawn on her that she'd made a terrible mistake. My first hint came when she addressed me as Captain. And later, you yourself supplied the clincher when you admitted to having an informant. Two and two went together: the answer was Cinana. All in all, very elementary.

"Yes, you're a weird breed of cat, Delphi. What other man would have sent his own flesh and blood out in the dead of night to commit murder? Hardly the Father of the Year. Even your hired help wander around like robots. What's your trick, Delphi? You sprinkle mind-deadening drugs in their cornflakes, or do you mesmerize them with those phony yellow eyes?"

Delphi looked unsure; Pitt wasn't acting like a man who'd come to the end of his string.

"You push too far." Delphi leaned forward and locked a hypnotic gaze on Pitt's eyes.

Pitt's deep green eyes never hesitated, meeting Delphi's stare with burning intensity. "Don't strain yourself, Delphi. I'm not the least impressed. As I've said, they're phony. Yellow contact lenses, nothing more. You can't cast a spell over a man who's laughing at you. You're a fraud from top to bottom. Lavella and Roblemann. Who're you trying to kid? You're not fit to wipe their blackboards. Hell, you can't even do a decent impression of Frederick Moran . . ."

Pitt broke off abruptly, dodging to the side as Delphi, clenched teeth bared in rage, leaped from behind the desk and swung in a wide, windmilling arc with his fist. The blow carried every ounce of Delphi's immense strength, but the blinding haze of anger blurred his timing and the fist soared past with-

out making a connection. He stumbled, recovered, and then lost his balance, going down on his hands and knees with a grunt of agony as Pitt's foot caught him on the side of his body. He stayed where he was, swaying from side to side.

There was a moment of stunned silence throughout the room as Delphi rose unsteadily, supporting himself on the top of the heavy desk. His breath was coming in gasps, his mouth a taut white line.

Pitt stood frozen, cursing himself for overplaying his hand. There was no doubt in his mind—there could be no doubt in the mind of all who were in the room—that Delphi meant to kill him and Al. Delphi reached behind the desk, pulling open a drawer and lifting out a gun. Not one of the projectile pistols, but an automatic, Pitt noticed uneasily—a heavy dark blue .44 Colt revolver—hardly the gun he expected Delphi to wield. Unhurriedly, Delphi broke the gun open, checked the shells, and snapped it shut again. The yellow eyes hadn't yet changed—they were as expressionless and icy as ever. Pitt turned and looked down at Giordino who met his eyes with a wry grin. They tensed their bodies, waiting for the end. But Delphi's yellow eyes strayed over his targets, toward the door.

"No, Father!" Summer implored. "Not that way!"

She stood at the door, wearing a green robe that came to mid thigh, her beautifully tanned and smooth skin radiating warmth and self-assurance. Pitt's blood began to pump rapidly through his veins. She moved into the room, her eyes touching Delphi with a confident, challenging gaze.

"Do not interfere," Delphi whispered. "This matter does not concern you."

"You just can't shoot them down here," Summer per-

sisted. "You just can't!" Her great gray eyes suddenly became soft and pleading. "Not within these walls!"

"Their blood can be washed away."

"It's no good, Father. You've had to kill to maintain our sanctuary. But that was outside in the sea. You must not bring death into your own house."

Delphi hesitated and slowly dropped the gun.

"You're quite right, Daughter." He smiled, "Death from a bullet is too quick, too merciful, and too unclean. We'll set them free on the surface. We'll give them a chance to survive."

"Fat chance," Pitt growled. "Hundreds of miles to the nearest land. Man-eaters waiting for a bite of human flesh. You're all heart."

"Enough of this morbid talk." The giant's face wore a sardonic expression. "I still wish to hear how you came to be here, and I haven't time for any more of your wit."

Pitt casually studied his watch. "About thirty-one minutes to be exact."

"Thirty-one minutes?"

"Yes, that's when your precious sanctuary caves in."

"Back with the jokes again, are we, my friend?" He walked over to the portal, staring at the moray eel, before turning abruptly. "How many other men were in your aircraft?"

Pitt snapped another question back. "What became of Lavella, Roblemann, and Moran?"

"You persist in toying with me."

"No, I'm dead serious," Pitt said. "You answer a couple of questions and I'll tell you what you want to know. My word."

Delphi thoughtfully looked at the gun. Then he laid it on the desk. "I believe you."

"To begin with, Major, my name really is Moran."

"Frederick Moran would have to be in his eighties to be alive now!"

"I am his son," Delphi said slowly. "I was a young man when he set out with Dr. Lavella and Dr. Roblemann to find the lost island of Kanoli. You see, my father was a pacifist. After the second world war had ended in the inferno of the atomic bomb, he knew it would only be a question of time before mankind destroyed itself in a nuclear holocaust. When countries arm for war, the arms never go unused, he once said. He began researching areas that would be safe from radiation and far from target sectors, eventually discovering that a base under the sea provided the ideal retreat. When the island of Kanoli sank into the sea many centuries ago, it dropped suddenly, without volcanic activity or major cataclysm. This indicated that the ceremonial caves and tunnels recorded in the legends might still be intact. Lavella and Roblemann sympathized with my father; they joined him in his search for the lost isle. After nearly three months of sounding the seafloor, they found it, and immediately began plans for pumping the passages dry. It took them nearly a year before they were able to set up quarters within the seamount."

"How was it possible to work so long in secret?" Pitt asked. "The records list the expedition's ship as missing only a few months after it left port."

"Secrecy was no great problem," Delphi continued. "The ship's hull had been modified so that divers and equipment would be able to pass in and out of the sea. A few alterations like changing the name on the bow, and painting the superstructure, and the ship simply became another unnoticed steamer plying the

Western trade route. Not secrecy, but financing, became the major problem."

"The rest I know," Pitt said with an unnerving degree of certainty.

Delphi looked up. Summer took a step forward, the identical expression of doubt showing in their faces.

"How odd you didn't catch onto the fact that the entire 101st Fleet, the entire Navy Department, discovered your setup."

"What purpose do you serve by lying?" Delphi demanded.

"You should have guessed, Delphi. Remember when you left my apartment? I mentioned Kanoli, yet you hardly batted an eye. Probably because you knew I was about to die so my little revelation was of no consequence."

"How ... how could you? ..."

"The curator at the Bishop Museum. He remembered your father. But that was only the beginning. The pieces are all there, Delphi, and they all neatly finish the puzzle." Pitt walked over and knelt down beside Giordino. Then he faced Delphi again. "You kill because of greed, nothing else. You've even imbedded the same cold-blooded philosophy in your own daughter. Your father might have been a pacifist, but what Dr. Moran began for strictly scientific and humanitarian reasons, unwittingly became, in your hands, the slickest hijack operation in maritime history."

"Don't stop," Delphi said grimly. "I want to hear it all."

"You want to hear it told from the other side?" Pitt asked, his tone neutral. "Want to hear how you're put down in the files? Very well. Before continuing, how-

ever, I'd appreciate it if you could make Giordino here a bit more comfortable. It's embarrassing for him to have to lie on the floor like an animal."

Delphi nodded reluctantly to the guards, who lifted Giordino by the arms and carried him to the red-cushioned couch. Only when Giordino was sitting more comfortably did Pitt continue. The next few minutes wouldn't make much sense unless he could guess enough of the plot behind Delphi's strange organization. If they were to have even one chance in a hundred of escaping the crush of the coming explosion, he'd have to get Giordino and Summer out of that room. The great crystal portal would be the first to go, unleashing a million gallons of seawater. He could only pray for an interruption. He took a deep breath, hoped his imagination was operating in high gear, and began.

"The *Explorer*, your father's ship, had outlived her usefulness by the time the scientists had made the seamount livable. Dr. Moran needed money to buy equipment in order to continue underwater construction, so he resorted to the world's most common con game—taking an insurance company. Screwing the establishment out of a few bucks in the name of science consoled his conscience. And what the hell did he care? He and Lavella and Roblemann had dropped out of society anyway. So he sailed the *Explorer* to the States, loaded the holds with worthless junk, insured the ship and cargo to the hilt, all this under a different name and registry, of course. Then he sailed the ship back to Kanoli where he opened the sea cocks and became the first victim of the Vortex. He immediately applied for the insurance.

"The scheme worked so smoothly, Delphi, that you couldn't resist opening up for business in a big way

after the good scientists died off and could offer no objections. Only this time, you refined the operation. You used ships that didn't belong to you. There was more loot in this method, as you weren't out the original cost of the ship. It must have been one hell of a profitable scheme. And still is, for that matter. It's almost ridiculously simple. You arrange for a few of your men to sign on as crew members on a merchantman heading west from the mainland to the Indies and the Orient. Why always west? The western steamer lane cuts right over your backyard, and not only does Kanoli lie near its path, but goods stamped MADE IN THE U.S.A. are easier to sell in the backwater black markets. All your clandestine crew had to do was deviate the ship a few degrees off its course, signal 'All Stop' to the engine room, and then stand by while you and your merry band of pirates climbed aboard and murdered the loyal crew.

"No trace of the vessel is ever found. How could it be? The bodies were weighted and dumped over the side, the hull was repainted from stem to stern, a few prominent areas of its superstructure were altered, and presto, you had a new ship. Then it was only the small matter of selling the cargo—unless it was easily traceable and too hot to handle, in which case it was expediently dropped in the sea. You made a few honest trade runs under a new registry before you then reinsured it, and then you sunk it on the summit of the seamount so you could always get at the remains for spare parts needed to make phony modifications on future acquisitions to your ill-gotten fleet. God, how all the buccaneers of the Spanish Main would have envied your organization, Delphi. Next to you, they were nothing but a gang of muggers. Why hell, you've got half the world fooled into thinking there's

almost thirty ships out there on the bottom, when
in reality, there's only half that many. Every one of
them was listed as missing twice. Once under their
original name, and again when you scuttled them
under yours."

"Very penetrating," the scoff in Delphi's tone was
belied by the deep absorption in his eyes.

"The *Lillie Marlene*," Pitt went on in a quiet voice,
"that was a clever hoax. Things were getting a little
too hot around the seamount; too many private
pleasure crafts cruising about, trying to treasure hunt
the missing ships. It was only a matter of time before
a Fathometer or sonar picked up the outline of the
hulks. So you cooked up the *Lillie Marlene* affair to
get the heat off your operation.

"The Coast Guard, the Navy, the Merchant Marine
were all taken in by the eerie discovery on board the
yacht. You'd make a great press agent, Delphi. That
description of the dead bodies with green skin and
burned faces put the fear of the unknown into every
superstitious seaman sailing the Pacific. Ships and
crews began avoiding these parts like the plague.
You had them all conned. No one considered the
notion of a trumped-up facade. You sent that phony
message from the *Lillie Marlene*'s radio. The operator
was already dead. The crew of the Spanish freighter,
the *San Gabriel*, had murdered him and everyone on
the yacht."

Pitt paused to let his words sink in. "That was a
neat touch, having the *Lillie Marlene* blow herself
and the boarding crew to shreds. In reality, there was
no explosion; the yacht had been captured and sailed
away to the seamount for a complete facelift. She
was too pretty a ship to scuttle. You've probably got
her tied up this minute at one of the Honolulu yacht

marinas under a new name and registered to the same outfit, on paper at any rate, that owns your other ships. What's the name again? The Pisces Pacific Corporation?"

Delphi suddenly stiffened. "You know about Pisces Pacific?"

"Doesn't everybody?" Pitt asked. "I can easily inform you that everything you own outside the seamount is under custody at this moment. Your amphibian aircraft, corporation offices, the radio transmitter on Maui, to mention a few." Pitt realized that his imagination had hit home. "You had a good thing going, Delphi. Every contingency was covered. Even if one of your victims managed to get off a Mayday signal, your transmitter on the island effectively garbled it and then rebroadcast a confused message that just happened to mention the ship's position, a position over a hundred miles away from where the actual act of piracy actually took place."

Delphi's face was a mask of malevolence. "You should have died, Pitt. You should have died in triplicate."

"Ah yes," Pitt shrugged. "The slimy crud in the gray panel truck for one. A damnably crude attempt for someone of your finesse. But I suppose you were pressed for time, especially since Cinana had informed you that I was placed on duty with Admiral Hunter and his staff that morning. After the botched job by Summer the night before, it would have been awkward if I'd launched an investigation of my own, or worse yet, if Adrian Hunter let slip a few choice remarks about her affair with Cinana. It all totaled to one conclusion: Pitt had to get flushed, and fast."

"You're a cunning man," Delphi said slowly. "Far more cunning than I gave you credit for. But it

makes little difference now. You've played a bluffing
game. Your guesswork is fairly accurate. You missed
target on my father, however. He was a good man.
He and his fellow scientists were all killed when a
pump failed and they drowned in a flood tunnel short-
ly before their work was finished. Credit for the
missing ships belongs only to me. I planned and conceived the entire operation beginning with the
Explorer. I made mistakes, but none that couldn't be
glossed over. Yes, Mr. Pitt, you are bluffing. Captain
Cinana kept me informed right up until his unfortunate passing. Admiral Hunter could not possibly
have put the entire story together in the last twenty-
four hours."

Delphi passed his hand over his brow and rubbed
his closed eyes. It was as though he was trying to
erase a past error. "You were my most inexcusable
mistake. Three decades of perfect isolation and you
nearly destroyed it."

"Thirty years is a long time to get away with so
awesome a crime," said Pitt. "You destroyed yourself,
Delphi. You bit off more than you can chew. Your
worst blunder was capturing the *Starbuck*. It's one
thing to hijack a merchant vessel or pleasure boat. The
Coast Guard seldom conducts any more than a surface
search in the area of the last-known position of the
missing ship. But when a naval vessel vanishes, the
Navy never stops scouring the sea, no matter how
far or how deep, until they find the remains."

Delphi stared out the portal for a long moment. "If
Commander Dupree had only kept on his original
course, instead of deviating and discovering our
sanctuary, he and his crew would still be alive."

Pitt's eyes were like round chunks of ice. "How did

you do it? How did you capture a nuclear submarine while it was underwater?"

"Really quite simple," Delphi answered. "My men stretched heavy steel cable in the sub's path, snagging the propellers. When she drifted to a stop, we forced open several of her outside ballast vents, allowing water to enter her air tanks while flooding two interior compartments. As the *Starbuck* sank to the bottom, its low frequency radio signals were jammed and the escape hatches were sealed from the outside. Months later, when the food stocks ran out and the crew were weakened by starvation, my people entered and disposed of them."

"Really quite simple," Pitt repeated grimly. "The *Starbuck* was the greatest prize of the century, the crowning zenith of criminal plunder. And you were home free. The Navy was searching hundreds of miles away. It took only a few days to clean out the flooded compartments, and there sat the *Starbuck* as good as new in only ninety feet of water. Except you had a problem, Delphi. I couldn't figure it at first; it didn't make sense. Here you have the world's most advanced nuclear submarine, including her missiles complete with warheads, sitting a few hundred yards from your doorstep, and you never moved her as much as an inch because you didn't know how to operate her. The *Starbuck* is a highly complex piece of machinery. After your father and the other scientists were killed, you were the only one left with any smattering of intelligence. Your entire organization is built on blind obedience to you. None of your people have one ounce of smarts. That's why you let Seaman Farris live—hoping he could be tortured into training your men to at least deliver the *Starbuck* to a

Russian or Chinese port where she could be sold. But Farris's mind was gone. The ordeal of watching his crewmates and officers either die or disappear until he was the only one left, was too much. He snapped. He'll never fully recover."

"A minor miscalculation," Delphi said tiredly.

"What happened to the *Andrei Vyborg*, Delphi? Did the Russians decide there was no honor among thieves and make a try at hijacking the *Starbuck* for themselves?"

"This time you are quite wrong, Major Pitt." Delphi delicately massaged the spot where Pitt had kicked him. "The captain of the *Andrei Vyborg* had his suspicions aroused when your ship, the *Martha Ann*, tarried too long in one spot. He came to investigate. I had no choice but to eliminate him as I had the others."

"It must have broken your heart to lose the *Martha Ann*," Pitt said acidly. "She spoiled your record by being the first and only victim to have gotten away."

"Unfortunately, our losses in capturing the ship were quite heavy," Delphi said. "The *Martha Ann* was activated to return to Pearl Harbor before my men could take the necessary steps to stop her."

"You could have blown her out of the water."

"Too late. Captain Cinana warned us of a new crew that was already flying from the islands to take command. We only had time to remove our dead and wounded."

"Nothing seems to go right for you, does it?" Pitt said conversationally.

"You were on the *Martha Ann*," Delphi said coldly. "It was you who shot down my men and spirited away the ship's crew in the helicopter. It has always been you who has corrupted my plans."

"Get screwed," Pitt said viciously. "You invited me to the party, remember. I didn't ask to find that phony message capsule."

Delphi bared his teeth. "Why did you come here?" he demanded. "What exactly is your mission?"

"To rescue Adrian Hunter," Pitt snapped back.

"You lie!" Delphi shouted.

"Suit yourself."

Delphi's eyes widened; suddenly he knew. He hit Pitt across the face savagely, as Pitt stumbled back against the wall, tasting the blood in his mouth.

"The submarine," Delphi said in a quiet, toneless voice. "You found the *Starbuck* operable, killed my men, and escaped with Farris. Now you've returned with a crew to reclaim it."

"As I promised," Pitt said. "Nothing less than the truth. You're right, Delphi. I brought a crew of Navy submariners with me to salvage the *Starbuck*. While we've been standing here discussing the sins of your criminal acts, the sub has been raised off the bottom." Pitt studied his watch. It was eleven minutes to 0500. "I should put her about twenty-miles south by now.

"How the fortunes of war swing from side to side," Pitt said quietly. "But it shouldn't come as a surprise really. You couldn't be fool enough to think you could get away with it forever. In eleven minutes, the missile cruiser *Monitor* is going to fire a small nuclear warhead on the center of your precious seamount. In eleven minutes we all die."

"Nothing can crush these walls," Delphi said calmly. "Look around you, Major. The base of this seamount is granite, a hard quartz-type granite. It's stronger than reinforced concrete."

Pitt shook his head. "One crack. All it takes is one crack and thousands of tons of water will come burst-

ing through these caverns with ten times the pressure of a fire hose. Everyone will be crushed from the water's force before they have a chance to drown."

"You're overly inventive," Delphi said. "Anyway, no missile will be fired as long as you, Captain Giordino, and Miss Hunter are here."

"Don't bet on it. The decision came from Washington, not Admiral Hunter. You underestimate Hunter. He won't plead for our lives against orders. Besides, he probably thinks Giordino and I are already dead. As for Adrian, no one will know until it's all over that his daughter was accidentally killed during a naval operation to destroy the Pacific Vortex. The man has an over-abundance of guts; he won't hesitate to sacrifice Adrian's life to put your operation out of business."

The calmness slowly faded from the giant's gaunt face, leaving it frozen in uncertainty. "Words. Nothing but words. You can prove nothing."

Pitt decided to throw out his last card. With ten minutes to go, it was now or never.

"I can give you absolute proof that what I've told you is gospel. Check with your radio facility. You'll find that your transmitter on Maui is in the hands of the United States Marines. You will also discover that Admiral Hunter has been trying to reach you for the last twenty minutes to negotiate your surrender."

Delphi suddenly started laughing, malevolently, angrily.

"You fool," he managed to gasp between uproars. "You stupid fool. Your desperate bluff has failed. You weren't as smart as you thought. You couldn't have known, could you? The transmitting station on Maui is no longer mine. I sold it out, lock, stock, and barrel, to the Russians six weeks ago. I haven't been monitoring your transmissions. The Russians have. The Soviet

Navy paid dearly to own a radio facility so close to the United States Naval Headquarters of the Pacific. And by monitoring the 101st Fleet's messages, they hoped to find the *Starbuck*'s whereabouts. A masterful deception, don't you agree, Major? They had no idea they were dealing with the organization that had already claimed the submarine." He looked at Pitt vengefully. "If you're waiting for a last minute reprieve, my dear Pitt, you're wasting your time. There will be no communication from Admiral Hunter; there will be no offer of surrender; there will be no atomic missile for the qualified reason that I am leaving the seamount. Its purpose has ended. Tomorrow I will begin moving my organization to a new location. My communication equipment here has already been dismantled and without that, there can be no contact with Pearl Harbor or anyplace else for that matter."

Pitt didn't answer. He simply stood in place, wondering if the next ten minutes would be his last.

"And that's only the half of it," Delphi sneered. "You put the *Starbuck* twenty miles south of here, indeed. How much practice does it take to inject so much conviction into your face when you spout so many lies?" He laughed out loud. "You were right about one thing, Pitt. I could not operate the submarine with a nonexperienced crew. But I did figure out her ballast system. At this moment every air tank is empty. Yet there she still sits imbedded on the bottom. Nothing short of a major salvage operation will pull the hull free. Months of resting in the same place has built up a suction beyond what her blown ballast is capable of breaking. Yes, a pity. Your crew of submariners are as good as dead, if they're not already dead by the hands of seven of my best men. I knew your Navy wouldn't give up so easily. I knew

they'd be back for another try at reclaiming their precious submarine, so I left my most trusted men on board—men who love to kill. Against them I wouldn't give your engineering crew one chance in ten thousand."

Pitt tried to leap at Delphi, to ram his fist into the teeth under the yellow eyes. But one of the guards quickly shot him, grazing him in the left shoulder. He crashed sideways into a wall where he slowly slid onto the stone floor.

Summer gave a half-retching, half-choking scream. Her eyes showed white around large gray irises; she made a move to go to Pitt, then looked hesitantly at her father. He shook his head and she shrank back in humble obeyance.

Giordino had not moved. He stared impassively at Pitt, but Pitt caught a warning millimetric nod of the head.

"You've won a battle," Pitt hissed through clenched teeth. "But you haven't won the war."

"Wrong again, Major Pitt. I win. Up and down the line, I win. The *Starbuck* was heaven-sent. As soon as I can transact her, shall we say, transfer of ownership, I can close out my venture here in the Pacific and retire to less taxing enterprises. I'm sure the new owners will take great delight in the Hyperion missiles."

"Nuclear blackmail!" Pitt spat thickly. "You're crazy."

"Nuclear blackmail? Come, come, Major. How common of you. That's for fictional spy novels. I have no intention of blackmailing the superpowers over the threat of a nuclear holocaust. My motives are strictly for profit. In spite of what you might think, I have

no stomach for murdering women and children need-
lessly. A man, that's different. Killing a man is the
same as killing an animal; there's no tinge of remorse
afterward."

Pitt pushed himself upright against the wall. "No
one knows that better than you."

"No," Delphi continued. "My plan is much more
subtle; ingenious in its simplicity. I have arranged to
sell the *Starbuck* and her weapons system to one of the
Arab oil countries. Which one makes little difference.
All that matters is that they are willing to pay a
healthy price without haggling."

"You're crazy," Pitt repeated. "Totally, hopelessly
sick in the head." But Delphi didn't look or act crazy.
Everything he said seemed logical. Any one of the
rich Arab oil nations would make the ideal buyer.

"We shall know soon enough, won't we?" He walked
over to the intercom receiver and spoke. "Prepare my
mini-sub. I'll be there in five minutes." Then he turned
back to Pitt. "A personal inspection trip to the *Starbuck*. I'll give the survivors of your crew, if there are
any, your regards."

"You're wasting your time," Pitt said bitterly.

"I think not," Delphi replied contemptuously. "The
submarine sits where I left her."

"The Navy will never give the *Starbuck* up; they'll
destroy her first."

"By this time tomorrow, they will have no say in
the matter. An Arab salvage fleet will be here to
raise the hull. These are international waters. Your
Navy would never attack another nation over a derelict and be condemned by every country in the world
for instigating an act of war. Their only prayer is a
deal with the Arabs for the return of the sub. By then,

I shall have my finder's fee—three hundred million British pounds—deposited to a Swiss bank, and be on my way."

"You will never leave this seamount," Pitt said, his face twisted in cold hate. "In eight minutes you will die."

Delphi's eyes caught Pitt's. "So? I am going to die, am I?" He turned as if he were ignoring an insect and moved to the door. Then he looked back. "Then I shall at least have the satisfaction of knowing you died first." He nodded to the guards. "Throw them into the sea."

"No last consideration for the condemned?" Pitt asked.

"None whatsoever," Delphi said with a satanic grin. "Good-bye again, Major Pitt. Thank you for a most entertaining diversion."

The sound of his footsteps died away and there was only silence. It was five minutes before 0500.

CHAPTER 18

Giordino writhed onto his elbows, his entire body leaping in a convulsive spasm as his eyes rolled upward. He fell from the couch, clutching his throat. He had held his breath until his face was nearly purple; he'd even saved a wad of saliva until this moment, letting it burst from his trembling lips in a cloud of spray between labored gasps. It was a masterful performance, and the incredulous and stunned guards were taken in completely.

Pitt watched the scene as the two guards, keeping their guns aimed in Pitt's direction, gathered about Giordino and lifted the limp arms across their shoulders. Still without speaking, they motioned for Pitt to walk ahead.

He nodded, crossing the room to stand in front of Summer.

"Summer," he said softly. He touched her shoulder gently and gazed into her tired face. "I have so much to say and so little time to say it. Will you walk with me?"

She nodded and motioned to the guards. They simply bowed their heads in mute understanding. Summer took Pitt's arm and led him out into a well-lit rock-hewn corridor.

"Please forgive me." Her voice was barely more than a whisper.

"For what? None of this was your doing. You've already saved my life twice. Why did you do it?"

She appeared not to hear. She looked up into Pitt's eyes, and her face radiated a softness and beauty that seemed to make everything else in the passageway dim and fade. "I have a strange feeling when I'm in your presence," she murmured. "It is not simply happiness or contentment but something else. I can't quite describe it."

"The feeling is love," Pitt said tenderly. He bent down, wincing from the pain in his shoulder, and kissed her eyes.

The guards on either side of Giordino halted and were stunned. Giordino's feet trailed on the floor, his head lay far across his right shoulder. He was moaning softly, his eyes seemingly shut. The guards did not notice his forearms slipping slowly up their shoulders until his hands rested loosely beside their necks. Then there was a sudden flexing of the great biceps and the guards were smashed together, bone against bone.

Giordino stood there unsteadily on his shredded feet sporting a satisfied grin. "Was that, or was that not, a work of art?"

"Every move a picture," Pitt grinned back. He took Summer's chin in one hand. "Will you help us get out of here?"

She raised her head slowly and looked up at him through her spilled red hair, like a frightened child. Then she reached around his waist and clung tightly to him. A wall of tears masked the gray of her eyes.

"I love you," she said, savoring the words. "I love you."

Pitt kissed her again, this time on the lips.

"I don't mean to come between you two," Giordino cut in. "But time is short."

Summer hurried ahead, peering in both directions at the unconscious guards. "We must go before one of my father's men finds us like this."

"Wait!" Pitt snapped. "Where's Adrian Hunter? We've got to take her with us."

"She sleeps in the room next to mine."

"Take us there."

She gently touched his shoulder. "But how? You are wounded and your friend cannot walk."

"I've borne his cross for years." Pitt kneeled down and Giordino, in silent understanding, grasped him around the neck. Then Pitt hooked an arm under one of Giordino's knees and staggered upright.

"I must look like a papoose," Giordino grumbled.

"You sure as hell don't feel like one." Pitt then nodded to Summer. "Okay, lead on."

Summer hurried ahead, peering in both directions at open corridors to see if all was clear.

They walked on, until someone approached from a side corridor; Summer waved them back. Pitt loosened his hold on Giordino and they ducked into a doorway. The footsteps of the intruder could clearly be heard along the corridor across the interchange.

For five seconds, the footsteps pounded along the cross passage. Pitt's heart was pounding from exertion, sweat pouring down his face. One fit man against two down-and-out derelicts. Two good legs against two wobbly ones. The odds, Pitt decided, were definitely not on their side. Then the footsteps passed the interchange and faded into the other direction.

"Come, come," Summer whispered from another doorway further down the passage. "It's safe now."

Pitt lifted Giordino again and struggled on.

"How's the time?" Pitt asked.

"We aren't going to make it," Giordino answered grimly, "providing the missile is on schedule."

"It'll be on schedule," Pitt panted. "Delphi was wrong about that. When the Navy receives no reply to the surrender offer, they'll take it as an act of defiance and blast the seamount anyway."

Summer took Pitt's arm and guided him, supporting his aching, overburdened body as best she could. Pitt staggered ahead, one foot in front of the other, telling himself one more, just one more step and they would be there. Finally, as he reached the last ounce of his endurance, Summer stopped at one of the side doors. She put her ear against the panel and listened a moment. Then she quietly pushed the door ajar and stepped inside. Pitt stumbled in behind her and sank to his knees, letting Giordino slide rump first onto a lush red carpet.

Summer ran up to a large bed carved into the far wall and shook the sleeping Adrian. "Wake up, Miss Hunter. Please wake up!"

Adrian's response was a soft moan; Summer took her by the wrist and dragged her naked body from the bed.

The sleep quickly receded from Adrian's eyes as she became aware of Pitt and Giordino on the floor. Making no attempt to cover her nakedness, she rushed across the room and knelt at Pitt's side.

"Oh my God, Dirk! What happened to you? How did you get here?"

"We've come for you," he said between labored breaths.

She shook her head slowly, disbelieving.

"No, no, it's impossible. There's no way out of this place."

"In the next room, Summer's bedroom, there's a passage to the sea . . ."

Pitt was interrupted by a heavy rumbling explosion. The room trembled from distant shock waves. The *Monitor*'s missile had struck the surface of the water above the seamount. The velvet curtains swept to and fro, and several coral ornaments on a stone table clattered from the unseen force.

"No time for a recital," Pitt snapped. "Everybody out."

Summer looked lost and confused, unable to move. "I can't . . . my father."

"Stay with us or die," Pitt said. "This whole mountain is going to collapse any second."

For a few seconds she didn't move, but then another tremor shook the room, shaking her back to her senses. She ran toward her room, Adrian right behind her, as Pitt and Giordino struggled painfully to bring up the rear.

They had barely entered Summer's exotic blue bedroom when a deafening roar and mountainous shock wave knocked them to the floor. The compression waves, rammed by a giant surge of seawater bursting through massive cracks and fissures on the top levels of the seamount, came rumbling through the passageways like an express train, crushing everything in its path.

Pitt scrambled to his feet, all pain forgotten. He slammed the corridor door closed, grabbed Adrian's arm, and pushed her through the curtain into the exit tunnel. Then he lunged at the fallen Summer, scooped her up, and threw her sprawling in a heap on top of Adrian. At that moment, the great mirror on the ceiling fell with a shattering crash to the room below, missing Pitt by inches. A cascade of water followed

the splintering glass, accompanied by a tearing, grinding rumble as the rock room tore apart.

"Al!" Pitt shouted through the deluge of rock and water.

"Over here!" Giordino yelled back. He waved an arm from under a stone dressing table.

Pitt waded through the rising milky froth of the slate-colored water and grabbed Giordino's upraised arm.

"Stay back!" Giordino cried. "If you carry me, you'll never make it."

"And ruin my big chance for a life-saving merit badge?" Pitt said curtly. "No way."

He threw Giordino's arm over his shoulder and then half carried, half dragged his friend to the escape tunnel. By the time they made the entrance, the water was up to their knees and swirling into the darkness beyond.

"You women run on ahead," Pitt commanded.

Without being told a second time, Adrian and Summer began splashing awkwardly through the narrow tube.

The process with Giordino was slow, and Pitt soon lost sight of the girls in the darkness. The rushing current of water hurtled down the ramp, causing him to stumble and fall. As he went down, his head was covered momentarily by the flow and he inhaled the saltwater. Choking, he pushed himself to his knees and managed to make it the rest of the way with the help of a strong, muscled arm that came out of nowhere.

Miraculously, it was Giordino, gnashing his teeth from the agony of his bruised feet.

"This is one good deed you're going to regret," Giordino muttered.

"Complain, complain," Pitt sputtered, coughing out

the seawater. "That's all you ever do. Come on, we've got a boat to catch."

The slippery stone ramp gradually broadened out into the stairway, and Pitt found the going a little easier. The yellow phosphorescent rocks were falling like hail, splashing around them in a flowing stream. The strange, glowing color of the rocks as they streaked from the cavern's vaulted dome created the eerie appearance of a ghostly meteor shower. Then, at last, the gushing river of water finally diminished as it fell over the side of the stairs to the pond below, enabling Pitt to see where he was stepping.

"Hold on, old buddy," Pitt said encouragingly. "We're almost there. The two statues should be around the next bend."

"See the women?" Giordino asked.

"Not yet."

They would be there; Pitt was sure of that. A wave of confidence coursed through his veins. They were too close to die now. They had survived the explosion. Once in the water, it was only a short swim through the outer caves to the surface. True, they might all find death waiting outside from sharks, from drowning, or from exhaustion. But as long as they were still alive, Pitt would keep pushing them until the final door was slammed in their faces. He hurried his pace and began dragging Giordino two steps at a time, trying to end this part of the claustrophobic journey as quickly as possible. If they were to die, it was better to die under the familiar touch of the sun and sky.

They were rounding the final bend now. Pitt could see Summer. She was standing at the edge of the pool like one of the sculptures under the yellow phosphorescent light.

Adrian also came into view, leaning wearily against the base of one of the statues. She looked up as they arrived, her eyes filled with terror.

"Dirk . . . it's too late," she mumbled. "He . . ."

Pitt cut her in mid-sentence. "No time for talk. The roof is starting to give way . . ."

The last word froze in his throat. His mixed feelings of fatigue, pain, joy, and hope melted into a twisted knot of defeat. From behind one of the sea god statues stepped Delphi. His right hand held the big Colt and the gun was aimed straight at Pitt's forehead.

"Leaving before the party's over?" he said, the hate spread across his face.

"I bore easily," Pitt said, shrugging helplessly. "You might as well kill me now. You don't have much time if you wish to save the others."

"How very noble of you, Major," Delphi said, his face a mask of cruel evil. "But you needn't concern yourself with details. My daughter and I are the only ones who will leave this cavern alive."

For a moment no one spoke. The only sounds came from the splashing of the falling rocks as they smacked the water. Deep within the seamount, a rumbling shudder shook the ancient-hewn chambers. Soon, very soon, Kanoli would be totally destroyed, never to be rediscovered again.

A sudden explosive cracking sound rolled through the cavern and vibrated into a thunderous crescendo as the tremors shook the hard rock walls.

For a fleeting instant, Pitt thought Delphi had fired the gun. Then he realized the cracking sound had originated from overhead. One wall had broken loose and was crumbling down the stairway in a sweeping avalanche. Pitt gave Summer a violent shove which sent her flying from the steps into the yellow

pool. In the same swift motion he threw himself on top of Adrian, blanketing her body with his.

The avalanche hit. Tons of gold-tinted rock bounded down the sloping wall burying the stairway. One of the carved, sphinxlike statues stood firm on its pedestal against the onslaught, but the second figure succumbed to the crushing force and toppled over, to Pitt's dazed mind looking like a cowboy who fell off his horse in the middle of a cattle stampede.

Pitt gritted his teeth and tensed his muscles as the rocks mercilessly rained down on his back. One tumbling boulder smashed into his side, and he heard, rather than felt, a rib snap. His face itched as blood trickled down his cheeks from a gash in his scalp. An odd piercing cry reached his ears over the rumbling din. It seemed far away, but then it dawned on him that it was coming from Adrian's lips only a few inches away as she screamed in uncontrollable hysteria. The rocks kept coming, covering Pitt's legs to his waist. He was pinned and unable to move. He clutched Adrian more tightly, as if his arm could squeeze the fear out of her.

It took almost a full minute before Pitt became aware of a heavy silence, broken only by an occasional small rock clattering down the slide and splashing into the water. He could now feel Adrian's spasmodic movements as she sobbed in numbed terror.

He slowly raised his head and peered over the jagged rubble. A veil of phosphorescent dust hung in the damp cavern air and slowly settled, like a swarm of glowing fireflies, to the stone floor. One statue still stood, staring coldly into nothingness while its base lay encircled by a thick layer of rocks. Its mate was missing, but on a closer inspection, Pitt could faintly see it on one side, a shattered and broken piece of antiquity.

Then something moved beneath the fallen sculpture. Pitt strained to penetrate the gloom. He freed one hand to rub the blood and dust from his eyes. The object rose slightly and turned, two glinting eyes staring in Pitt's direction. It was Delphi.

The great body lay crushed beneath the broken statue; only the head and one shoulder were visible above the broken mound of sculpture. Blood oozed from his mouth, but he seemed unaware of it. Then the gold, venomous eyes narrowed when they recognized Pitt.

It was becoming lighter now, and Pitt and Delphi saw the Colt at the same time, its steel blue barrel poking up from a pile of debris about four feet from Delphi's head. Pitt cursed his helplessness while Delphi's hand crawled toward the gun. Pitt struggled with every ounce of his ebbing strength to pull free, but his legs were pinned too tightly beneath the rubble. His breath came in great gulping pants; his mind raced with a growing sense of hopelessness. The gun was a good two feet closer to Delphi.

Delphi's face was contorted with the strain; his skin glistened with sweat. He said nothing, conserving every gram of his diminishing strength. He looked at Pitt again, shook his head as if gripped by an enormous spasm of hatred, and willed his fingers on toward the Colt. To Pitt, the seconds decelerated until time slowed to a sluggish halt. He frantically began pushing the boulders from his buried legs, but each try was a tremendous agony, and he had precious little left to give the effort.

Delphi's fingertips touched and clawed at the Colt. The barrel tilted slightly and he hooked two fingers around the muzzle tip and pulled. The gun gave an eighth of an inch, but Delphi lost his fragile grip.

Again and again he tried, until at last the .44 fell within reach of his palm. Then he clutched the handgrip with such force his knuckles turned bone-white.

Delphi coughed and a wave of blood spilled from his mouth, staining the rocks beneath him. But his intent never wavered; his face twisted fiendishly as he raised the gun barrel. He thumbed the hammer back. A grin swept his face, revealing a set of crimson-coated teeth as he leveled the sights at a point between Pitt's eyes.

Suddenly there was a movement a few feet in front of Delphi. Pitt watched in stunned fascination as another arm snaked upward from the rubble. Like a ghostly apparition rising from the grave, the arm and its attached hand rose and swung in an arc toward Delphi. Slowly the hand doubled up and closed into a fist except for the little finger which remained extended. Next, in one lightning motion, the fist fell and rammed against the gun muzzle, imbedding the little finger up to the first knuckle inside the barrel.

Giordino could not quite reach far enough to grasp the gun; he had jammed his finger in the barrel, knowing that if Delphi squeezed the trigger, the stoppage would momentarily expand the charge and the breech would blow up in the giant's face.

Incredulous surprise cast its shadow over Delphi's eyes. He feebly jerked the Colt from side to side—his strength was gone; he could hardly hold the gun level, much less engage in a struggle to dislodge the obstruction. The finger stayed. Delphi seemed to ponder the situation, but blackness was seeping into his mind. For the last time he flashed his blood-covered grin, and pulled the trigger.

The muffled crash shook the cavern; several small rocks broke and tumbled from the vaulted ceiling.

The right side of Delphi's face dissolved. The mangled gun dropped from his hand, and he fell forward, his head striking heavily on the rocks.

Giordino had uttered no sound. His arm and hand were still erect as he unclenched the fist and revealed a thumb and three fingers—the little finger was smashed to its base.

Pitt renewed the fight with his rock prison. He finally managed to tear himself free. Then he lifted Adrian from her confining position and leaned her against the standing statue. She had passed out cold.

"If you're up to it," Giordino murmured through tight lips, "how about excavating me from the ruins?"

"Hold on," Pitt answered.

He crawled over the rubble to Giordino. Together they shoved away the boulders that had entombed all but Al's face and right arm.

"Any other bones broken besides your missing pinkie?" Pitt asked.

"No," Giordino answered tersely, grimacing from the pain in his hand. "How about you?"

"A bent rib or two." Pitt slipped out of his torn swimming trunks and began tearing them into strips. "Here, let me wrap your hand."

"I've heard of giving a friend the shirt off your back," said Giordino, smiling gratefully, "but this is a new twist."

Just as he finished, Pitt heard a low gasp where the rock slide ended in the pond. Summer was pulling herself out of the water, her eyes dazed and glassy. She looked vacantly at Pitt.

"My father . . . what? . . ." Her voice trailed off and the words became jumbled and incoherent.

"Rest easy," Pitt said. "We'll be out of here and safe in a few minutes."

He reached over and pulled her to him, cradling her head in his arm. His fingers gently pushed the dripping hair from her face; he could see a dark red cut on her temple which was starting to swell. He whispered a few words in her ear and kissed her lightly on the mouth.

The water was rising rapidly throughout the cavern, creeping up the stairway, but Pitt wasn't aware of it. His face was tight with pity for Summer. He wanted to cry out that he loved her, but his lips moved soundlessly. She looked up into Pitt's eyes with an expression of faraway detachment. Her lips moved; she reached up and placed her hand on his chest.

"He's dead, isn't he?"

"Yes, the rock slide," he lied, but it was only a little lie. The exploding Colt only hastened Delphi's end. His crushed and broken body would have given up the fight within the hour.

"I hate to keep coming between you two," Giordino said, "but I think we better make our getaway, if you'll excuse the expression, before the roof falls in."

Pitt kissed Summer once more and then rose unsteadily to his feet. He was about to ask Giordino to revive Adrian when she appeared, naked, covered with golden phosphorescence, looking like a gilded nymph.

"Do you think you can swim?" Giordino asked her.

"I'll try," Adrian muttered weakly.

"Al, you and Adrian go first," Pitt said. "Have her hold onto your shoulders. Summer and I will follow." He nodded reassuringly at Giordino. "We'll meet you in the next chamber."

Giordino looked around. "Too bad some of our equipment isn't still around."

"Even if it was, we'd never find it under all this."

"Come along," Giordino said to Adrian. "The Albert Giordino Great Western and Pacific Underwater Express waits for no one." He led Adrian gently into the water. He had trouble walking, but swimming came easily. He guided her arms around his bull-like neck and she buried her face on his back between the shoulder blades. "Now hold tight and take a deep breath," he ordered. Then they both disappeared, leaving only a spreading circle of ripples.

Summer gazed back at the mound of rocks surrounding the fallen statue. "There's nothing that can be done?" she asked.

"Nothing."

Grief is a strange emotion. Summer's sad and lovely face suddenly became a mask of haunting serenity, edged by an icy expression of determination. "I love you, Dirk, but I . . . I cannot go with you."

Pitt stared at her. "That's nonsense."

"Please understand," she pleaded. "This seamount has always been my home. My mother lies buried here and now my father."

"That's no reason to die here too."

She laid her face against his chest. "I once promised my father I would never leave his side. I must honor that promise."

Pitt had to fight to overcome an urge to order her to dive into the water. Instead he stroked her hair and tenderly said: "I'm a selfish man. Your father is gone and now you belong to me. I want you. I need you. Even he wouldn't wish you to die to fulfill a young girl's promise." He hugged her tightly. "No more arguments. We're leaving together and we're leaving now."

Summer was still softly crying when hand in hand they slid beneath the yellow-tinted water.

Giordino and Adrian were sitting on the ledge in the outer chamber when Pitt and Summer broke the surface.

"What took you two so long?" asked Giordino. "This waiting around is making me hungry."

Pitt remained in the water, holding onto the ledge, unable to pull himself onto its dry surface. "We're halfway home now," he said confidently. "A quick swim to the surface and then it's off we go for Honolulu."

"We'll go up in the same order," Pitt said firmly. "And remember, exhale as you swim toward the surface. There's no sense in any of us getting an air embolism after coming this far." He turned to Summer. The water had turned her green robe into a transparent veil, and the clinging wetness of the material revealed every contour of her body. He had known many women of all shapes and sizes, but they all seemed colorless when compared to this woman from the seamount. His mind was so occupied with Summer that he hardly noticed Giordino and Adrian sliding into the water.

"See you topside," Giordino said, smiling. But the concern in his eyes was obvious. There was no telling what they might find on the surface. If anything.

Pitt managed to smile back. "Good luck. Keep a sharp watch for sharks."

"Don't worry. If I see one, I'll bite first." He waved his good hand, and, with Adrian securely draped around his neck, dove down and out of the underwater entrance.

A strange stillness gripped the chamber. The murky

water lapped gently at the walls and spilled around the tiny sealife attached to the rock. Dim light from the outside danced upon the roof, throwing fleeting shadows across the broken surface.

"There's a new life for both of us up there," Pitt said softly.

Summer gazed into Pitt's green eyes and caressed his face lightly with her fingers. Then she wept; her mind and being torn between love for her father and new love for a man she barely knew. She struggled within her heart to reach a decision, her long sunset hair lifting and falling with the gentle waves, tears mingling with the saltwater on her cheeks. Then she knew what she must do.

"I am ready," she said. "You are sorely hurt so you must go first. I will follow."

Pitt nodded silently, yielding to her logic. He brushed his lips over her hand. Then he smiled and ducked under the surface and was gone.

Summer watched his naked form glide beneath the rocks and vanish into the sea.

"Good-bye, Dirk Pitt," she murmured to herself and the empty chamber. She climbed up on the ledge, arched her supple body, and dove cleanly into the water. For a brief instant she stared at the sunlit entrance to the outside world. Then she turned and swam back toward the yellow cavern and her father.

The water became warmer as Pitt rose upward. Fifty feet, he thought, that's what Giordino's depth gauge had read when they had entered the small, air-pocketed chamber. He peered through the bluish-green liquid, just making out the rhythmic sway of the sun-dazzled surface above. He exhaled bits of breath slowly, erasing the pressure on his lungs and watching with loose curiosity as his air bubbles trailed

alongside his head during the ascent. It was as if they were hanging motionlessly in space.

He bobbed to the surface, met by the burning tropical sun. The breath rasped in and out of his lungs like air cycles from a pneumatic stamping press. He relaxed a few moments, as much as his aching and exhausted body would allow, floating in the gentle rise and fall of the swells. His eyes blinked clear, and he searched for Adrian and Giordino, spotting their heads twenty feet away as they rose on the crest of a wave just before they dropped and disappeared momentarily in the trough.

Suddenly there was a thunderous rumbling sound below as a great spreading swell of bubbles carpeted the sea. Then the depths gave up a clutter of debris containing shattered pieces of wood, slicks of oil, and bits of torn cloth. It was the final end of Kanoli; the final end of the Pacific Vortex.

Pitt looked for Summer, desperately searching each wave crest. But there was no sign of her flaming red hair. He shouted her name. But his only answer came from the distant rumble on the seafloor. Burying his head in the water, he dove back to find her. But his body would not respond—it had long reached its limits of endurance. Somewhere in the watery distance he thought he heard the distorted sounds of voices and he feebly fought to regain the surface.

A monstrous fish, that's the only description his numbed brain could offer, a monstrous black fish rose up from the sea and towered above his head, threatening to devour what was left of him. Pitt didn't care; he was ready. The sea had offered him someone to love, only to steal her back within its depths.

Then something caught his arm and gripped firm. Nearly insensible with exhaustion, he looked up. A

maze of blurred faces came down from the monstrous black fish, gently lifting his nude and badly injured body and wrapping him in a blanket. One of the faces detached itself from the rest and leaned closely over Pitt.

"Christ!" Crowhaven said in awe. "What's happened to you?"

Pitt tried to talk, but he choked and coughed instead, spitting up saltwater and vomit on the white blanket. Hoarsely he whispered: "You ... the *Starbuck* ... you raised her?"

"The Crowhaven luck," he said patiently. "The *Monitor's* missile exploded on the opposite side of the seamount so we were partially shielded from the main force of the underwater shock waves. The concussion was just enough to pop the bottom suction and up we came. The Navy won't take too kindly to what I've done to their submarine though. The starboard prop is sheared off and the port prop looks like a sick pretzel."

Pitt leaned his head up. Giordino and Adrian were also on board, similarly encased in the heavy white woolen U.S. Navy blankets. One of the seamen was attending to Giordino's hand.

"A girl ... there's another girl out there."

Crowhaven hovered over Pitt. "Rest easy, Major. If she's out there, we'll find her."

Pitt coughed again and fell back. He felt drained and shrunken. His mind was empty, surrounded by a creeping cover of black mist.

Crowhaven's men searched endlessly, but no trace of Summer was ever found. The mysteries of Kanoli were buried forever.

EPILOGUE

The tide of Kaena Point was coming in; the surf swept the sands just before it touched the feet of the overlooking bluffs. As each wave receded, the clear, tide-washed sand reappeared while tiny sand crabs burrowed new holes in the firmly packed grains.

Pitt stood on the bluffs of Kaena Point and watched the restless waters. He stood for a very long time, even after the tide reached high water and started to ebb. This is where it all began, he thought. And, for him, this is where it would end. Yet there were some things, he knew, that stay with a man until his heart hits the last rhythmic beat.

An albatross lazily circled overhead in ever-widening arcs. Then, as if sensing danger, it broke and winged away toward the north. Pitt studied the great white and black feathered bird until it became a small winged speck, finally vanishing in the flat blue sky.

The fragrance from the wisp of plumeria in his hand pierced his nostrils; from somewhere beyond the horizon a soft voice seemed to say: "*A ka makani hema pa.*" The words were carried on the light breeze that drifted in from the ocean.

Pitt listened intently but heard no more. He stared at the bouquet for a moment and then cast it into the

sea, watching as the surf rolled over the white blossoms, scattering them in the foaming sand.

As he turned away from the shoreline, Pitt sensed a vast feeling of relief. He began to whistle as his AC Cobra leaped down the winding dirt road, leaving a thin vapor of dust to slowly settle over the empty beach.

ABOUT THE AUTHOR

CLIVE CUSSLER lives the same sort of adventurous life as his hero, Dirk Pitt. Tramping the Southwest in search of gold mines, diving in isolated Rocky Mountain lakes for missing aircraft, heading an expedition to salvage John Paul Jones' ship, the *Bonhomme Richard*. Most recently Cussler discovered and excavated a sister ship to the *Monitor*, as well as finding artifacts from its famous nemesis the *Merrimack*. A noted collector of classic automobiles, Cussler lives in the foothills overlooking Denver, Colorado. Here he writes his bestselling thrillers: RAISE THE TITANIC!, ICEBERG, THE MEDITERRANEAN CAPER, VIXEN 03, and NIGHT PROBE!

Now that you've experienced the thrills of
PACIFIC VORTEX!,
read the following pages for an exciting
further glimpse into the remarkable life of

CLIVE CUSSLER'S

unstoppable hero

DIRK PITT

Lightning stabbed the night air again, a jagged fork splitting the clouded sky. Gene Seagram watched it strike somewhere behind the Balboa Island rooftops, and in almost the same instant, the roar of the thunder thrust against his eardrums like a cannon barrage.

Everyone else had nervously moved inside the dining room, and Seagram soon found the terrace deserted. He stayed, enjoying mother nature's display of fireworks. He finished off the cognac and leaned back in his chair, watching for the next flash of lightning. It soon came and illuminated a figure standing beside his table. In that instant of light, he made out a tall man with black hair and rugged features staring down at him through cool, piercing eyes. Then the stranger blended into the darkness again.

As the thunder rumbled away, a seemingly disembodied voice asked, "Are you Gene Seagram?"

Seagram hesitated, waiting for his eyes to readjust themselves to the dark that followed the flash. "I am."

"I believe you've been looking for me."

"At the moment, you have the advantage."

"I'm Dirk Pitt."

The skies lit up again and Seagram was relieved to see a smiling face. "It would seem, Mr. Pitt, that dramatic entrances are a habit with you. Did you also conjure up this electrical storm?"

Pitt's answering laugh came to the accompaniment of a clap of thunder.

"I haven't mastered that feat yet, but I am making progress at parting the Red Sea."

He's the man who dared to accept the challenge of raising the Titanic. *He's the man who took on an unknown enemy to salvage a devastatingly deadly cargo*

from a sunken airplane. He's the man who had to face down Britain's most cunning secret agent to attempt to capture a long-lost treaty for his country. He's Dirk Pitt, Special Projects Director for the National Underwater and Marine Agency (NUMA).

As the previous excerpt from RAISE THE TITANIC! proves, Clive Cussler's hero has an uncanny sense of the dramatic and it is this sense that makes Dirk Pitt one of the most exciting adventurers in fiction—the man the United States government calls on to accomplish virtually impossible underwater missions—usually with millions of lives hanging in the balance.

In the following episode from NIGHT PROBE!, an operation worth billions of dollars to an energy-starved, economically-hobbled America has met with seemingly insurmountable resistance. But there's still one hope left. . . .

It had to be bad news. From the sour look on Harrison Moon's face, the President knew it couldn't be anything else. He laid aside the speech he was editing and sat back in his chair.

"You look like a man with a problem, Harrison."

Moon laid a folder on the desk. "I'm afraid the British have tagged the game."

The President opened the file and found himself staring at an eight-by-ten glossy of a man who gazed back at the camera.

"This was just flown in from the *Ocean Venturer*," explained Moon. "An underwater survey vehicle was probing the wreck when it was ripped off by a pair of unknown divers. Before communications were broken, this face appeared on the monitors."

"Who is he?"

"For the last twenty-five years he's been living under the name of Brian Shaw. As you can see in the report,

he's a former British secret agent. His record makes interesting reading. Achieved quite a bit of notoriety back in the fifties and early sixties. He became too well known to operate; couldn't step on the sidewalk without a Soviet agent from their SMERSH assassination unit waiting to cut him down. His cover, as they say in the intelligence circles, was blown. Forced his secluded retirement. Their secret service buried his old identity by listing him as killed on duty in the West Indies."

"How did you put a make on him so fast?"

"Commander Milligan is on board the *Ocean Venturer*. She recognized him from the monitors. The CIA tracked down his true identity in their files."

"She knew Shaw?" the President asked incredulously.

Moon nodded. "Met him at a party in Los Angeles a month ago."

"I thought she was shipped out to sea."

"A foul-up. It never occurred to anyone to check out the fact that her ship was ordered to lay over three days in Long Beach for modifications. Also, nothing was said about not allowing her on shore."

"Their meeting? Could it have been a setup?"

"Seems so. The FBI spotted Shaw when he arrived from Britain. A usual procedure when embassy staff members greet overseas visitors. Shaw was escorted to a plane bound for LA. There the party was thrown by Graham Humberly, a well-known jet setter on the payroll of British intelligence."

"So Commander Milligan spilled her knowledge of the treaty."

Moon shrugged. "She had no instructions to keep her mouth shut."

"But how did they get wind of our knowledge of the treaty in the first place?"

"We don't know," Moon admitted.

The President read through the report on Shaw. "Odd that the British would trust an assignment of such magnitude to a man crowding seventy."

"At first glance it seems MI6 has given our treaty search low priority. But when you think about it, Shaw might well be the perfect choice to operate undercover. If Commander Milligan hadn't recognized his face, I doubt if we'd have tied him to British intelligence."

"Times have changed since Shaw was on the active list. He may be out of his element on this one."

"I wouldn't bet on it," Moon said. "The guy is no slouch. He's pegged us every step of the way."

The President sat very still for a moment. "It would appear that our neatly hatched concept has been penetrated."

"Yes, sir," Moon nodded somberly. "The stakes are too high for the British to gamble on us not finding the treaty."

"Then we write off the *Empress of Ireland* as a lost cause."

"Unless . . ." Moon said as if thinking out loud. "Unless Dirk Pitt can find the treaty in what precious time he has left."

Pitt's specialty: underwater salvage missions of the ultimate danger and consequence. In VIXEN 03, Pitt's talents are desperately needed to track down an airplane that plummeted to the sea over thirty years before. On board the plane is a cargo that must be destroyed—the most potent germ warfare weapon ever created (Pitt will soon discover that the cargo has been partially depleted by a terrorist group bent on holding the world at bay).

In the following excerpt, Pitt makes his first horrifying dive upon locating the sunken plane. . . .

In spite of the chilling morning air, Pitt was sweating inside his wet suit. He checked his breathing regulator, gave the thumbs-up sign to Giordino, and dropped over the side of the boat.

The icy water, surging between his skin and the interior lining of his three-sixteenths-inch-thick neoprene suit, felt like an electric shock. He hung suspended just below the surface for several moments, suffering the stabbing agony, waiting for his body heat to warm the entrapped water layer. When the temperature became bearable, he cleared his ears and kicked his fins, descending into an eerie world where wind and air were unknown. The line from the marker buoy angled off into the beckoning depths and he swam along beside it.

The bottom seemed to rise up and meet him. His right fin trailed through the mud before he leveled off, creating a gray cloud that mushroomed like smoke from an oil-tank explosion.

Pitt checked the depth gauge on his wrist. It read one hundred forty feet. That meant approximately ten minutes' bottom time without worrying about decompression.

His primary enemy was the water temperature. The icy pressure would drastically affect his concentration and performance. His body heat would soon be drained by the cold, pushing his endurance beyond its borders and into the realm of excessive fatigue.

Visibility was no more than eight feet, but that factor did not hinder him. The marker buoy had missed the sunken plane by mere inches and he had but to extend a hand and touch the metal surface. Pitt had wondered what sensations would course through him. He was certain fear and apprehension would raise their tentacles. But they did not appear. Instead, he felt a strange sense of accomplishment. It was as though he'd come to the end of a long and exhausting journey.

He swam over the engines, the blades of their propellers gracefully bent backward, like the curled petals of an iris, the finned cylinder heads never to feel the heat of combustion again. He swam past the windows of the cockpit. The glass was still intact but coated with slime, cutting off any view of the interior.

Pitt noted that he had used up nearly two minutes of his bottom time. He quickly kicked around to the shattered opening of the main fuselage, squeezed through, and switched on his dive light.

The first thing his eyes distinguished in the somber gloom were large silver canisters. Their tie-down straps had broken in the crash and they lay jumbled about the cargo-cabin floor. Carefully he snaked in and around them and glided through the open door to the control cabin.

There were four skeletons sitting in their assigned seats, held in their grotesque positions by nylon seat belts. The navigator's bony fingers were still clenched; the one at the engineer's panel leaned backward, its skull cocked to one side.

Pitt moved forward, more than a touch of fear and revulsion in his chest. The bubbles from his air regulator cascaded upward and mingled in one corner of the cockpit's ceiling. What made the scene all the more unearthly was the fact that although the flesh of the bodies was gone, the clothes remained. The icy-cold water had held back the rotting process over the decades, and the crew sat as properly uniformed as at the instant they had all died.

The copilot sat stiffly upright, his jaws open in what Pitt imagined to be a ghostly scream. The pilot drooped forward, his head almost touching the instrument panel. A small metal plate protruded from his breast pocket, and Pitt gently retrieved it, pushing the small rectangle up one of the sleeves of his wet suit. A vinyl folder hung from a pocket next to the pilot's seat, and Pitt took that also.

A glance at his watch told him his time was up. He didn't need an engraved invitation to head for the surface and the friendly rays of the sun. The cold was beginning to seep into his blood and mist his mind. He could have sworn the skeletons had all turned and were staring at him through the empty sockets of their skulls.

He hurriedly backed out of the cockpit and turned around when space permitted in the cargo cabin. It was then he spied a skeletal foot behind one of the canisters. The body that belonged to the foot was secured by straps to several of the cargo tie-down rings. Unlike the remains of the crew forward, this one still had remnants of flesh adhering to its bones.

Pitt fought the bile rising in his throat and studied more closely what was once a living, breathing man. The uniform was not Air Force blue but rather a khaki similar to the old Army issue. He went through the pockets, but they were bare.

An alarm began to go off in his head. His arms and legs were losing all feeling and turning stiff from the relentless cold, and his movements came as though he were immersed in syrup. If he did not get some warmth to his body soon, the ancient aircraft would claim another victim.

Danger and action for Pitt are not limited to his explorations underwater, however. In the following excerpt from ICEBERG, Pitt engages in a deadly on-the-water battle in his attempts to thwart an unthinkable conspiracy. . . .

Everything had to go perfect the first time. There could be no second chance. The radar operator on the hydroplane was probably at this instant reacting to the fact that the blip on his scope had lost headway and had stopped dead in the water. By the time he notified his commander and a decision was reached, it would be too late for a course change. The hydroplane's superior speed would have put its bow almost on top of *The Grimsi*.

Pitt rechecked the containers lying in a neat row beside him for perhaps the tenth time. It had to be the

poorest excuse for an arsenal ever concocted, he mused. One of the containers was a gallon glass jar scrounged from the galley. The other three were battered and rusty cans in various sizes that Pitt had found in a locker aft of the engine room. Except for their contents, the cloth wicks protruding from the cap openings and the holes punched through the top of the cans, the four vessels had little in common.

The hydroplane was close now—very close. Pitt turned to the wheelhouse and shouted, "Now!" Then he lit the wick of the glass jar with his lighter and braced himself for the sudden surge of acceleration he prayed would come.

Admiral James Sandecker pushed the starter button. The 420-hp Sterlings coughed once, twice, then burst into rpm's with a roar. He swung the wheel over to starboard hard and jammed the throttles forward. *The Grimsi* took off over the water like a racehorse. The admiral held on grimly, clutching the wheel and half expecting to collide with the hydroplane bow on. Then suddenly as a spoke flew off the wheel and clattered against the compass, he became aware that bullets were striking the wheelhouse. He could still see nothing, but he knew the crew of the hydroplane were firing blindly through the fog, guided only by the commands of the radar operator.

To Pitt the tension was unbearable. His gaze alternated from the wall of fog in front of the bow to the jar in his hand. The flame on the wick was getting dangerously close to the tapered neck and the gasoline sloshing behind the glass. Five seconds, no more, then he would have to heave the jar over the side. He began counting. Five came and went. Six, seven. He cocked his arm. Eight. Then the hydroplane leaped from the mist on an opposite course, passing no more than ten feet from *The Grimsi*'s railing. Pitt hurled the jar.

The next instant stayed etched in Pitt's memory the rest of his days. The frightful image of a tall, yellow-

haired man in a leather windbreaker gripping the bridge railing, watching in shocked fascination that deathly thing sailing through the damp air toward him. Then the jar burst on the bulkhead beside him and he vanished in a blast of searing bright flame.

Pitt had no time to reflect. Quickly he lit the wick on one of the gas cans as Sandecker swept *The Grimsi* on a hard-a-port, hundred-and-eighty-degree swing into the hydroplane's wake. The worm had turned. The hydroplane had slowed, and a pulsating yellowish-red glow could be easily seen through the gray mist. The admiral headed straight for it. He was standing straight as a ramrod now. It was certain that anybody who might have been shooting at *The Gimsi* thirty seconds ago would not be standing on a flaming deck in the hope of drilling an old scow full of holes. Nor was there now any possibility of the hydroplane ramming anything until the fire was out.

"Hit 'em again," he yelled to Pitt through the shattered forward window of the wheelhouse. "Give the bastards a taste of their own medicine."

Pitt didn't answer. He barely had time to throw the flaming can before Sandecker spun the wheel and turned across the hydroplane's bow for a third running attack. Twice more they raced from the fog, and twice more Pitt lobbed his dented cans of searing destruction until his makeshift arsenal was used up.

And then it hit *The Grimsi,* a thunderous shock wave that knocked Pitt to the deck and blew out what glass was left in the windows around Sandecker. The hydroplane had erupted in a volcanic roar of fire and flaming debris, instantly becoming a blazing inferno from end to end.

The echoes had returned from the cliffs on shore and left again when Pitt pushed himself shakily to his feet and stared incredulously at the hydroplane. What had once been a superbly designed boat was now a shambles and burning furiously down to the water's edge. He staggered to the wheelhouse—his sense of

balance temporarily crippled by the ringing in his ears from the concussion—as Sandecker slowed *The Grimsi* and drifted past the fiery wreck.

But Pitt isn't always engaged in the most deadly activities. Pitt is also quite a man with the ladies and in each of his adventures, he meets up with at least one stunning and remarkable woman. In THE MEDITERRANEAN CAPER, a Greek island provides the setting for one such meeting. . . .

"Please allow me to introduce myself; my name is Dirk Pitt."

"I'm Teri." She didn't offer her last name, and Pitt didn't press for it.

He pointed to the beach sand. "Won't you join me and help raise the sun?"

She laughed. "Thank you, I'd like that. But then again, for all I know you might be a monster or something." There was a note of whimsy in her tone. "Can I trust you?"

"To be perfectly honest, no. I think it only fair to warn you that I've assaulted over two hundred innocent virgins right here on this very spot." Pitt's humor was overly forward, but he knew it was a good system for testing a female's personality.

"Oh blimey, I would dearly have loved to have been number two hundred and one, but I'm not an innocent virgin." There was enough light now for Pitt to see the white of her teeth arched in a smile. "I certainly hope you won't hold that against me."

"No, I'm very broadminded about that sort of thing. But I must ask you to keep secret the fact that two hundred and one wasn't pure as the driven snow. If it ever leaked out, my reputation as a monster would be ruined."

They both laughed and sat down together on Pitt's

towel and talked while the hot sun reluctantly began its climb over the Aegean Sea. As the blazing orange ball threw its first golden rays over the shimmering horizon, Pitt gazed at the woman in the new light and studied her closely.

She was about thirty and wore a red bikini swim suit. The bikini was not the exaggerated brief kind, even though the lower half began a good two inches below the navel. The material had a satin sheen to it and clung tautly to her body like an outer layer of skin. Her figure was a beguiling mixture of grace and firmness; the stomach looked smooth and flat and the breasts were perfect, not too small but not too large and out of scale. Her legs were long, creamy colored and slightly on the thin side. Pitt decided to overlook this faint imperfection and swung his eyes to her face. The profile was exquisite. Her features possessed the beauty and mystery of a Grecian statue and would have rated near perfection except for a round pockmark beside her right temple. Ordinarily the scar would have been covered by her shoulder length black hair, but she had thrown her head back as she watched the sunrise and the ebony strands angled back behind her shoulders, touching the sand and revealing the thin blemish.

Suddenly she turned and caught Pitt's examining stare.

"You're supposed to be watching the sunrise," she said with a bemused smile.

"I've seen sunrises before, but this is the first time I've ever come face to face with a lovely, genuine Grecian Aphrodite." Pitt could see her dark brown eyes flashing with enjoyment at his compliment.

"Thank you for the flattery, but Aphrodite was the Greek goddess of love and beauty, and I'm only half Greek."

"What's the other half?"

"My father was German."

"In that case, I must thank the gods that you took after your mother's side."

She gave a pouting glance. "You'd better not let my uncle hear you say that."

"A typical kraut?"

"Yes, indeed. In fact he's why I happen to be on Thasos."

"Then he can't be all bad," Pitt said, admiring her hazel eyes. "Do you live with him?"

"No, actually I was born here, but I was raised in England. I suffered through school there, and when I was eighteen I fell in love with a dashing motorcar salesman and married him."

"I didn't know car salesmen could be dashing."

She ignored his sarcastic remark and continued. "He loved to race cars on his time off, and he was good at it too. He won trials and hill climbs and sporting car events." She shrugged and began drawing circles in the sand with her finger. Her voice became strange and husky. "Then one weekend he was racing a supercharged MG. It was raining, and he skidded off the course and hit a tree. He was dead before I could reach his side."

Pitt sat silent for a minute, staring at her sad face. "How long ago?" he asked simply.

"It's been eight and a half years now," she replied in a whisper.

Pitt felt dazed. Then anger set in. What a waste, he thought. What a rotten waste for a beautiful woman like her to grieve over a dead man for nearly nine years. The more he thought about it the angrier he became. He could see tears welling in her eyes as she lost herself in the remembrance, and the sight sickened him. He reached over and gave her a hard backhand slap across the face.

Her eyes jerked wide, and her whole body tensed from the sharp blow. It was as if she was struck by a bullet. "Why did you strike me?" she gasped.

"Because you needed it, needed it badly," he snapped. "That torch you carry around is as worn out as an overcoat. I'm surprised someone hasn't taken you over a knee and spanked it off. So your husband was dashing. So what? He's dead and buried, and mourning over him for all these years won't resurrect him from the grave. Lock away his memory somewhere and forget him. You're a beautiful woman—you don't belong chained to a coffin full of bones. You belong to every man who turns and admires you as you pass by and who longs to possess you." Pitt could see his words were penetrating her weak defenses. "Now you think about it. It's your life. Don't throw it away and play 'Camille' until you're withered and gray."

Her face was distraught in the morning sun, and her breath came in sobs. Pitt let her cry for a long time. When she finally raised her head and turned it toward him, he could set that her cheeks were streaked with tears, mixed with tiny grains of sand, clinging to the wetness. She looked up at him, and he caught the gleam in her eyes. They were soft and scared-looking, like a little girl's. He lifted her in his arms and kissed her. Her lips were warm and moist.

"When was the last time you had a man?" he whispered.

What kind of man is this daring adventurer? In this brief passage from VIXEN 03, Pitt's longtime friend and invaluable aide, Al Giordino, offers his insights. . . .

Colonel Steiger watched him for a moment and then turned to Al Giordino. "Have you known Pitt long?"

"Since the first grade. I was the class bully. When Dirk moved into the neighborhood and showed up for his first day at school, I worked him over pretty good."

"You showed him who was boss?"

"Not exactly." Giordino reached up and opened the

cargo door. "After I bloodied his nose and blackened one eye, he got up off the ground and kicked me in the crotch. I walked lopsided for a week."

"You make him sound devious."

"Let's just say that Pitt has a ton of balls, the brains to go with them, and an uncanny knack for knocking the shit out of any obstacle, man made or otherwise, that gets in his way. He is a soft touch for kids and animals, and helps little old ladies up escalators. To my knowledge, he's never stolen a dime in his life nor used his sly talents for personal gain. Beyond all that, he's one helluva guy."

"Do you think he might have gone too far this time?"

"You mean his stock in a nonexistent aircraft?"

Steiger nodded.

"If Pitt tells you there's a Santa Claus, hang your stocking on the mantel, because you better believe it."

Clive Cussler's Dirk Pitt adventures have thrilled and captivated millions of readers. If you enjoyed PACIFIC VORTEX!, plunge even further into the remarkable world of Dirk Pitt through these great Clive Cussler novels:

RAISE THE TITANIC! (22889-7 * $3.95)

NIGHT PROBE! (20663-X * $3.95)

VIXEN 03 (23092-1 * $3.95)

ICEBERG (14641-6 * $3.95)

THE MEDITERRANEAN CAPER
   (22875-7 * $3.50)

All of these books are on sale now wherever Bantam paperbacks are sold.

P9-AZX-589

DEEP IN THE VORTEX, A SUPER-SUB VANISHES...
DIRK PITT'S MISSION:
FIND IT. SAVE IT. BEFORE THE SEA EXPLODES!